# CHOCOLATE CAN BE DEADLY

## Cupcake Catering Mystery Series Book 7

### KIM DAVIS

Cinnamon & Sugar Press

---

# Chocolate Can Be Deadly

---

Cupcake Catering Mystery Series
Book 7

By Kim Davis

## Chapter 1

"Emory, I've got the contract for you to sign!" Tillie walked onto her patio and waved two sheets of paper in front of my face. "The committee finally decided the Valentine's dessert theme will be Dying for Chocolate. I told them you'd come up with a slew of chocolate desserts for us."

"Given my track record for finding bodies, is that really the best theme?" I wasn't kidding, either.

Tillie chortled. "As long as the victim is that old biddy Frances Allain, I'm good with it."

I ignored her comment, took the contract for the Society of Women for Arts and Literature event, and quickly glanced over it. "But this says the party is next Saturday. Six days from now."

She shrugged off my concerns and bent down to ruffle Piper and Missy's ears. The two dogs had been napping in the sun. "You can blame Frances. She kept voting against awarding you the contract until it was too late to hire another caterer. I know you're up for the challenge."

Octogenarian Tillie Skyler was my friend and my mentor. Not only did I live in her two-bedroom pool house across the alleyway from her Newport Beach bayside McMansion, but I also dated her grandson, Brian. And did I mention my half sister, Vannie, was Tillie's granddaughter? That practically made us family. Had it been anyone else wanting to hire me this close to Valentine's Day, I would have declined... like the rest of the caterers that Tillie's nemesis, Frances, had probably approached.

Sighing, I sank onto the cushy patio chair. Ignoring the seagull that had perched on the supporting post for the glass wall that shielded the patio from bay breezes, I scanned the contract.

"Fifty people and ten chocolate desserts?" I gulped. Valentine's Day was the coming Friday, and owning a cupcake catering business meant that I had a slew of orders to fulfill this week. And that was in addition to the six dozen cupcakes I provided to Oceana, Brian's award-winning restaurant in Laguna Beach, on a weekly basis. "Am I expected to not sleep at all this week?"

"You don't have to make fifty servings of each dessert." Tillie fluffed her platinum hair and turned her pale blue eyes toward me. "You know more than half of the women attending won't even take a single nibble. Sugar is bad for the waistline."

I tried not to grimace. Buttercream and cupcakes weren't my friends when it came to trying to make healthier food choices. But given a lot of my recipes were originals I created from cocktail flavors, I had to sample. A lot. And my waistline attested to that fact.

Starting a series of self-defense classes was supposed to take place at the beginning of March, which would provide me more exercise. After suffering a broken arm a few months before, I'd wanted to give my bones extra time to heal and become strong enough to withstand whatever rigors the instructor had in store for me. I wasn't looking forward to it.

Turning my attention back to the contract, I continued reading.

"Whose house is it being held at?" The address listed on the contract was in the Newport Coast area, a swanky enclave of mansions.

"Frances gets the honor." Tillie scowled. "The entire committee would like to see her kicked out, but no one has the guts to do it."

"Tell me what the plan is for next Saturday?" I gave up trying to read the contract. I'd get to it later.

"You need to be at Frances's house at one. Her staff will let you in and show you where to set up the desserts. They'll be assisting you in serving the champagne and attending to the guests."

"What time will you be arriving?" I knew the group would attend a performance at the local children's theater, which was the recipient of the large check the committee had fundraised for the previous year.

"We'll be at the children's theater from one until three for the *American Tail* musical performance. We should arrive at Frances's house around three thirty for the champagne and the Dying for Chocolate buffet."

"And who else will attend the dessert buffet? There's only ten of you on the committee, right?"

"We are each bringing a guest. Vannie is attending with me." Tillie tapped her perfectly manicured index finger on her pursed lips. "Then the theater's board of directors and their spouses, and the production team for the theater."

"No actors?"

"No. Frances wanted to keep this an 'adults only' event." Tillie curled her index and middle fingers downward in the quotation sign. "She also didn't want to mingle with the plebeian actors. Her words, not mine."

I snorted. "Seriously?"

"I tell you, her snobbishness has gotten worse these last

few months. She's probably got a new man on the hook and wants to impress him."

I'd had the misfortune of meeting Frances a few times. Not to be catty, but she wasn't what I'd consider a prize catch unless the man in question was after her considerable wealth.

I picked up the pen Tillie had placed beside the contract. After making sure the fee they offered would cover whatever ingredients I'd need and a reasonable hourly wage for myself —I wouldn't put it past Frances to sneak in a miserly sum—I signed it.

I handed her the contract then rubbed my temples. "Did any of the committee members have specific dessert requests?"

"I hate to break the news to you, but there need to be several vegan and gluten-free desserts. There seems to be quite a few attendees with food sensitives or at least lifestyle choices this time around."

I opened the notes app on my phone and started a list. "I can make a couple batches of cocktail-themed cupcakes and some nonalcoholic cupcakes."

"And we'll definitely want some cookies. Those are easy to nibble on during a party."

I tapped the information into my phone. "I'll plan on making at least two kinds of cookies, and one of those can be vegan and gluten-free. Plus, I'll come up with something more decadent for those who can't enjoy the rest of the dessert buffet."

"Let's talk about the cocktail cupcakes." Tillie mimed tossing back a drink. "We should probably sample some chocolate cocktails before we make a decision."

I couldn't help but laugh despite the gnawing sensation growing in my stomach that this was a catering job I should have turned down. A Dying for Chocolate theme hit just a bit too close to home, and I knew, without a doubt, Frances was going to make my life miserable between now and even several weeks after the event was over. She was just that kind of person.

"I had a chocolate mudslide cocktail on our trip." My face heated as I thought back to the romantic trip Brian and I had taken after the holidays. "I've been wanting to re-create it in cupcake form."

"What's in a mudslide? It doesn't sound all that appetizing." Tillie's brows drew together, but nary a wrinkle could be found on her smooth skin thanks to having the best cosmetic surgeon on speed dial.

"It's a light chocolate and coffee-based cupcake with Bailey's Irish Cream and Kahlúa."

"Oh goodness. That sounds marvelous." Tillie rubbed her hands together. "Let me make a pitcher for cocktail hour tonight instead of my usual gimlet."

I held my hand up, palm facing her. "That's not going to work. I've got to go grocery shopping for all the ingredients since I need to tinker with the recipes if I'm going to pull this off in time for Saturday."

"You'll have more fun tinkering with a cocktail or two first."

"I'm sure you're right, but then I'd lose my focus, and trust me, the cupcakes won't be pretty." I patted her hand. "We can't give Frances any ammunition to hold my desserts over our heads."

Tillie stuck her lower lip out. "You're right. She's such a sour lemon. We have to find a way to get rid of her."

"You mean kick her off the committee, right?" The party theme still didn't sit easy with me.

"Of course, that's what I meant." She winked at me. "But you really don't have to worry. Your desserts are always fabulous, and there won't be a single thing she can gripe about."

# Chapter 2

"You're ten minutes late, young lady." Frances Allain glared at me before tapping her diamond-encrusted wristwatch with her bloodred nail, which looked like a talon.

Shifting the boxes of cupcakes I held, I tried to look contrite instead of annoyed. "I apologize, but there was an issue at your security gate. They didn't have my name, and they couldn't reach anyone to authorize my entrance."

Given that Frances was here instead of at the play with the committee, I would bet money that she purposely left me stranded at the gate so she'd have something to complain about.

"You should have allowed extra time for that." Her sharp voice cut through the air.

"Of course, and I apologize. May I come in and start setting up?" I shifted the cupcake boxes again. They were cumbersome, and I would have taken the time to place them in a tote had Frances not been waiting at the front door already when I'd pulled up in front of her imposing house. Mansion was really more of an apt description than a house.

The creamy-ivory Greek revival edifice had imposing

columns flanking the twenty-foot-high wrought iron arched door. There were two double-story wings on the house, each second floor hosting large covered balconies supported by more columns.

"If it weren't too late to hire another catering company, I'd send you on your way and tear up your final payment." She grudgingly pulled the massive door all the way open and allowed me to step into the foyer.

What was with this woman? I had done nothing to incur her wrath.

Two sweeping marble staircases, with bronzed filigreed banisters, led from the foyer to the second floor. Overhead, a stained glass ceiling let in filtered light from the rotunda, while an upside-down Christmas-tree-shaped crystal chandelier hung from the top of the rotunda down to the center of the large room. The chandelier had to have been at least ten feet long, and I hoped the supports held.

Frances shut the door with a loud bang, and I jumped.

"Follow me, but touch nothing." She brushed past me and tottered down the wide hallway on four-inch heels. Her tight black skirt swished around her bony knees while her skeletal-thin arms poked out from frilly silk cap sleeves. "As soon as you're done unloading, move your vehicle to the staff's space behind the house. You should have parked there first."

"Yes, Mrs. Allain." I couldn't help but wonder if she treated her staff this horribly as well.

The décor was overly fussy, more ornate than tasteful. She led me to a dining room large enough to accommodate at least seventy-five guests, and a long rectangular dining table stood beneath another elaborate crystal chandelier that was at least six feet in diameter. The lights reflected off the gleaming crystals. I'd hate to have been one of the housekeeping staff in charge of keeping all the chandeliers dusted.

"You can set up here, but don't scratch the table. If you didn't bring a tablecloth, ask Laurie to supply you with one."

I eyed the twenty-foot gilded table and shuddered. It was a monstrosity but probably cost more than I made in a year or even two. "I'll need to ask Laurie for a tablecloth, if that's not a problem?"

"Humph. I should have known Matilda's protégé would be sorely lacking." She flicked her hand toward the entrance on the far side of the room. "You can find Laurie in the kitchen."

"I have tablecloths for two eight-foot tables, which is what the contract stated. Had I been notified otherwise, I would have made arrangements." I had a feeling the event would only go downhill from here. Frances seemed to go out of her way to sabotage me.

"There's no need to take that tone with me, *Emory*." She leaned in until her beak-like nose stopped a mere few inches from my face. "You and Matilda will get your due, mark my words."

I reared back at the venom in her voice. "What are you talking about? I've done nothing to you—neither has Tillie."

With a parting glare thrown my way, Frances spun on her heels and marched out the door. I couldn't help but blow out the breath I'd been holding in. What was going on? I wished I could call or at least text Tillie and ask her. But I didn't even try since I was certain she'd have her cell phone turned off during the performance. There wouldn't be time to talk before the event, so I'd have to find patience and wait until later.

Finding Laurie turned out to be a challenge as well, and I fumed as the minutes ticked away. I gave up, returned to my car, and unloaded the boxes of desserts. It wouldn't hurt for them to be stacked on the floor until I could find a tablecloth. Surely critters or insects wouldn't dare live in Frances's house. And I dared not stack the boxes on the table. Frances would find a miniscule scratch and blame it on me.

Pulling my car behind the house to park in the staff's lot, I spotted an older woman dressed in a black maid's uniform. Crossing my fingers it was Laurie—or at least someone who knew where to find her—I made my way over to where she swept the ivory-colored travertine-paved walkway.

"Excuse me. Are you Laurie?"

The woman, who looked to be in her fifties, lifted her head. She nodded, and her tight iron-gray curls bobbed with the movement. "How can I help you?"

"I'm catering the event this afternoon, and Mrs. Allain said you could provide me with a tablecloth for the dining table."

Her pale blue eyes narrowed for a moment, and deep creases appeared on her forehead. "Ah, yes. Shall I meet you in the dining room, Ms...."

"I'm Emory. And yes, I'll meet you in the dining room." I pointed over my shoulder. "Am I parked in the right spot? Mrs. Allain was vague about where I should put my car."

Laurie's light-toned skin seemed to pale. "If you leave your keys with me, I'll park it in the appropriate spot. You're in Mrs. Allain's personal assistant's spot, and she's very particular."

I didn't know if she was talking about Frances or the personal assistant being particular, but I didn't need any more issues. I quickly handed over my keys. "Thank you. Would you mind getting the tablecloth first? I need to get the desserts arranged before the guests arrive."

"Of course. I'll meet you in a moment."

Just as I turned to head back into the house, a sporty red convertible Mercedes roared into the parking lot. It screeched to a halt just a few feet from my SUV. The driver, a young blonde woman wearing oversized sunglasses, honked the horn then gestured at Laurie. It wasn't difficult to see that the woman was annoyed and expected Laurie to do something about it. Was this Frances's personal assistant? It seemed hard to believe. I had expected a dour, middle-aged woman to hold that position. Not a frivolous blonde who seemed just as demanding as her employer.

Laurie dropped the broom and hastened toward my vehicle. She turned her head and hissed over her shoulder. "I'll meet you in the dining room. Go quickly. Now."

Whatever Frances was paying Laurie, it couldn't possibly be enough. And I fervently wished I hadn't let Tillie talk me into taking this job.

# Chapter 3

It took another ten minutes before Laurie walked into the dining room, carrying an extra-large plastic-wrapped package.

"I hope I didn't get you in trouble with…" I wasn't sure what the woman's name was, and I couldn't see her being a personal assistant.

"Paris. Paris Allain is Mrs. Allain's great-niece and personal assistant." Laurie pursed her lips together before her expression became bland again. She placed the package on the table. "It'll take the both of us to spread the tablecloth. Had I known ahead of time, I would have steamed the fold lines out."

"I'm so sorry to cause you extra work. I was told there were two small tables for the desserts, and I brought my own tablecloths for those."

"No matter. I'll pick some flowers from the garden and put them in vases to help hide the worst of the lines." Laurie peeled the lightweight plastic off and began unfolding the white tablecloth.

The lines were minimal thanks to the generous amount of tissue paper used when packaging the clean tablecloth.

Frances would predictably find cause to complain about them anyway, but it was too late to worry about that now. When Laurie left to pick the flowers—and I fervently hoped there weren't any bugs on them—I began unloading the desserts. I arranged the three Tunnel of Fudge Bundt cakes down the middle of the table, spaced two feet apart. After arranging the cupcakes, cookies, tarts, fudge, and chocolate-dipped straw-berries on platters and tiered stand trays, I positioned them around the table. The monochromic shades of chocolate needed some splashes of color, so I'd garnished some desserts with fresh raspberries and strawberries, and sifted confection-ers' sugar on others. After the desserts had been placed around the table, I sprinkled organic red and pink rose petals around the desserts and onto the tablecloth.

Laurie reappeared, carrying a tray covered with small bud vases filled with red and pink rosebuds that had just started opening.

"Those are beautiful." I picked up one of the vases after she'd settled the tray onto the far end of the table. "How are they already coming into bloom? It's not the right season yet."

"We have a small greenhouse on the south side of the property. The gardener keeps them blooming year-round." Laurie smiled, showing a gap between her two front teeth. She began placing bud vases around the desserts and rear-ranging the rose petals to strategically cover any hint of fold lines.

I thought it looked beautiful and told her so before taking out my phone and capturing several photos from a variety of angles. I'd add them to my online website, the one my best friend, Brad, had so generously designed for me as a Christmas gift. Or, I should say, had one of his tech people design for me. As a result, my business had grown, and I finally felt like I was financially secure after being decimated by my snake of an ex-husband.

"Let me know if you need anything else. I need to get

back to my chores." Laurie turned to leave, but I stopped her by placing my hand on her arm.

"I was told that there would be staff to pour the champagne and help pick up dirty plates during the event. Are they here yet?" I glanced over at the sideboard and didn't see any champagne flutes set out yet, nor any ice buckets.

Laurie's salt-and-pepper eyebrows shot up toward her hairline. "No, miss. I have heard nothing about that."

"Aren't you the head housekeeper? Or is there someone else I should speak with?"

"I'm it. I bring in extra people from an agency once a month to do a deep clean, but it's only me."

"Would Paris have made the arrangements and forgotten to tell you?" I checked the time on my phone. We had forty minutes, if we were lucky, to get this resolved.

"I don't know." Laurie tried to leave again, and once again I stopped her.

"Where can I find Paris? I need to find out where the champagne flutes are and get them set up. Do you know if the champagne has been chilled?" The more I thought about everything that needed done, the more panicky I felt.

Laurie jerked away from me. "I wouldn't interrupt her if I were you."

"I don't have a choice. Fifty people will be here in about a half hour, and nothing is ready except my desserts. There should be coffee brewing, the mudslide cocktails should be in a pitcher, all the serving accouterments and barware should be in place, and most of all, champagne and glasses should be ready to serve."

She hesitated a moment. "You'll find her office on the other side of the kitchen. I'd be cautious if I were you."

Before I could reply or ask any further questions, Laurie scurried away. Had Frances intentionally set up me up to fail, or had she, or Paris, simply overlooked their part of the event? I practically had the contract memorized and marked up so I knew it hadn't been my responsibility to provide the serving items or drinks, aside from the mudslide cocktails.

I practically ran through the kitchen and down the hallway that I hoped led to Paris. There were several closed doors, so I began knocking on each one then opening it to peek into the room. On the fourth try, I found her sitting at a glass desk, a sleek Macintosh computer prominently displayed, flipping through a fashion magazine.

"Paris? I'm Emory Martinez, the caterer. I think we have a problem."

"You're the caterer. Fix it." She kept her eyes glued to the page and flicked her fingertips my way.

"I've been hired to provide desserts and mudslide cocktails only. The champagne, glasses, and plates were to be provided by Mrs. Allain." I didn't have a liquor license, nor did I want one—I only got by with providing the cocktails because I didn't charge for them and Tillie had provided the booze—so I knew I couldn't have overlooked being responsible for the champagne. "The contract clearly states that the hostess will provide those items."

Well, it didn't clearly state that, but it had certainly been implied.

"I told Frances you would screw this up, and voilà, here we are." She flipped the page and began studying a dress that barely covered the skinny model.

"I suggest you do something to fix the problem, or at least let Mrs. Allain know about it before guests arrive in thirty minutes." My face felt hotter with each passing second.

"Not my problem, so I suggest you do something about it." Paris flipped to a new page.

"Where can I find Mrs. Allain?" I knew I shouldn't have taken this job. It was going to give me ulcers before the day was over.

"She's probably in her office."

"Which is where?"

She huffed. "Go back through the kitchen, take the first entryway on your right. Her office is the second door on the left."

I didn't bother saying thank you as I sprinted for Mrs. Allain's office. I followed the directions then knocked on the door. Without waiting for a reply, I barged in… and I wished I could scrub my retinas. Frances was lip-locked with a man who had to be twenty years her junior. He was on the pudgy side, with a comb-over to cover his balding pate. His face was red, but I couldn't tell if it was because my entrance had embarrassed him or if that was his normal coloring. I had to admit, his suit seemed to be custom made and fit him well, even if his hot-pink tie was askew.

"Oh! Excuse me. Uh, Mrs. Allain, we have a problem with the champagne and, uh, stuff."

"That's not my problem. Paris warned me you'd make this event a disaster." Frances patted down her short-bobbed dark-chestnut-brown hair. She used to tint her hair blue. I guess she was trying to appear younger and more appealing to her companion.

"The contract stipulated I was hired to provide the desserts. Everything else was to be provided by the hostess." Their runaround exhausted me—on top of being up until three that morning, baking everything needed. I'd hoped to have had at least an hour or two with Brian—it being Valentine's Day the day before—but it never happened. His swamped restaurant had kept him just as busy as my cupcake and dessert orders had kept me.

"Get Laurie to figure it out. There should be several cases of champagne in the wine cellar. Just tell her what you need." Frances raised one eyebrow. "Now, if you don't mind, leave us be and get back to work. I don't need or want Matilda's spy getting into my business."

## Chapter 4

Hastily, I closed the door and went in search of Laurie again. I found her in the kitchen and relayed everything she needed to help me get done. After confirming with Frances that yes, she was to get the champagne and all the drinks, she got to work.

The coffee had just been set to brew and I'd just finished drying the cocktail glasses and champagne flutes—who in their right mind kept cases of barware stacked in a pantry?—when Tillie and Vannie arrived. A steady stream of guests followed them into the dining room, and soon the chatter of committee members and the clink of glassware filled the air. Frances and her companion were conspicuously absent.

I quickly explained to Tilly and Vannie about the lack of serving staff and the hoops I'd had to jump through to get refreshments set up.

"Don't worry, dear. I'll get Andrew to pour the champagne, and Laurie can focus on cleaning up and serving coffee. Let people help themselves to the mudslide cocktails." Tillie patted my cheek. "You've done a marvelous job, and I just know you'll get a lot of business from this event."

"Are you sure Andrew won't mind? I can try to do it along

with assisting with the desserts." Andrew was Tillie's longtime driver and cherished employee. He'd come along with us on our many misadventures, and I was pretty sure he would do anything Tillie asked of him.

"He won't mind a bit. I think he gets a bit bored at times, waiting for my events to finish."

I wasn't sure that was the case. Andrew was an avid reader, and we'd talk from time to time about what books we were reading. He always had a book with him in the car, and I knew he passed the time diving into the latest thriller or mystery. It doesn't get much better than being paid to sit around and read.

"I'm happy to help too," Vannie said. "Just point out what you need me to do, and I'll do it."

"That'll be a tremendous help." I gave my sister a one-armed hug. "Thank you."

Tillie sent Andrew a text just as Frances and her companion strolled in. Frances looked like the cat that just swallowed the canary, and an enormous diamond sparkled on her ring finger. It was a new accessory that hadn't been there when I'd arrived.

Frances pulled her new fiancé over to the champagne, glowered at me, and poured them each a glass. She found a spoon and clinked it against the crystal.

"Can I have your attention, please? I want to make an announcement." She beamed at the man while she waited for the room to quiet. I heard a gasp coming from the back of the room. "I want to introduce you to my fiancé, Ian Hesser. Please join us in celebrating our news."

Most people raised their glasses and congratulated the pair. Tillie was not one of them. Instead, she leaned in and whispered, "Frances must have a death wish. That's Rebecca Hesser's ex-husband. Their divorce was finalized only two weeks ago."

The front door of the mansion slammed loud enough to

echo in the dining room. I looked up just in time to see Frances smile with glee.

Lowering my voice so no one could overhear, I whispered, "I take it that was Rebecca Hesser who just left?"

"You got it, cupcake."

"Who is she? The name seems familiar, but I can't place it." Vannie rested her hand on Tillie's arm.

"She'll be the next chairwoman of our committee, starting next quarter. Frances was vying for the position, but thankfully, Rebecca put her name in and handily won." Tillie shuddered. "We don't need someone as vindictive as Frances leading the group."

"Is that why she went after Ian?" I didn't see the marriage taking place, and if it did, it wouldn't be a happy one.

"Bingo. Ian's had some financial difficulties the last couple of years. I'm sure Frances's fortune lured him in."

"But he's got to be twenty years her junior." Not that there was anything wrong with a wide gap in ages when it came to romance, especially amongst mature adults.

"I'm sure Frances counts that as another feather in her cap." Tillie waved for Andrew to join us. "Show him what needs to be done. I need to circulate and see who's willing to join me in forcing that old biddy out of the committee. She's gone too far this time."

Tillie was a force of nature, and if anyone could accomplish it, she'd be the one.

"I hear you need an extra pair of hands to help." Andrew, cover-model worthy, sidled up to me. He kept his blond hair trimmed short, and his broad shoulders filled out the black suit he wore. Knowing Tillie, I was pretty certain the suit had a designer label, given how it fit his toned body perfectly. Several women in our vicinity eyed him like the dessert they forbade themselves.

"If you could pour the champagne and then walk around refilling flutes as needed, I'd be grateful."

"Sure. Point me toward the kitchen, and I'll wash my hands first."

I gave him directions then had Vannie assist me in plating cupcakes, cookies, and tarts while answering questions about the desserts and pointing them to the pitcher containing the cocktail mixture. There was a flurry of activity when word spread that I had vegan and gluten-free chocolate raspberry tarts, chocolate chunk cookies, and brownie cookies. Several women clustered around me, wanting to try the special desserts. Once the rush around the table subsided, Vannie made her way around the room, collecting dirty dishes and ferrying them to the kitchen. I couldn't have asked for a more diligent assistant.

Tillie seemed to keep out of the way of Frances and Ian as they made their rounds to collect well-wishes from the guests. As attendees began to depart, the newly engaged couple left the dining room as well. Within moments, Tillie stood by my side and plucked a brownie cookie from the container I'd just placed it in.

"I have about three-quarters of the committee members on board with kicking Frances out. We plan on putting it to a vote at our next monthly meeting."

"I'm glad you're finding the support you need." I handed her an empty pastry box. "You can help me finish boxing up the desserts. You were right. We only needed about half of what I brought."

She nudged me with her elbow. "You should listen to your elders more often, dear."

"I'd rather have too much than run out. Frances probably would withhold my final check had we run low."

"Bah. She's the one who fell through with her end of hosting the event." Tillie carefully placed the chocolate mini tarts into the box. "What was she thinking when she neglected to get the champagne and servers like she promised when fighting to host the event? It was the only reason she was given the honor."

"She has it in for both of us." I flashed Tillie a side eye. "I know I have done nothing to deserve her ire. What did *you* do?"

She waved off my question with a flip of her hand. Before I could pry any further, a scream pierced the air.

I whipped around to find out where the scream came from. The dining room was empty, aside from me, Tillie, and Andrew. Where was Vannie? The scream came again, clearly from a woman who, thankfully, didn't sound like my sister. I darted for the hall with Andrew on my heels. Paris backed out of her great-aunt's office, her hand over her mouth. More screaming ensued from inside. It had to be coming from Frances.

Pushing Paris aside, I stepped through the doorway. Ian had collapsed onto the floor, his sightless brown eyes staring at the ceiling. His face was even redder than the last time I'd seen him in the dining room, but what made my heart stop was the foam mixing with chocolate frosting coming from his mouth. A half-eaten mudslide cupcake lay crumpled next to his outstretched hand.

"You! You killed him, you monster." Frances had her bony finger outstretched and pointed in my direction. "Paris, call the police this instant and tell them to arrest Emory. She's the killer."

## Chapter 5

Pandemonium soon ensued. Paris started screaming and wouldn't shut up. Laurie tried to take the young woman back to her office, but instead, Paris collapsed in the hallway on the white marble floor. Guests who had lingered in the front entrance rushed to see what had happened and their pushing to see inside the office kept me from retreating from Frances's shouted accusations.

Andrew finally gave an ear-piercing whistle. "Listen up. You all need to return to the dining room and clear the way for emergency personnel. They'll be here momentarily."

"Don't let her leave. Someone make a citizen's arrest." Frances jabbed her red talons in my direction. "She killed Ian."

Andrew gripped my arm and pulled me from the office. Vannie stood in the hallway, her face ashen. She reached out and took hold of my arm then pulled me to follow Andrew. He shouldered his way through the still-milling crowd and led the way to the dining room while we stayed on his heels. We found Tillie at the dessert table, taking the desserts out of the boxes and arranging them on the platters.

"I thought people would need to nibble while we wait for the police. I called them when I heard Frances accuse you of murder." She gave me a side hug after Vannie released my arm. "And I'm sure the detectives and crime scene techs will get hungry. I guess it's a good thing you made extras, Emory."

My face must've shown the shock I felt at seeing Ian's body and then being accused of being a killer in such a public fashion.

"Andrew, get a chair for Em. She looks like she might pass out." She pressed a glass of bubbly champagne into my hands. "Drink up and then I'll find some brandy for you. It'll be good for your nerves."

I pushed it away. "No. I think some water would be better."

"If you say so, dear. But brandy is always a restorative beverage, in my opinion." Tillie waved Laurie over. "Can you bring a glass of cold water for Emory? She's had quite the shock."

"Of course." She hurried away, her rubber-soled shoes squeaking on the cold marble floor.

"Maybe Laurie should check on Frances. She's probably more in shock than I am." I rubbed my eyes, trying to unsee the crumbled mudslide cupcake lying next to Ian. I thought back to the room and seemed to recall there had been a plate with three more cupcakes sitting atop the desk. There had been a red heart-shaped box of chocolates there too. I hoped that had been the means of poisoning Ian—the frothing at the mouth could only be one thing unless he had rabies, which was highly doubtful—instead of my cupcakes. The detectives would figure it out.

"I don't think Frances knows what shock means. She's too self-absorbed."

Tillie might have a point. Instead of trying to get medical aid for Ian, she'd only wanted the police so they could arrest me. Had Frances killed Ian just so she could frame me and harm Tillie's reputation? Could she really be that awful?

I gulped the water the second Laurie placed it in my hands. Some dribbled onto my white silk blouse, and when I tried wiping it away, I smeared chocolate into the fabric. I hadn't even known my hands were dirty.

Sirens interrupted the quiet murmurings, and I tried not to notice the surreptitious glances the guests were giving me. Paramedics tromped down the hallway toward Frances and Ian's body. One of the ambulance crew pushed a gurney after them, but I knew it wouldn't be needed. Within a couple minutes, he pushed the empty gurney back past the dining room entrance toward the front door, with the paramedics following close behind.

Next came two uniformed police officers. They stayed in Frances's office for about five minutes, then one of them came to stand at the entrance to the dining room.

"I'm sorry, folks, but I'll need you to stay put until the detective arrives." He glanced around the room until his gaze came to land on me then on Vannie. He pointed. "Emory Martinez?"

Biting my tongue to keep from crying, I raised my hand. Tillie gave my free hand a hard squeeze.

He crooked his finger. "I need for you to come with me."

I stood on wobbly legs and slowly made my way across the room. It felt like a spotlight was on me as every pair of eyes followed my progress. Following him down the now-empty hallway, he led me to the kitchen and gestured for me to sit on the island barstool. I practically collapsed then rested my head in the palms of my hands.

"Detective Gabe O'Neill is on his way to secure the crime scene."

My mood brightened at Gabe's name. He was married to my BFF Brad and would know, without a doubt, that I wasn't a murderer. I wouldn't have anything to worry about aside from, perhaps, some bad online reviews about my cupcakes, even if the poison had surely come from the chocolates. But I wouldn't let that cause me concern because Brad could get rid of those reviews once his hackers—er, employees—scrubbed them from the internet.

"That's great. He's a good detective." I wondered if it would be rude to help myself to another glass of water. Now that the shock and worry had receded, my mouth felt dehydrated.

"He asked that, given Mrs. Allain's accusations, you be kept on your own until a replacement detective can be sent to interview you."

"What?" That didn't sound good. How could Gabe not believe that I was one hundred percent innocent?

I peered at his nameplate pinned beneath his gold badge. "Why can't Gabe talk to me, Officer Bennett? He knows I'm innocent."

"That's exactly the problem. He said it's a conflict of interest given your close friendship, and an impartial detective needs to be involved." He looked at his watch. "Hopefully, the new detective will be here within an hour."

I dropped my head back into my hands and slumped over the black marble island. My phone chimed with a text from Tillie.

**Vannie, Andrew, and I will wait for you to be questioned, no matter how long it takes. I'm calling my attorney.**

I thumbed a quick reply.

**No attorney yet. Gabe is coming for crime scene, but a new detective is coming to question me.**

Tillie sent a palm-over-face emoji.

I couldn't help but berate myself for not listening to my instinct telling me to not get involved in the Dying for Chocolate party. I couldn't help but think Frances had something to do with the murder, but I didn't see how it would be possible to prove it.

I knew my family and friends would come together to support me and help me come up with a plan to prove my innocence and find the real killer.

## Chapter 6

While waiting for the new detective to show up, I began washing dishes and cleaning the kitchen for Laurie, after obtaining permission from Officer Bennett, who'd had to get permission from Gabe.

"Crime scene techs will bag up the remaining food in the dining room and, of course, the cupcakes and chocolate found in Mrs. Allain's office." He shuffled his feet and looked bored. I couldn't blame him. Watching me wash dishes and scrub counters had to be mind-numbing, to say the least. To give him credit, though, he finally offered to dry the champagne flutes after I'd washed them.

I tried to engage him in conversation, but he only responded with monosyllables. Giving up on trying to chat with him, I made a mental list—the officer would have been horrified if he knew my thoughts—of all the suspects who might have wanted Ian dead. Naturally, Ian's recently divorced wife headed my list. Tillie could probably find out the gossip about what instigated the divorce and maybe even information about Ian's financial trouble. Although Brad's hackers—er, employees—would probably be a better source for that.

Despite the animosity between Tillie and Frances, I couldn't see the old biddy killing her fiancé just to frame me and shame her nemesis. But what if Ian had somehow betrayed Frances? Maybe she was distraught or so angry she decided to kill two birds with one stone, so to speak. I had to wonder if Ian was the intended victim. Perhaps the killer planned that the poisoned chocolates—I refused to believe that my cupcakes were the vehicle for the poisoning—would kill Frances, and Ian turned out to be an innocent bystander who died instead.

Shaking my head, I tried to gather my thoughts. Anyone and everyone knew Frances barely ate, and never, ever ate sugar. It was how she kept her sticklike figure, which, to be honest, was worse than having a few extra pounds. That was my personal opinion, and I was sticking to it.

"Are you okay, Ms. Martinez?" Officer Bennett looked at me with concern. His amber eyes seemed to turn even more golden as the late-afternoon sun filtered through the kitchen windows. "You seem to be doing a lot of head bobbing and shaking."

"Uh, yeah. I'm fine. Just listening to some internal music to pass the time." I felt my face flush hot. "Sorry for causing you to worry."

"I can find a Spotify list to play."

"That won't be necessary, Officer Bennett." The deep, stern voice caused me to startle, and I almost dropped the glass I'd been washing. "Your job is to keep the suspect from escaping. Not to keep her entertained."

I had a strong hunch that this was the new detective, and I was beyond certain I would not like him. I slowly turned to face the man who would surely interrogate me. He was squat, and his face resembled a bullfrog. The only redeeming physical feature I could see was his thick golden mane of hair that swooped over his forehead and brushed the tops of his ears.

Even though he looked to be in his late fifties, there wasn't even a touch of gray in his locks.

"Ms. Martinez, I presume?" His thick New York accent hung in the air.

"Yes, that's me." I carefully placed the dripping-wet flute on a towel and dried my hands on the apron I'd donned before starting dishes.

"Officer Bennett, you can excuse yourself. I'll take it from here." The detective drew his bushy, light-brown eyebrows together and glowered at the officer.

"Of course, Detective Reece." He swiftly departed, and the detective turned his glare toward me.

"Sit. We need to have a frank discussion about what happened this afternoon." He pointed his thick, stubby finger at the barstool.

"Um, sure, but I don't know anything except Ian passed away." I couldn't help myself and twirled one of my red— practically a clown's dream red color—corkscrew curl around my finger.

"You're the caterer, and your cupcakes were found in the office where the deceased expired, with remnants of your cupcake in his mouth."

"There was also a box of opened Valentine's chocolates next to the plate of cupcakes. Maybe the poison came from there." I felt relieved to get my suspicions out in the open. Too late, I realized I might have jumped the gun.

"Aha! You know it was poison that killed Mr. Hesser." He dangled a set of handcuffs from his fingers. "That right there is enough to place you under arrest."

Oh, good lord. Gabe was going to get an earful from me. Where did Newport Beach dig up this archaic detective, and why did they keep him around?

"Excuse me, Detective Reece. I think it's common knowledge amongst anyone who watches crime and mystery shows that when someone is frothing at the mouth, it probably means poison. Unless they have rabies, of course." I hoped he'd listen to my reasonable explanation. The last thing I needed was to be led out in handcuffs. I should have listened to Tillie and had her call an attorney before I spoke with the detective.

"Maybe you watch these kinds of shows to get information on how to avoid being caught?" Had the detective sported a handlebar mustache, he would have twirled it at this point. Seriously, where did this character come from? I hadn't heard Gabe mention someone with this attitude on the force, so perhaps he was new to the area. Or did they bring him in from another division, given Gabe's friendship with me?

Standing, I waved my hand toward the door. "I've given you all the information I can, so I'll be going now."

"Not so fast, little lady."

I rolled my eyes so hard I was surprised I didn't see stars. "If you want to question me further, you can schedule an appointment when my attorney is available. My contact information is on record if you don't already have it."

"Is everything okay in here?" Gabe strode into the room, and his piercing eyes met my gaze.

Detective Reece sputtered. "I'm still questioning our suspect."

"Like I told the detective, here, I've answered all his questions, and I don't know anything else." I crossed my arms. "I'll be happy to sign the statement when it's ready, but until then, I'd like to be done here, especially after being falsely accused."

Gabe jerked his head toward the doorway. "Go ahead and leave, Emory. We'll be in touch later."

I spun on my heels and practically trotted from the room. Detective Reece's voice boomed as he berated Gabe for interfering in his investigation. Keeping my instinct to run in check, I tried to appear like I was calm and in control. Once the detectives were no longer within hearing distance, I picked up the pace and half jogged to find Tillie and Vannie. We needed to get out of here before Detective Reece produced his hand-cuffs and clipped them on my wrists.

Tillie and Vannie were waiting in the foyer. With one look at my face, Vannie threw the front door open and grabbed Tillie's arm. The three of us scurried onto the landing then down the five steps and rushed to where Andrew waited by the town car. I jumped into the front seat and scrunched down so my head wasn't visible through the windows while Andrew helped Tillie into the back seat. Vannie was already seated in the back and buckled in before Andrew even closed Tillie's door.

I stayed in the scrunched position—Andrew knew better than to ask questions—until we reached the Pacific Coast Highway, or PCH, as locals called it.

"What happened, Emory? You're not on the lam, are you?" Tillie giggled then patted my shoulder. "I felt like we were Bonnie and Clyde getting out of Dodge the way we ran from the house."

"Gram, you're mixing your metaphors." Vannie's green eyes examined my freckled face that bore a strong resemblance to her own. "Are you all right, Em?"

"I'm not sure. Gabe's replacement detective is a misogynic mess, and I think he's determined to prove I killed Ian." I shuddered. "I left my SUV back there but I had to get away from that man. Can one of you bring me back tomorrow morning? I don't want to risk running into him."

"Andrew, will you be so kind and make arrangements to pick up Emory's vehicle tonight and return it to her house?" Tillie patted my shoulder.

"I don't want to cause any trouble for Andrew," I protested.

"It's not a problem. I'll be happy to do it." Andrew held his hand out to me, palm up. "Give me your key fob and I'll take care of it."

"Thank you. It really means a lot to me." I dropped the

fob into his hand then turned in my seat to face the back. "Tillie, I'm going to need the name and number of your attorney. I told Detective Reece I wouldn't talk to him without an attorney present, and I'm not sure Gabe will be able to talk any sense into that horrible man."

"You did the right thing, dear." Tillie rummaged in her handbag and drew out her phone. "I'll text her contact information to you."

My phone chimed with an incoming text from Tillie with her contact information for Irene Cumberland, attorney-at-law. "Thanks. I'll call her when we get home, and then we need to figure out how to catch a killer."

# Chapter 7

As soon as we returned to Tillie's house, I took our dogs, Piper and Missy, for a walk. They tugged on their leashes, trying to lead me to the beach to romp in the sand—their favorite place. Not having the energy to bathe and groom them to remove all the sand that seemed to stick in their fur like Velcro, I pulled them to the main road. Even though the sun had already set and it was dark, there were plenty of streetlights to see clearly by.

While the dogs sniffed every tree and bush we passed, I called my boyfriend, Brian. Being a Saturday evening, and the day after Valentine's Day, no less, I knew he wouldn't be able to answer his cell. His popular Laguna Beach restaurant, Oceana, had a waiting list for every table from Friday through Sunday night. But I wanted to hear his voice, even if it was only his outgoing voice mail message. When his voice mail came on, I left him a message.

"It's me, just checking in. In case gossip is hitting your restaurant already, I wanted to let you know that we're fine, but there was a murder at Tillie's committee event this afternoon. I know you're swamped, but call me when dinner service is over. Maybe we can get together tomorrow? Love and miss you. Bye."

By the time I returned home with Piper and Missy in tow, my best friend, Brad had arrived. I'd texted him during the drive, telling him we needed him for an emergency meeting. Being married to Gabe, I hoped he'd be able to glean information about the investigation to pass on to us.

"What kind of trouble have you gotten yourself in now, cupcake?" Brad wrapped his arms around my waist and gave me a tight hug then reached down to give the begging dogs their due attention. "It's almost like you shouldn't go out in public anymore."

I mock-slapped his muscular arm. "Don't start that, Ruller. Next thing you know, you'll be calling me a murder magnet."

He grimaced. "I won't stoop to your ex-husband's level, I promise."

"I'll hold you to it." The dogs scampered ahead, eager to get some treats, as I pulled him toward Tillie's kitchen. "By the way, I have a huge issue with your husband bringing in another detective to investigate. His name is Detective Reece, and he's just awful. Have you heard of him?"

"Gabe might have mentioned him. A transplant from New York, if I'm not mistaken."

"Yeah, from his accent and attitude, I think you're right. And he's misogynistic to boot."

Tillie appeared at the entry to the kitchen, a filled cocktail glass in her hand. "You two need to come take a seat so we can start our investigation."

I looped my hand through the crook of Brad's arm and tugged him forward. "You'll be our mole and pass on anything you find out from Gabe."

"Oh, gee, thanks. It's been my life's goal to become a mole." Brad took the gimlet from Tillie's hand then bent to kiss her cheek. "Thanks, doll. I think I'm going to need this."

"Not a problem. Vannie made a pitcher of them, so

there's more where that came from." She pointed at me. "Em, do you want one, or shall I make you a cup of tea with brandy? You're probably still in shock."

"I'll skip the alcohol tonight. What if Detective Reece comes to question me?" I shuddered. "Or arrest me? I need to have all my wits."

"Why would he arrest you?" Brad took a sip of his cocktail. "What haven't you told me?"

Actually, I hadn't told Brad much of anything, so I quickly gave him the short version. "Detective Reece was quick to accuse me of the murder. He even had his handcuffs out, ready to arrest me while questioning me."

"You need to tell Gabe exactly what Reece said and what happened." Brad rubbed his palm over the light-golden stubble that covered his cheek. "I'm not sure I should publicly get involved in helping you. I'd hate for this Reece guy to create some kind of problem for Gabe at work because of something I did. He sounds like a jerk."

"See? I told you, being a mole is the best plan." I nudged him with my elbow. "Should I call Gabe right now?"

"Why don't you wait until tomorrow morning? That'll give him a better idea of what's going on with the investigation and what Reece is doing."

Vannie placed a plate of chocolate-chunk cookies on the table. "I spoke with Carrie to let her know what happened today and sent Mother a text. Carrie can't make our meeting, and Mother wants you to send her a detailed email later tonight."

Our mother and stepdad, Lars, were on a Greek isles cruise. With the time difference, we'd been mostly communicating via emails.

"Thanks for letting them know." It didn't surprise me that my twin sister, Carrie, wasn't available. She had three young children, two kittens, and a husband and ran a successful catering company. Managing it all had to create a sleep deficit for her, but she always looked put together and polished, unlike me even on my good days.

My mother had become a happier woman since locating and connecting with Vannie, the daughter she had given up at birth after the father, Tillie's eldest son, had abandoned her. To her everlasting heartbreak, Tillie had never been told about the pregnancy or birth until just a couple of years before.

My mother had even become more accepting of my penchant for finding murder victims. We'd grown closer over the last couple of years, and she'd occasionally help gather information for our investigations. Even though Frances had been one of Tillie's contemporaries, my mother still had a lot of society connections, which might provide useful information… That is, if she were home and not on a cruise ship.

"I'll take notes while we talk." Vannie put her iPad on the long wooden farm-style table and sat down on the bench seat across from me. "Emory, do you have a list of suspects in mind yet?"

"I think Frances should be at the top of the list."

Tillie gaped at me. "Really? I think she was the intended victim."

"At first I thought that too." I held up an index finger. "But think about it. Anyone who hated her enough to murder her had to have known she never eats sugar. Heck, I'm not even sure she eats… ever."

"You make a good point." Tillie took a sip of her gimlet. "Still, you have to admit there are probably at least a few hundred people who would be happy to see her gone."

"What if someone who didn't know her well just snapped and tried to kill her on the spur of the moment?" Brad picked up a cookie and shoved the entire thing in his mouth.

"With poison involved, it had to have been premeditated." I eyed the cookies, chose one, and took a small nibble. It was every bit as good as I'd remembered. The buckwheat flour gave it a nice nutty flavor that complemented the dark chocolate chunks. "Is it possible she found out Ian betrayed her or was only after her wealth when he proposed?"

"I doubt Frances had any illusions about why Ian was with her." Tillie shook her head. "She would have known she was buying his companionship. But maybe something else set her off, if she did indeed do the deed."

"If it was premeditated, then why go through with the farce of announcing the engagement?" Vannie tapped the iPad and entered a note.

"Maybe to throw people off the scent? Now everyone is feeling sorry for her over the loss of Ian, especially since it happened right after their announcement." Tillie furrowed her brows, but nary a wrinkle appeared on her forehead. "We need to talk to Laurie and find out how long their relationship had been going on, especially since his divorce only happened a couple of weeks ago. Emory, you and I can take some cookies and our condolences and drop by to chat with Laurie tomorrow morning. Does eleven work for you? Hopefully, we'll have the opportunity to question Frances while we're there, although she's more likely to toss us out on our ears than talk."

I made a note on my calendar after giving my assent. "Back to our suspect list. If Ian was the intended victim, I think we need to consider Rebecca Hesser, his ex-wife. Even though she departed during the big announcement, she might have left the box of chocolates in Frances's office during the reception. Maybe she didn't care if it were Ian or Frances or both that she poisoned."

"What's the size of the box of chocolates?" Brad asked. "Small enough to fit into a handbag or pocket?"

I twisted my lips as I tried to recall the heart-shaped box. "It definitely wouldn't fit into a pocket, but a large handbag might work. I don't even know what Rebecca looks like. Did either of you notice what kind of bag she was carrying?"

Vannie gazed at Tillie. "Is she the dark-haired woman who wore the blush-pink sheath? It looked a couple sizes too large for her."

"That's the one. She's lost a lot of weight since the last time I saw her. It's probably because of the divorce." Tillie twisted an emerald ring that sat on her middle finger. "She looked pretty anxious and on edge all afternoon long. Maybe she knew Ian and Frances were going to make their announcement, and she wanted revenge. It would explain her anxiety—worrying about whether she could pull it off."

My sister entered the information. "Who else do you think could have killed Ian?"

"There's Paris Allain, great-niece and personal assistant to Frances." My phone rang, and I glanced down at the screen. It was the Newport Beach Police Department. I held my phone up so that everyone could see the caller ID. "Uh-oh. I think I have to answer this, even though I don't want to."

Brad squeezed my arm and motioned for me to answer the call. I did so and put it on speaker.

"Hello?" My voice squeaked, and I berated myself for making my greeting sound so tentative.

"Ms. Martinez, this is Detective Reece. I'm on my way to your house to finish up the interview and want to make sure you'll be there." His gruff voice told me I didn't have a choice.

"As I stated before, I won't talk to you until my attorney can be present." I chided myself for having put off calling her. "Can we schedule something for tomorrow morning, and we'll meet you at your office?"

"It's your prerogative to have legal counsel present, but if you insist on delaying our interview, I have every right to take you into custody now. You can wait for your attorney in a holding cell." His vehicle's blinker sounded tinny over the phone. "And trust me, there will be handcuffs involved if I take you in."

Tillie gasped then slapped her hand over her mouth.

Hopefully, he would think I'd made the noise. "Have it your way. I'm staying with Tillie Skyler, so you can meet me here."

"I'd rather question you at your house."

"There's a killer on the loose, and I don't want to stay alone." I took a deep breath then recited her address. "Press the gate bell, and I'll come let you in."

He snorted. "Fine. Have it your way. I'll be there in five."

# Chapter 8

I wanted to slam my phone onto the table after the detective disconnected the call. Instead, I carefully put it into my pocket and blew out a long breath. "That didn't go very well."

Tillie stood, her fists clenched into balls. "I'm calling Irene right this minute. If she's not available, then I'm sure she'll send one of her associate attorneys right away."

Brad squeezed my shoulder. "I'm sorry to bail on you, but I really can't let Reece find me here. He sounds like a person who'd do something to jeopardize Gabe's career if he thought I was meddling."

"I understand and don't want to put you in a bad position with Gabe." I stood and gave him a hug. "You'd better hurry and sneak out if you can. I wouldn't put it past him to be outside waiting to pounce on me should I try to leave."

Brad's normally tan face paled. "Do you really think he could be out there?"

I shrugged. "Maybe? Just in case, we can get a hat, sunglasses, and a coat for you to wear when you leave."

"Yeah, wearing sunglasses when it's dark outside is not going to be suspicious."

"Good point." I thought for a moment. "I think John left a tweed coat and a wool tam hat in the coat closet. At least wear those and keep the cap low on your forehead. Maybe hunch over a bit and walk with a limp when you leave."

"Okay. Let's suit me up, and I'll get out of here before the detective shows up." Brad led the way to the coat closet.

I pulled John's coat from the padded hanger and handed it to Brad. Next, I fetched the cap from the closet wall hook and placed it on Brad's wavy honey-blond locks. I looked him up and down. "You look pretty dapper."

Brad ran his fingers down the lapel of the coat. "This is really nice. I'll have to get John to bring me one from London next time he comes to visit."

John was Tillie's *special* friend. A real-life baron, he lived in London but frequently traveled to California to spend time with her. John would be happy to have Tillie move across the pond to be with him full-time, but she had her family and life here and wasn't willing to give them up. Nor was he willing to give up his businesses and London lifestyle. Somehow, they'd made their relationship work for over a year.

"I'm sure he'll be happy to do so." I followed Brad as he made his way back to the kitchen. "Don't you need to get out of here?"

"Yes, but I don't want to go barging out the front door. What if Reece is already at the gate? I think I should go out the back and do some reconnaissance before I open the front gate."

"Good point." I slid the glass patio door open. "It's too bad there isn't any other way to leave Tillie's property."

"I could also hop her neighbor's fence and leave by their front gate."

"Better not. They might have their yard and side gates alarmed. You don't want to risk setting one off with the detective already in the area."

"You're right, as always." Brad kissed my cheek then jogged toward the side of the house. "Wish me luck!"

I held up my hand and crossed my index and middle fingers. "Call me later."

He waved and disappeared around the corner.

When I stepped back into the kitchen, Vannie and Tillie were sitting at the table, the dogs curled up beneath.

"Did that detective scare Brad off?" Tillie's mouth turned down at the corners.

"Yes. He didn't want to put Gabe in a bad position by flouting his involvement in our investigation." I picked up another cookie and, this time, crammed the whole thing into my mouth. Maybe the chocolate would calm me. "Did you reach the attorney? Is she on her way?"

Tillie's shoulders slumped, and my heart fell. "What's wrong? Why can't she come?"

"Irene is on vacation in Bali. The answering service will try to contact Irene's assistant, but the service isn't sure when they'll hear from her. Apparently, the assistant's daughter is in labor, and she's at the hospital." Tillie rat-a-tat-tatted her nails on the tabletop. "You know what it's like at the hospital. No cell phones allowed on. I left a detailed message asking that another attorney from Irene's firm call me back immediately, but who knows if the messages will be passed on."

"Is there another attorney from a different firm we can call?" I really didn't want to face the detective without some legal advice.

"Let me go make some calls and see if I can get any recommendations." Tillie pushed back from the table and left the kitchen.

Vannie pushed the plate of cookies toward me. "It's been ten minutes since the detective called. Maybe something else came up and he won't come."

"I hope that's the case." I plucked another cookie from the plate and took a nibble. "For whatever reason, he seems determined to arrest me. There can't be anything but circumstantial evidence, and even then, it could only be since I baked the cupcakes found in Frances's office."

"Maybe you should go down to Brian's and hide out there for a while."

"You mean so the detective can't find me?" I couldn't believe Vannie suggested that course of action.

"That's a splendid idea, Emory." Tillie walked in, rubbing her hands together, and a gleeful grin on her face. "We'll help you go on the lam. Brian can be our go-between and bring you meals and whatnot until the case is solved."

I put my hand up in the stop position. "Even though I'm innocent of the murder, I'm pretty sure I could be arrested later for obstruction of justice. Thanks, but no thanks."

"Irene will be back before that can happen. If anyone can get you out of a jam, it'll be her." Tillie sat beside me and dribbled a bit more gimlet into her glass from the half-full pitcher.

"I will not go on the 'lam,' as you put it." I crooked my fingers to mimic a quote sign. "Besides, if I go into hiding, how am I going to investigate and clear my name? It might take months for the detective to solve the case if we don't help."

"You'd have us to be your eyes and ears." Tillie stuck her lower lip out, as if pouting. "But I see your point."

"Gram, did you have any luck getting a recommendation for another attorney?" Vannie asked.

"I've left messages for just about everyone I know, but so far, no one has come through."

"Thanks for trying. Hopefully, I won't need it." I crossed my fingers beneath the table, adding an extra layer of wishful thinking.

Vannie stood, went to the refrigerator—alerting both dogs —opened it, and gazed in. "What should I fix for dinner?"

I looked at the remaining few cookies left on the plate and

realized I wasn't that hungry any longer. "I'm fine with a salad with some chicken or whatever protein you have."

Piper and Missy jumped to their feet, and with tails wagging, trotted to sit beside Vannie. She patted their heads then shook her finger at them. "You've both had dinner and a treat. No more for you tonight."

Missy barked while Piper sat up, her two front paws perched in front of her body.

I couldn't help but giggle when Tillie jumped up and retrieved their treats from the doggy cookie jar and tossed a couple to them.

"Gram, you really need to stop spoiling them so much. The vet isn't going to be happy with us."

"They're fine. Besides, I cut the treat into quarters, so they didn't eat as much as you think." Tillie scratched their ears. "Right, babies? You cuties are doing just fine."

My mood lightened with the happiness my family and dogs brought to my life. And then the gate bell rang.

# Chapter 9

Heart thumping, I opened the gate cameras on my phone app. It was Detective Reece, and he didn't look happy.

"It's him. What do I do?" Panic gripped me, and my hands shook.

"Go sit in the living room, dear. I'll deal with him." Tillie rose from the chair and stood ramrod straight. "He can't push us around just because he wants to."

I wasn't so sure about that. I took Vannie's hand and pulled her to the living room with me. "Please stay. I really don't want to be alone with that man."

"Gram and I will be right here. He can't kick us out." Vannie gave my hand a squeeze before plopping down on the sofa. When Piper and Missy started barking, she jumped back up. "I'd better take care of them and put them in my room. We don't need to give him any more reasons to be nasty."

Left alone with nothing but my worrisome thoughts, I chewed my thumbnail. I'd rather have had the dogs sitting next to me, providing comfort. They were both experts at it.

Tillie entered the living room, Detective Reece right on her heels. His deep scowl looked thunderous. A wave of revulsion swept over me. He wasn't even respecting her personal space.

"Gabe will be here in a moment. He's in the powder room." Tillie made her way to sit by my side, her posture held regally. "We'll wait until he joins us to have any discussions."

Did that mean that Gabe was still in charge? Was he this man's supervisor? I hoped that was the case. I also couldn't help but notice the conspicuous lack of hospitality being offered. Had it been only Gabe coming to question me, Tillie would have offered coffee, or tea, and Vannie would plate cookies. Detective Reece didn't seem to be worthy of such niceties.

"Gabe! I'm so glad it's you who came instead of that other detective." Vannie's voice came from just outside the room. She froze as she walked through the doorway when she spotted Detective Reece. "Oh. You're both here."

Gabe patted her arm and directed her to sit. "We have a few questions for Emory, but since you're all here, you might be able to answer some questions about other attendees."

"Can I offer you something to drink? Or I have extra chocolate chunk cookies." Vannie started to stand back up.

"We're not here for a social call, Ms. Crawford." Detective Reece practically snarled. "Keep seated until we've finished with you."

"Reece, that is completely unnecessary." Gabe's voice was steady, but his jaw muscles clenched, as if trying to hold in his anger.

"Well, excuse me for doing my job." The detective puffed out his chest, making him seem even more like a bullfrog. "I didn't realize a coffee klatch was called for when interrogating suspects in California."

It took all of my willpower to not bark out a laugh, especially when Vannie looked like she was about ready to do the same. Where did this Neanderthal come from?

Gabe didn't respond immediately. Instead, he remained

silent, seeming to calm himself. Maybe he was counting to twenty? He finally turned to face the arrogant detective. "Didn't the captain just have a conversation with you before we came here? I'd recommend you recall his exact words, or you can leave. Do I make myself clear?"

"I'll let myself out, but mark my words, I'll be letting Internal Affairs hear how this department is operated. It's a disgrace to the uniform." Detective Reece practically stomped from the living room, and within moments, the front door slammed.

"Well, I just…well…" Tillie, never at a loss for words, seemed to flounder for something to say.

"Do you mind if I let Piper and Missy out? They're not too happy about being cooped up in my room, but I was afraid they wouldn't like that guy. Who knows what he would have done if they'd barked and growled at him." Vannie didn't wait to be given permission to stand, and was halfway to the entryway before she'd even finished her sentence.

"Dogs have a good sense about people, don't they?" Gabe's delivery was dry and monotone, but then he broke out in a chuckle. "By all means, let the girls out. I'd love to see them."

While Vannie ran upstairs to release our fur babies, I couldn't help but question Gabe. "Where did he come from, and why is he involved in the case?"

Gabe ran long, elegant fingers through his short golden hair. His amber-colored eyes flashed—with resentment? Irritation? Annoyance? I wasn't sure what emotion he was feeling at the moment. Me? I was feeling all three emotions and more.

"He moved here from New York or Brooklyn or something. He's vague about exactly where. But apparently, it's because his ex-wife got a job out here, and since she has sole custody of their two teen kids, he followed them so he'd be able to see them once in a while."

"It doesn't take a rocket scientist to see why she divorced

him and received sole custody." Tillie rolled her eyes. "Poor woman and kids."

"Yes, well, he's here and resenting every single aspect of it. He hates California, he hates surfers, he hates our feel-good vibes and kumbaya fests. His words, not mine." Gabe dropped his head into his hands. "You get the picture. Anyway, he wants the easiest solution to solving this murder, which seems to be you, Emory."

"What are we going to do about that?" Vannie came back into the living room, following the yips and prancing of two dogs happy to see one of their friends.

Gabe bent down and gave each of them their due adoration. When he sat back up, he seemed more at ease. "Thanks, I needed that. They're instant stress relievers."

"You and Brad should get a dog or two. He can take them to the office so they're not left alone at home all the time," Vannie said.

Brad owned a very successful software gaming company and, as boss of his own firm, could do what he wanted.

"I agree. You need a dog. Maybe even two." I bent over to kiss Piper's head. I'd adopted her when I'd still been married to my ex-husband, but given the long hours he'd worked as a police officer, it made more sense that I took her when we split. Plus, Piper had chosen me over him, which gave me immense pleasure, probably more than it should have. Tillie adopted Missy when a tragic death took her owner. The two dogs instantly became best friends, and in the end, not wanting to separate them, Tillie, Vannie, and I became co-doggy parents. It worked well for all of us.

"We've been talking about taking that step lately." Gabe's cheeks turned a dusky pink. "We thought it might be good practice, you know, being responsible for someone, uh, a pet. Something other than ourselves."

"Oh-em-gee. Are you saying what I think you're hinting

at?" I practically leaped off the sofa and ran to hug Gabe. "Please tell me I'm reading the situation right."

"Maybe? It's early days still." Gabe wouldn't meet my gaze, and his cheeks turned even pinker.

"What are you talking about, Emory?" Tillie's gaze darted from me to Gabe and back again.

I looked at Gabe. "It's up to you. Or would you rather wait?"

"Brad and I only started talking about it. It seems too premature, but we're not getting any younger." He threw his hands up in the air. "In for a penny, in for a pound, right?"

I nodded my encouragement.

He turned his attention to Tillie and Vannie, who seemed mesmerized by our dialogue. "Fine. Here it goes…"

Except Gabe kind of froze. I nudged him. "You can do this. Once it's out, you can get excited."

"Excited about what? Are they having a baby or something?" It finally dawned on Tillie what Gabe's news might be, and she jumped up, clapping her hands. "Should I break out the champagne? Where's Brad? We need to celebrate!"

"Slow down, Tillie." Gabe bounced his hands, palms downward. "We're in the discussion-and-research stage right now. We thought getting a dog first might be a good step in the right direction."

Tears trickled down Tillie's cheeks. "It would make me so happy to hold a great-grandchild of my own."

Technically, Brad and Gabe weren't her grandchildren, but she'd said on many occasions that they were her adopted family, and she treated them as such.

"I'm sorry. I can't say it's going to happen right away, but it could be a reality in the future."

"Make sure it happens sooner rather than later, since my other grandchildren aren't cooperating." She glared at me.

"You have two other grandchildren besides Brian. I don't know why you're pressuring us instead of them." I'd thought

Tillie had given up on trying to get us to 'tie the knot' and procreate, but with Gabe's news, it seemed he'd unleashed her impatience.

"You and Brian are the only ones in a relationship." She shook her finger at me. "Don't go dragging Vannie and Theodore into this. You're responsible for yourself and my grandson."

Behind Tillie, Vannie smirked at me. She'd tolerated my moaning and groaning about feeling pressured to at least move in with Brian—and I really wanted to—but none of the houses we'd looked at suited our needs. I didn't want to be far from Tillie and Vannie. Not only did I love them and the time we spent together, but Brian worked super long and late hours at his restaurant. I didn't want to be so far away that I couldn't pop over for dinner or a movie night without having to spend forty-five minutes driving home. Brian agreed that we both wanted to be within walking distance of Tillie's house, but real estate in the coastal area was scarce and at a premium.

"We're working on finding a house, Tillie." I glanced at Vannie and Gabe, wishing they'd jump in to take the pressure on me. No such luck. "These things take time, and the holidays put us behind, and Brian's restaurant has kept him super busy."

"You both have too many excuses. You just need to take the plunge and get it done."

# Chapter 10

I'd had enough of my relationship with Brian being fussed about, so I changed the subject... back to murder. Which was entirely preferable as long as I wasn't a suspect.

"How is the investigation coming along, Gabe? Aside from Detective Reece thinking I'm a killer." I massaged my temples, the stress of the day finally pushing the tension into a headache.

"It's too early to say. With so many people at the party, it's going to take time." He took out his phone, tapped a few times, then set it on the table beside him. "Do you mind if I record our conversation? It'll be easier for me to reference the details later without having to spend so much time taking notes at the moment."

"You look exhausted, dear." Tillie stood. "Let me get you some coffee, and Vannie can make you a sandwich or something."

He waved her offer away. "I'm fine, thank you. I'd rather get through the interview so I can make it home before midnight."

"Have it your way, but Vannie can package up some

cookies for you to take." Tillie nodded at Vannie, who smiled at Gabe.

"Emory, tell me what you experienced when you arrived at the Allain residence and all the way through when you finally left. I understand you got there a couple hours before the guests?" Gabe crossed his ankles and relaxed back into the armchair.

"Yes. I arrived at one. Well, actually, I entered the house at one ten since Frances never told the guard at the gate that I was coming."

Tillie snorted and muttered, "That figures."

Gabe stopped the recording on his phone, smiled, and winked at Tillie. "Please, no interruptions from the peanut gallery."

Tillie guffawed and, as soon as she settled, Gabe started the recording again. "What happened next, Emory?"

I talked almost nonstop for around ten minutes. Gabe questioned me several times about people I'd seen—specifically Laurie and Paris—at different times of the day. Did he consider them viable suspects? I didn't think they should be at the top of his list.

"Personally, I think the ex-wife, Rebecca Hesser, is the strongest contender for being the killer. She seemed angry enough to leave early and slam the door on the way out. Plus, her handbag was probably large enough to hide a poisoned box of chocolates."

"We'll be questioning her as well, but given the status of the recent divorce, I'm not sure she would have had the opportunity to access Mrs. Allain's office without calling attention to herself." Gabe pointed at Tillie. "Tell me about your relationship with Mrs. Allain. I'm hearing that you had quite a few volatile arguments."

"Does that mean you think she was the intended victim?" Tillie practically rubbed her hands together.

"We're looking into that possibility. But back to my question. Tell me everything you can about her."

And boy, did Tillie have a lot to say. By the time she finished her monologue, I'd almost started feeling sorry for Frances. It sounded like she was a bitter woman who had no friends and had instead racked up more enemies than Tillie could recall.

Gabe tried to keep a passive face, but it seemed like he was a bit shell-shocked. If Frances had been the intended victim, it would be impossible to narrow down a list of suspects, especially if the chocolates were the method of delivering the poison. The chocolates could have been mailed, or hand delivered, or brought to the party by persons unknown. It was daunting to think about, but the alternative of having my cupcakes bearing the poison wasn't something I wanted to dwell on.

"You've given me a lot of information to look into. I'll cross-reference the names with those who attended the party." Gabe rubbed his jaw, and his light beard stubble made a rasping sound. "Vannie, is there anything you saw at the party that was out of place? Or someone acting odd?"

"Not at all. I was helping serve desserts and ferry dirty dishes back to the kitchen. There wasn't much time for me to linger and watch the guests."

"If any of you can think of anything that might be pertinent, no matter how insignificant it might seem, please reach out to me." Gabe stood and stretched his neck sideways. "I'll have another word with the captain and make sure Reece doesn't harass you. For all our sakes, I hope he goes back to where he came from."

After Gabe departed, Vannie started dinner. I poured us glasses of chardonnay, settled at the table, and opened my cupcake catering email app to look through the several emails that had come in during our conversation with Gabe.

I frowned as I read the first email from a customer that

had contracted for two dozen cupcakes the following Saturday. She no longer needed them, and wanted to cancel, and would I please refund her deposit? I nearly dropped the phone when the next two emails were almost verbatim, aside from the date and the customer. The fourth email I opened made me yelp when I read the first paragraph.

*I cannot jeopardize the health and safety of my family and friends by purchasing cupcakes from a poisoner. I demand a full refund of my deposit and expect you to comply within twenty-four hours, or I'll sue you.*

"What is it? Good news or bad news?" Tillie asked as she settled down beside me.

Handing her the phone, I gulped down half the wine.

She scrolled down the email until she got to the end. "That Winifred is such a witch. She's probably the closest anyone has gotten to being a so-called friend with Frances. I'll bet money that Frances is the one spreading the rumor that your cupcakes were poisoned."

"What am I going to do?" I took my phone back and looked at the remaining eight unopened emails. "If the rest of the emails are the same, it'll mean I have twelve order cancelations."

"We can sue Frances for defamation. It would give me great pleasure, and I'd be happy to foot the attorney bill." Tillie swiped on her phone and brought up her attorney's contact information.

"There's only two problems with that." I held up my index and middle fingers. "First, we don't know for sure that someone didn't poison my cupcakes at the party. And two, your attorney is in Bali on vacation."

Somewhere I wished I could be. Right now, warm sun, golden sand, and turquoise waves with Brian by my side sounded heavenly. Instead, I was facing a tanking business and a murder charge.

Tillie clinked her wineglass to mine. "Then our only recourse is to find the actual killer and then sue Frances."

## Chapter 11

A warm arm encircled my waist while a cold, wet nose nudged my hand draped over the side of the bed. Piper whined and nuzzled my hand again.

"Is it morning already?" Brian mumbled against my neck. He'd stumbled in around one in the morning, exhausted after a long day at the restaurant. Typically, after such a busy day, he'd sleep at his own house, which was close to the restaurant. However, after listening to my voice mail message, he'd decided I needed some comfort. He wasn't wrong.

"Go back to sleep. I'll take the girls for a walk then come back and fix breakfast." I rolled out of bed, checked the time —it was only six—and scratched behind Piper and Missy's ears. Their tails wagged, and they pranced off toward the French doors that led to the patio.

"Gram won't be happy unless we join her and Vannie." He threw an arm over his eyes.

"It's still too early for that." I pulled on a pair of leggings and a sweatshirt that extolled the virtues of coffee. "I'll let them know we'll be over around seven thirty."

Brian was already gently snoring by the time I opened the French doors and let the dogs out. We had a doggie door, but after an opossum wandered in during the middle of the night, I kept it closed. Only when we were out for the day and the dogs needed to come and go as needed did I leave it available for them.

The girls ran around the yard, sniffing to see if any critters had visited overnight. Once they'd made their rounds, I snapped leashes onto their collars and headed out for a walk. The morning was chilly, with lingering beach fog that left a misty dampness on my clothes. Scents of salt and seaweed filled my nose, and the bark of a seal, swimming in the harbor behind Tillie's house, was answered by cawing seagulls. The dogs pulled me at a fast clip for the first mile, and then after that, they slowed to sniff every blade of grass and every shrub we passed.

By the time the four of us had gathered in Tillie's kitchen with the two tired dogs, I felt exhausted. More cupcake-order cancelations had come in, although none had been as nasty as Winifred's email. Still, the sting over losing customers was there.

My mood worsened as I picked at the omelet Brian had whipped up and managed only a bite or two of the applesauce muffins I'd baked after coming home from the walk. Vannie refilled my coffee cup without asking, and I didn't even scold Tillie for feeding bacon to the dogs.

"What time do you have to go in to the restaurant?" Tillie placed her well-manicured hand on Brian's muscular forearm. He took the dogs for runs when he had time, as well as surfed every chance he could, to keep fit.

"Not until one. I swapped shifts with our lunch chef, so he's covering brunch for me this morning, and I'll work his shift next Friday."

"That'll be a brutal sixteen-hour day for you." Vannie shuddered. "I thought it was bad enough teaching high schoolers for six hours a day and then coming home and working another two or three hours grading papers and organizing lesson plans. I'm glad I never wanted to be a chef."

"Brutal is right, but it's getting better now that the new chef is on board and up to speed." He downed the rest of his coffee. "I should be able to have more time off, at least during the day."

As much as I wished Brian had regular work hours, I couldn't help but admire his commitment to making Oceana a success.

"How about you, Emory? What are your plans?" Tillie's sly gaze made me suspicious.

"I *had* planned on baking cupcakes, but with all the cancelations, I'm not sure what I'm going to do." I narrowed my eyes at her. "Why? What do you have going on?"

"Maybe you should make some cupcakes or muffins, and we can pay a condolence call on the widow."

"You mean the ex-Mrs. Hesser?"

"I certainly don't mean the newly engaged Frances. She'd kick us to the curb if we showed up."

"Gram, I don't think an ex-wife is called a widow. Will she even want condolences? Maybe she's celebrating." Vannie refilled our coffee cups. Well, actually, they were delicate china teacups, so they needed constant refilling for those of us who needed a lot of caffeine this morning. Tillie preferred the elegant teacups, and we accommodated her desire, for the most part.

"I hate to bring this up, but she will not want any baked goods from me." I scrunched my face up. "Everyone already thinks that I poisoned the cupcakes, so she'd either slam the door in my face or toss the cupcakes in the garbage as soon as we left."

"That's a good point, Em. Then we'll take her a bouquet of sympathy flowers." Tillie took a sip of her coffee.

"Or celebration flowers," Vannie added.

"Here's the plan. We'll leave here at eleven to visit her,

then we'll go out to lunch." Tillie pointed at Brian. "Can you join us?"

"I'm going to pass this time. It would be best if I get to Oceana earlier than I'd planned." He ran fingers through his tousled blond hair that curled at the ends. "Valentine's celebrations have decimated our supplies, and I need to place orders and go through all the paperwork that's piled up."

Disappointment flooded my body, but I tried to hold back from expressing it. I'd hoped Brian and I could spend some time together before he had to go back to work. Instead, I was being pulled away for an investigation to clear my name. I knew it was important, but I couldn't help but feel like it wasn't fair. Would we ever catch a break?

"All right then. I'll text Andrew and have him pick us girls up, and we'll head over to visit Rebecca." Tillie pulled out her cell.

I placed my hand over her cell phone, blocking her access. "Let Andrew have a Sunday off. I'm happy to drive, especially since I have nothing else to do today."

"If you're sure?"

"I'm positive." I pushed back from the table and began stacking plates. "I'll load the dishwasher, then I need to hop into the shower."

Vannie took the dishes from my hands. "Go spend some time with Brian, and we'll see you at eleven."


I WAS a few minutes late meeting up with Tillie and Vannie. Brian had distracted me while I'd been trying to get dressed in something appropriate for a condolence call, and I'd lost track of time. Tillie smirked as I pulled my cherry-red SUV out of the garage and headed toward the PCH.

"You misbuttoned your blouse. Or did my grandson do that?"

Heat flared across my face, and when I came to a full stop

at a traffic light, I saw she wasn't kidding. Both Tillie and Vannie giggled as I pulled to the curb at the first opportunity I found. My fingers fumbled while attempting to rectify my apparel mishap, and I tried to ignore their laugher.

Heading south on the PCH, we made our way to Laguna Beach then turned inland on the 133. I turned right and followed a twisty road as it climbed toward the houses perched on the edge of a cliff. I kept my eyes firmly fixed on the asphalt in front of me, but I knew the ocean views were spectacular the higher we climbed.

"Did you call Mrs. Hesser to let her know we were dropping by?" I gripped the steering wheel tightly as I turned a sharp corner.

"I think it's best if we simply show up. That way she can't decline our visit and won't have a chance to get her story straight if she has something to hide." Tillie dabbed some pale-pink lipstick onto her lips, even though they already appeared fully colored. She wouldn't admit it, but I suspected she'd had color tattooed on since the color never wore off, even when eating and drinking.

"So we're ambushing her." Vannie, sitting in the back seat, said it as a statement and not a question. She shifted the vase of flowers on her lap and leaned forward. "You're taking the lead on this, aren't you, Gram?"

"If you think I should."

"Yes," Vannie and I chorused together.

"She knows you and will hopefully be freer answering your questions." I turned my attention to the residential street I'd just turned onto. The houses were large, although not in the huge mansion category Frances's house was. Rebecca's house was a modern box-style, and from the street, where we parked, it didn't look all that impressive. The smooth concrete walls were painted bright white, while the double garage door and front door were painted midnight black.

We stood in the Mexican-tiled entryway, in front of the

solid wood door. Vannie had pressed the doorbell twice, but still no one came to answer.

"She must not be home." I took Tillie's arm and turned to guide her back to the car. "We'll have to try another time."

A dog yapped, and I thought I saw movement beyond the large, narrow rectangular window at the right of the door. Tillie must've seen the same thing because she marched to the doorbell, pressed it several times, then used her fist to knock. Her persistence was a bit embarrassing, but I hoped it gave us results.

# Chapter 12

T he front door inched open, and a nose and a tumble of dark hair was all that could be seen from where we stood.

"Matilda, what are you doing here?" Rebecca's voice was low, raspy, and she seemed to be trying to keep her volume down.

"We're here to pay our condolences, of course." Tillie grabbed the flowers from Vannie and thrust them at Rebecca. Rebecca's hands instinctively came up to take the vase, and that's when Tillie pushed the door open and stepped into the house.

As daylight hit Rebecca's face, it became apparent she was much older than I'd thought, given her dark-brown hair. Despite the Botox, obvious fillers, and other surgeries she'd had done to stop the ravages of time, she still looked elderly and frail. Or perhaps the angst of going through a divorce had aged her, and then to lose her ex-husband to murder wouldn't have been easy. I couldn't help but wonder if she'd been left in financial difficulty from the divorce, then remembered Ian had been having money troubles before he'd died.

Maybe the ex-Mrs. Hesser had her own fortune and hadn't needed to rely on her husband.

"Why don't you come in and make yourself comfortable, Matilda?" Rebecca's icy voice dripped with sarcasm. "And while you're at it, you might as well bring the entire Scooby-Doo gang with you. I'd been warned you'd show up, but honestly, I thought you'd have a little more decorum than this."

"Whatever do you mean, Rebecca?" Tillie raised her shapely eyebrow. "It's simply good etiquette to bring flowers or food to the recently bereaved, even for the death of an ex."

"I appreciate you skipping the food since the last time your…"—she lifted her nose and swept her haughty gaze over me—"your people delivered food, someone ended up poisoned."

"There's no proof Emory brought poisoned cupcakes. It very well might have been the box of opened chocolates that killed Ian." Tillie's tone matched the haughtiness of our reluctant hostess. "Anyway, we've brought flowers and would like to offer our condolences."

"Thank you." She flicked her fingers toward the still-open door. "Now you can leave."

This wasn't going according to plan, and I didn't see how Tillie could maneuver us into a sit-down conversation. As for me, I wanted to slink out the door and head back home. Vannie seemed to have felt the same, if her hangdog expression was any sign.

"Trust me. You're going to want to hear what we have to say." Tillie tapped the side of her nose. "In case you didn't know, the detective in charge is a very close friend, and we spent some time with him last evening. It was very enlightening, if you know what I mean."

I'd been at that conversation with Gabe, and I had no idea what Tillie was talking about.

Whatever it was, Rebecca seemed to bite. She moved to

the front door, closed it—rather forcefully, in my opinion—and motioned for us to follow her deeper into the house.

As we walked toward the back of the house, the open floor plan rooms held stunning views of the distant ocean. The house, from the front, hadn't looked all that large, but now that we were inside, I could see that the appearance had been deceptive. A staircase led up to another level, and another staircase led downward. Rebecca showed us to a dining room that opened onto a patio. Hillside views filled most of my vision, but a sliver of the ocean and Catalina Island could be seen from the room. I imagined that from the patio, the view would be even grander.

"I suppose etiquette dictates I offer you some coffee, or would you prefer tea?" Rebecca's mouth pressed into a grim, straight line.

"We'd hate to impose, but tea sounds lovely." Sweetness practically oozed from Tillie's mouth. "I've heard you have a delightful tea blended specifically for you, if it's not too much trouble."

"It would be a pleasure, *Matilda*." From her gritted teeth and the narrowing of her eyes, I was certain it was anything but a pleasure. Still, Rebecca left us and went to the kitchen where the sounds of a teakettle being filled with water and crockery clacking together could be heard.

"What are you doing, Gram? You should've jumped in with the questions while you had the chance instead of wasting time on tea." Vannie glanced over her shoulder toward the kitchen area then lowered her voice. "If she's the one who poisoned Ian, I don't want to drink any of her tea."

I gulped. Vannie had made an excellent point.

"She'll pour from a teapot in front of us, so wait for her to take the first sip." Tillie put her index finger to her lips for a moment then sat back against the sofa cushions as if relaxed.

Rebecca appeared in the doorway. "I suppose you'll want some shortbread with the tea?"

"Please don't go to any trouble, dear. We're meeting some friends for lunch after our visit with you."

She trudged back to the kitchen, but not before throwing eye daggers at Tillie.

It seemed to take an inordinate amount of time for Rebecca to show back up, carrying an ornate tea tray. Besides a silver teapot, she'd stacked pink floral china teacups and saucers, along with cream, sugar, and lemon. After setting the tray down on the glass dining table in front of us, she poured amber liquid into four tea cups. Once I had the teacup in hand, I waited impatiently for Rebecca to take a few sips before I tasted the tea. Instead of drinking her tea, she added milk and sugar then lazily stirred it before setting her cup and saucer onto the table.

Vannie gave me a quick glance, her eyes wide. Had Rebecca poisoned the tea?

"Well, aren't you going to drink your tea, Matilda? I made it especially for you."

"It's still a bit too hot for me, dear, and I really don't want to dilute the lovely fragrance with milk or lemon." Tillie lifted the cup to just below her nose. "There's a hint of jasmine and rose. Can you tell me where you purchase the tea?"

"Oh, for heaven's sake, Matilda. I didn't poison the tea, and I didn't poison my ex-husband either." Rebecca picked up her teacup and took a healthy swallow of the floral tea. "See? It's safe to drink."

"I didn't think you poisoned Ian. Whoever did it wanted to make it seem like either you did it or poor Emory here." Matilda took a tentative sip of tea then set her cup down. "They went for trying to frame obvious suspects."

Rebecca glared at me. "For all I know, your girl did it, but maybe she was targeting Frances for you and accidentally killed Ian instead."

I'd just taken a small mouthful of the still-hot tea. At her words, I sputtered and choked as I tried to swallow, but most of the tea dribbled down my chin. My voice wheezed as I struggled to get the words out. "I didn't poison my cupcakes."

"Of course you didn't, dear." Tillie handed me a linen napkin from the tray. "Everyone who knew Frances knew she didn't eat sugar, so Ian must've been the intended victim. Did you deliver those poisoned Valentine chocolates to Frances's office, Rebecca? The box would have fit nicely into your Hermès handbag, and then you could have snuck it into the office and left the chocolates for him to find."

"Of course I didn't do that. Don't be trying to pin the crime on me."

"If not you, then who else would have wanted to kill your ex-husband?" Tillie picked up a clean napkin and dabbed at her lips. I noticed neither Tillie nor our hostess had sipped more tea. Was something wrong with it? Vannie hadn't bothered drinking any of it either. I set my cup down just in case.

"He financially ruined his former business associate, William Dalton, by making extremely risky investments. Maybe his wife, Geri, did the deed."

"Would either of them have been in contact with Ian recently?" I asked.

She shrugged. "I've had as little to do with my ex as possible over the last ten months, but I seem to recall Geri was on a committee with Frances some time ago. I don't recall what it was, but that might have been a way for the Daltons to connect with Ian."

Rebecca pointed at Tillie. "Did the police confirm he ingested the poison during the event, or could he have consumed something earlier and he just happened to have died at the party?"

Hope sprang in my chest. Maybe we'd jumped to the wrong conclusion, and no one at the event had anything to do with his death. My name would be exonerated, and my clients would come back for cupcakes. Still, since we were here and had Rebecca talking, we needed to ask as many questions as possible.

"We haven't heard the official cause of death yet, nor the delivery method of the poison," Tillie capitulated.

Afraid I'd put Rebecca's guard up, I tried to be as delicate as I could. "How long did Frances and Ian know each other?"

"You mean how long did it take for Ian to snare Frances and her wealth?" Rebecca chortled. "He started wooing her about six months ago, probably thinking he'd land the goose that lay the golden egg and all his money troubles would be over. I may not care for Frances, but she's no dummy. There's no way she'd let Ian get his paws on her money and she'd have had him on a very short leash had the wedding gone through. It would have been a very rude awakening for him, had he lived."

"Can you think of any reason Frances might have wanted Ian dead?" I asked.

Rebecca practically cackled. "Maybe not this early in their relationship, but given enough time, she would have eventually wanted to kill him."

## Chapter 13

After her declaration, Rebecca had all but thrown us out. She'd made a good point that we couldn't jump to the conclusion that Ian had been poisoned at the party. I crossed my fingers, hoping she was right. It would solve so many problems.

"After lunch, let's check in with Gabe and see if they've determined how Ian had been poisoned and with what." Tillie looked down at her phone and tapped several times. "After that, I say we try to drop in on William and Geri Dalton and see what they have to say. I'm texting an acquaintance to see if they can track down their address."

"Gram, do you even know them? We can't just go barging in." From my vantage from the rearview mirror, Vannie's face appeared pinched.

"I know Geri from the philharmonic fundraiser a few years ago. We can use the excuse that we're looking for sponsors for next year's annual event."

"But weren't they financially ruined by Ian?" Rebecca had imparted more information than I'd thought she'd provide, given her reception when we'd first shown up. I was pretty certain I'd heard that bit of information correctly.

"There's financially ruined and then there's financially inconvenienced for a while. I'm guessing it's the latter."

"But what if Ian left them destitute? Mrs. Dalton is going to slam the door on your face when you ask for a sponsorship." Vannie placed her hand on my shoulder. "We should probably pick up more flowers to take if Gram is insistent about barging in."

Tillie picked up her phone and read an incoming text. "Hmm… I might be wrong. They're not living in Laguna Beach any longer. Looks like they've downgraded and are living in Chino Hills."

"Isn't that a forty-five-minute drive or longer if traffic is bad?" I saw my afternoon slipping away, not that I had much of anything going on.

"Yeah, Gram. We really don't want to drive all the way out there if they're not home or don't want to talk to us."

I glanced at my sister from the rearview mirror again. Her mouth had turned downward, and her brows had drawn together. Generally, she was very amiable to whatever hijinks Tillie planned, and this was the first time I'd heard her disagree.

Tillie sighed. "You girls might have a point. Fine. We'll head back home after lunch, and I'll connect with some of my contacts to see if I can learn anything about the Dalton's financial woes and how best to interrogate them."

I glanced back at Vannie. She seemed a bit happier, and her face had relaxed.

"You okay back there, sis?" I asked.

"Yep." Vannie looked out the side window and refused to meet my gaze in the mirror.

Something was definitely up with her, but now wasn't the time to pry. I'd ask Tillie first before I questioned my sister, who was a very private person. Tillie had hinted that something tragic had happened to Vannie—besides her adoptive parents being murdered—but so far, my sister had never shared with either of us.

"Do you want fajitas for lunch, or should we stop for burgers and milkshakes?" I pulled my attention back to the road.

"I'd be happy with In-N-Out," Vannie answered. "Is that okay with you?"

"You won't catch me turning that choice down." My mouth watered at the thought of a juicy cheeseburger and an ice-cold creamy chocolate shake.

"It's fine with me, but I'll skip the milkshake," Tillie said.

After a highly satisfying lunch, I took the dogs for an extra-long walk to the beach. They loved chasing the gulls, digging in the sand, smelling clumps of dying seaweed, and splashing in the waves. I'd have to spend an hour bathing them then combing out their curly fur to remove all the sand, but it was worthwhile after seeing their happiness.

As we walked, I couldn't help but worry about my sister, especially when Tillie said Vannie wouldn't talk to her about whatever had been bothering her. After watching the dogs and their antics for a while, I felt the tension fall from my shoulders. I should have invited Vannie to join me. Instead, I'd watched as she hurried to her car and drove off, claiming she had errands to run.

Tillie sent me a text letting me know she had scheduled a meeting with a 'contact' for dinner to get the scoop on the Daltons. She couldn't reach Vannie but would appreciate if I could go with her.

I whistled for the romping dogs, then I clipped the leashes on when they came and hurried home to prepare for another round of interrogations.


AFTER INSISTING I drive us to dinner so that Andrew could continue to enjoy his Sunday—Tillie paid him handsomely to be on call, but I still felt guilty bothering him—we arrived at the Newport Cove Country Club. It boasted an imposing wood, stone, and glass edifice outside, while the inside held richly detailed wood and sumptuous brocades that reflected the feel of a colder climate. Almost the entire back wall of the clubhouse had been fashioned from glass and overlooked the rolling green grass of the golf course.

Tillie wouldn't tell me who we were meeting, so after being seated, I scanned the room of diners. Most were at least middle-aged or much older, but there were a few younger couples out for romantic dinners. These couples sat in cozy corner banquettes with sparkling crystal and fluttering candles.

"Mrs. Skyler, it's so good to see you." A handsome man in his late-twenties stopped by our table. He wore a black suit with a white button-down shirt. A dimple appeared in his cheek as his smile widened.

"Vince! You rascal. I haven't seen you in ages." Tillie stood and kissed his cheek. "You remember Emory, don't you?"

"How could I forget those delectable muffins and breakfast while discussing murder?" Vince winked at me then brushed his long wavy dark-brown bangs away from his eyes. "Do you have another investigation going on?"

"You know it, kiddo." Tillie looked around the dining room. "Why aren't you behind the bar? Or are they having their most talented bartender fix cocktails tableside now?"

"You've been out of the loop, haven't you?" He tugged his coat sleeve down. "I finally graduated with my restaurant management degree, and when the dining room manager position opened, I got the job."

"Congratulations!" Tillie gave him a hug. "I've been here off and on for bridge, but I've been pretty busy, especially with the holidays and family. I'm sorry I missed hearing about your promotion."

"They kept it under wraps until Friday, which was my first

day on the job, so it's no wonder you hadn't heard yet." Vince walked around the table and began clearing the extra place setting.

"You can leave that. We're waiting for Edwina Gertz. She'll be joining us tonight."

He deftly put the flatware back in its correct positions. "I'll let them know at the front, but in the meantime, can I bring you a cocktail or a bottle of wine?"

Since I was driving, I ordered sparkling water, but Tillie ordered her usual gimlet.

"You got it, Mrs. Skyler. I'll bring it right over." Vince turned to leave but then stopped and waved to someone at the entrance of the restaurant. "Your victim just got here. Do you need me to get her liquored up so she's freer with her information?"

Tillie jokingly slapped his hand. "You naughty boy. She's my informant, so let's keep her coherent tonight."

"Your wish is my command." Vince waited until Edwina reached the table then pulled her chair out for her. "Mrs. Gertz, I'm so glad you could join us this evening. May I bring you a cocktail or the wine list?"

"A cup of black coffee will be sufficient." She turned her back on him without even a thank you.

I'd forgotten how entitled some members seemed to be, especially after spending so much time with Tillie. She was nothing but gracious and kind to everyone she met, no matter their station in life. Well, she could dish out the attitude when called for, but that was rare. I had a feeling it was going to be a long, uncomfortable dinner with me biting my tongue to keep from being rude to Mrs. Gertz.

# Chapter 14

After an awkward introduction to me—awkward because Mrs. Gertz barely acknowledged me, and not because of Tillie—Tillie carefully broached the subject of William and Geri Dalton.

"I haven't seen the Daltons at the club in a while. Are they still members?" Tillie thanked Vince for the gimlet as he delivered all three of our beverages to the table. I smiled at him and thanked him as well. Mrs. Gertz remained stone-faced.

When Vince was out of hearing distance, Mrs. Gertz turned her gaze to Tillie. "Really, Matilda. You don't need to be so familiar with the staff. And please, never gossip in front of them. They're all terrible about keeping confidences, and everything they hear gets spread around like a communicable disease."

I stifled a giggle. No one gossiped more than the country club's bridge-playing matrons.

"But back to your question about the Daltons." A sly smile crossed Mrs. Gertz's face. "They had to sell their membership and their gorgeous home in Laguna about six months ago. Apparently, William made some terrible investments, and then his mother, bless her soul, had major medical expenses that weren't covered by insurance, so they had to pay, and they lost just about everything."

"That's terrible." Tillie placed a hand over her heart. "Where did they move to?"

"You'll never believe it, but they slunk off to Chino Hills." Mrs. Gertz covered her mouth with her hand, and her heavily penciled-in eyebrows rose toward her thin bleached-blonde hair line.

She was a bit overly dramatic for my tastes, but if she gave us some good insights into who killed Ian, I could endure.

"Why there?" Tillie took a sip of her gimlet.

"They moved in with his mother, of all things. A small three-bedroom tract home." Mrs. Gertz shuddered. "Can you imagine?"

"Poor dears," Tillie tsked.

"Geri invited me over for a visit, but truly, I can't think of anything ghastlier." She sipped her cooling coffee. "His mother is hooked up to oxygen and just sits around waiting to die. I don't need to be around that kind of negativity."

Tillie would get a piece of my mind when we left this enti-tled witch. She must've read my mind because she squeezed my knee beneath the table then gave me a firm pat.

"Such a tragedy." Tillie hesitated a beat, perhaps to see if Mrs. Gertz would add anything else, but when she didn't, she continued her questioning. "I heard William had been a busi-ness partner with Ian Hesser, who also had financial difficul-ties lately. Is that what happened with the Daltons?"

"I've heard rumors that there's a connection." Mrs. Gertz leaned in, and her eyes lit up. "Was it Ian who instigated the investment? Tell me what you know."

"It's all speculation at this point." Tillie rolled her wrist until her palm faced upward. "I've heard so many versions it's difficult to tell what is fact and what is fiction."

The way Mrs. Gertz gripped Tillie's arm, I didn't think she cared what version she received. "And with Ian murdered, you think William had something to do with his death? Am I right, or am I right?"

"You may be on to something, Edwina." Tillie waited until our server passed out the menus, recited the dinner specials, and left to attend to other guests before continuing the conversation. "We're looking into a variety of scenarios, but since you're friends with Geri, I thought you might shed some light on their relationship with Ian."

"I know you like to stick your nose in where it doesn't belong, Matilda, but shouldn't the police be handling this matter?" Mrs. Gertz tsked. "It's truly unseemly for someone of your standing in the community to get involved in something so tawdry."

"I was there when the murder happened, along with Emory and my granddaughter, which makes this personal." Tillie glanced over at me and paused a moment, as if to collect her thoughts. "The police are looking at the wrong people, so I feel like I'm doing my duty to the community to unearth information so that the police can do their job properly."

Mrs. Gertz noticed Tillie's gaze on me. She snapped her fingers. "You're that cupcake baker who killed her husband's lover. And now you're involved in another murder?"

Technically, I'd been involved in investigating a lot more murders than just Tori's, my ex-best friend and yes, my ex-husband's fling. But I wasn't about to admit to it now. "No, I absolutely did not kill her, or anyone, for that matter. The perpetrators were caught and are serving a long prison sentence."

Mrs. Gertz narrowed her pale, washed-out blue eyes at me, causing her wispy fake eyelashes to flutter against her skin. "Your son must be quite distraught over the company you keep, Matilda. If you were my family, I'd be doing something about the riffraff hanging on. I'm sure she's after your money, so you'd better watch your purse and your back."

I'd put up with this attitude on multiple occasions, so I liked to think I'd developed a thick skin and could ignore it. Tillie, on the other hand, suffered no fools and always stood up to their condescending attitudes and protected my reputation. I could see Tillie getting ready to lay into Mrs. Gertz, which I feared would jeopardize any chance we had of getting information on the Daltons.

"I'm sorry my past circumstances have caused you distress, so I'll excuse myself. My intent is nothing but gratitude for Tillie's friendship, and I would do nothing to abuse her trust." I nudged Tillie beneath the table then stood. "I'll leave you to enjoy your dinner together."

"Thank you, Emory. Tell Vince to order your dinner to go and charge it to my account." Tillie's cheeks had turned vivid red, and I could tell she was struggling to keep her anger at bay.

"Don't rush dinner on my account. Just text me when you're ready for me to drive you home." Without waiting for a reply, I slowly made my way to the front of the restaurant. I wouldn't give Mrs. Gertz the satisfaction of seeing me scurry away like a rodent.

Vince waved me over to the bar. His brows drew together until lines appeared in the middle of his forehead. "I take it Mrs. Gertz didn't approve of you socializing with her?"

"Something like that. She took exception to me being suspected of murdering my ex-husband's lover." I held up my hand in the stop position. "Which I was completely exonerated for."

"I'm surprised Mrs. Skyler didn't tell her where to stick her opinion." Vince chuckled. "Mrs. S. sure is a firecracker."

"You can say that again." I gazed around to make sure no one was listening to our conversation. "Tillie would've laid into her, but we're after information about the death of Ian Hesser. If I have to suffer some humiliation to get it, then so be it."

"You're a better person than I." Vince tilted his chin up to acknowledge a server trying to get his attention. "What would you like for dinner? You can sit at the bar, and I'll keep you company while you eat."

"I'll take the quesadilla with an extra side of guacamole." I pulled out a barstool and sat. "But don't worry about keeping me company. I have a book on my phone to read until Tillie is ready to go."

"I'll leave you to it, then." Vince hurried away to take care of whatever issue had cropped up with the server while I opened my phone and got lost in the latest cozy mystery I'd been reading.

# Chapter 15

On the drive home, Tillie told me about her interrogation of Mrs. Gertz. "I can't tell you how much I wanted to throw my gimlet in her face. The nerve of that woman treating you like that."

"It's all right. I hope you contained yourself and could use her attitude against me to your advantage." I pulled to a stop at a traffic light and studied her profile. Her lips were in a grim line, and her shoulders hunched over. "Don't stress out. I had a relaxing dinner at the bar and Vince took good care of me. Tell me what you found out about the Daltons."

"Edwina drove a hard bargain, but she eventually made an appointment for me to have lunch with Geri tomorrow. You'll be able to join me, won't you?" Tillie checked her phone screen. "I sent a text to Andrew. He'll drive us out there."

"What did you have to promise to Mrs. Gertz?" I hoped it wasn't anything too onerous.

Tillie blew out a raspberry. "I'm sponsoring a table at her fundraising gala for the Spinnaker sailing club. Don't get me wrong, I love contributing to worthy causes, but this is nothing more than a bunch of wealthy people raising money to send their wealthy kids and grandkids to a pretentious sailing camp that shuns diversity."

"I'm sorry. Is there any way you can fill the table but skip the gala yourself?"

"Edwina considered that factor and made me promise I'd attend."

Tillie was a considerable force in the community, and it would be a feather in Mrs. Gertz's cap to have her touted as sponsoring the event and then attending in person. She'd probably even garner new contributors on Tillie's name alone.

"When is the event?" I hoped it wasn't anytime soon. We had enough on our plate.

"Not until October. They're fundraising for next year's summer camp."

"Maybe there's a way to get out of it before then." The light turned green, finally, and I followed the line of cars as we merged onto the PCH. For a Sunday evening, traffic was busy. "Did you find out anything else about the Daltons?"

"William is not well-liked. He's brash and pushy in demanding his own way on anything and everything. Losing his financial independence was a tremendous blow to his ego, and he actually took a baseball bat to Ian's car shortly after their investments were decimated."

"Whoa. It sounds like he has anger management issues." Pressing down on the blinker stalk, I switched lanes to get around a slowpoke. "I'm very interested in finding out if he's had any recent interactions with Ian."

"According to Edwina, she thinks he's buried himself out in Chino Hills, drinking himself to death, and has cut all ties with everyone he knows. She thinks he's depressed and should check into rehab." Tillie huffed. "As if that doesn't cost money."

"What about Mrs. Dalton? After losing her home, their financial independence, and her husband in a funk, could she have exacted revenge?"

"That, my dear, is why we're having lunch with her tomorrow." She checked her phone again. "Andrew just confirmed. He'll pick us up at ten thirty. Wear a nice, professional outfit. We'll say you're my assistant, so hopefully you won't get tossed out from another meal again."

When we got home, we found Vannie's car parked in its usual curbside spot. I'd offered to let her share the garage with me, but she declined, saying she didn't want her comings and goings to bother me with the garage door going up and down all the time.

"I think I'll go in with you and check on Vannie." I gazed longingly toward my charming pool house and wanted nothing more than to pull on some cozy flannel pajamas, pour a glass of wine, and finish my book. But my sister took priority. As long as she'd talk to me. She wouldn't tell me to get lost, would she?

I opened the door from the garage that led into my home and called for the dogs. They were sitting by their food bowls, tails wagging. I'd fed them dinner before Tillie and I left for her club. They were simply trying to make me feel guilty. "Come on, you two. You can have a treat at Tillie's."

They shot past me and trotted to sit at Tillie's feet. The words Tillie and treats were synonymous. She bent to give them scratches then clipped on the leashes I handed her. While it was probably safe enough to let them follow us across the alleyway unleashed, we'd seen an increase in coyote sightings in our area, and I didn't want to risk one of our sweet girls getting attacked.

"Vannie's been out of sorts for a couple of weeks, even though she tries to hide it." Tillie punched in the security-gate code. "She hasn't responded to any of my questions, but maybe you'll have better luck getting her to open up."

"You don't think she regrets moving here, do you?" Having Vannie living and working close by was the best thing that had happened to our family. I'd be devastated if she decided she wanted to move back to her teaching position in Spain. Maybe she missed being abroad.

Piper and Missy scurried to the kitchen for treats. Instead of following, I climbed the stairs and made my way to Vannie's bedroom. Light shone from beneath the door, so I gently knocked.

"Come in." Her voice was faint, but I took comfort that she at least answered.

Opening the door, I stuck my head into the room. Vannie sat at her desk, halfway turned toward the door. "Are you busy? Can I come in?"

"I'm just grading essays and can use a break." She gestured at the twin armchairs upholstered in shades of turquoise and blue. They sat in the corner, next to a large window that overlooked the bay. She stood and stretched her arms overhead before coming to sit next to me. "Did you make any more progress on the case?"

"We had dinner with one of Tillie's acquaintances at the club. What an odious woman, but at least she got us a lunch appointment with the wife of Ian's business partner." I surreptitiously studied my sister. Her eyes were a little red-rimmed, but she didn't seem as tense as she'd been earlier in the day.

"When are you meeting her?" Vannie stood and pulled two bottles of water from the minifridge built into the morning kitchen and handed one to me. Her room was an extra-large suite, complete with the morning kitchen, a huge walk-in closet, and a spa-like bathroom. She'd decorated it in cool, soothing ocean hues and had two seascape paintings hanging on her walls. I found it relaxing.

"Tomorrow. Andrew is picking us up at ten thirty." I swallowed a swig of water. "I wish you could join us."

"Me too. Investigating a murder sounds a lot more fun that handing out the graded essays." She rolled her eyes. "Most of the students won't be thrilled with their grade, but I gave them fair warning the test was coming and what I expected from them."

Vannie taught high school English, and she was less impressed by American students than the kids she'd taught abroad. I think she'd called her current students spoiled and entitled a time or two. Given the treatment I'd received at the club that evening, it was easy to see where the kids learned that attitude from.

"Are you doing okay?" I reached over and grasped her hand. "You seemed tense and upset this afternoon."

She shrugged but wouldn't meet my gaze. "I'm fine."

"You know you can tell me anything. I'm a good listener and hugger, even if I don't have an answer or know what to say."

"I know, and I appreciate hearing that." This time, Vannie lifted her gaze to meet mine. Tears glittered in her eyes, but she blinked them away. "It's just that it's the anniversary of my parents' death this week. It's bringing back a lot of terrible memories of that time, and then I feel guilty about grieving them when I've found such a loving family with all of you. I don't want you, and especially Tillie, to think I'm ungrateful for you."

I lifted my arms and pulled her into a hug. "It's natural for you to grieve for the people who gave you a wonderful home with love and affection for so many years. In no way does that take away from what we feel for you or you being a part of our family."

"I know, but it's hard to not get emotional about it. The last couple of years, I've traveled and kept myself so busy I didn't have time to dwell on the memory." She swiped her palms over her eyes then grabbed a tissue. "But now I'm here with all of you, and I didn't want to talk about it because it makes their loss feel more real. Even after all this time."

"I can't imagine how devastating it must've been to lose your family like that. If they were still alive and we'd connected with you, I know for certain your parents would have become as much a treasured part of our family as you have." I handed her another tissue and took one for myself. "Maybe by talking about them and not bottling up your memories and emotions, it'll get easier over time."

"Maybe. I'll try." Another tear rolled down her cheek.

"Would it be easier to talk to a professional? Someone who doesn't have an emotional connection to you or the situation?"

"That might be a good place to start. It's time to admit to myself that I've been doing nothing but running from what happened without resolving how it impacted me." Vannie leaned over and gave me a quick hug. "Gram will know who I should talk to."

I let out a giggle. "She knows everything and everyone."

She smiled at me. "Thanks for listening. You gave me good advice, and I'm sorry I've caused worry for you and Gram."

"We only worry because we love and care about you." I stood when Vannie's stomach growled. "Why don't you come down to the kitchen with me? I'll fix you some dinner, or if you'd rather, I'll bring you something up to eat."

"I'll come down. It's time I put Gram's mind at ease and let her know what's been going on with me."

By the time Vannie ate and had shared her confidences with Tillie, she'd relaxed even more and seemed almost back to her cheerful self. And Tillie, just as we'd predicted, knew exactly who Vannie should talk to and had an appointment set up before we said good night.

## Chapter 16

Our lunch appointment with Mrs. Dalton didn't get off to a good start. She'd given us the name of the restaurant to meet her at Bella Napoli but neglected to tell us there were two locations in town. We sat in a red pleather booth for thirty minutes, waiting for her to show, when Tillie received a text from Mrs. Dalton.

Riddled with misspellings, the message was quite curt.

**Are you coming to restrant or knot? Ive been wating long thyme.**

Tillie quickly sent off a reply. It took a bit longer to receive an answer, giving us what we hoped was the correct address. We double-checked with the hostess just to be sure before we got into the car.

By the time we made it across town to the correct restaurant, Mrs. Dalton appeared to have consumed several glasses of red wine and no food. No wonder her text message had been chaotic.

She was a diminutive woman and, as typical amongst her former country-club peers, her face had endured multiple visits to a plastic surgeon. Her bleached-blonde hair would have been better suited to someone half her age or younger.

Her hands, which gripped a nearly empty wineglass, showed age spots, and the wrinkles on her chest gave a more accurate measure of her true age. I guessed she was at least in her early seventies.

"I apologize, Geri. It was our error by not confirming the address." Tillie tilted her head toward the hostess and mimicked bringing a utensil up to her mouth. I got the hint.

I left Tillie at the table, where she began pouring water into glasses and urging the intoxicated woman to drink. Intercepting the hostess before she could tend to a group walking through the front door, I quickly ordered lasagna, tortellini Alfredo, and a Caesar salad with garlic bread for the three of us to split, along with some coffee. If Mrs. Dalton wanted something else, we could order it when they brought the food to our table. Most important was getting some food and water down her before she became incoherent, if it wasn't already too late.

Quickly, I used the ladies' room, and when I returned to the table, I was happy to see that the coffee, salad, and bread had already been delivered. Mrs. Dalton's voice was overly loud, and her words slurred around the edges. Hadn't Mrs. Gertz told us that Mr. Dalton had a drinking problem? Had she meant Mrs. Dalton, or had both of them succumbed to alcohol as an escape from their problems? In any event, we couldn't let her get behind the wheel of a car in this state.

"There you are. I've been waiting to introduce you." Tillie's tone was a bit imperious, but I knew better than to take it seriously. She was playing her part of a snobbish socialite while I was the downtrodden assistant. However, given the level of Mrs. Dalton's intoxication, I wondered if it was even necessary.

"I apologize for the delay. I wanted to make sure the kitchen rushed the order after making you both wait so long for lunch." With my eyes downcast, it was difficult to see if Geri had any reaction to my presence.

"Well, sit down now and stop dillydallying." Tillie motioned at the dark wood chair that had been positioned at the far edge of the table. The two women sat in plush, over-stuffed chairs on opposite sides of the table. Leather-bound menus sat to the side of them. This was the classier restaurant than the first one we'd waited at. "You can serve our salads."

"Yes, Mrs. Skyler." I quickly added Caesar salad to two plates along with a slice of garlic bread and placed it in front of them. After they'd been served and began eating, I carefully served myself.

"I'm so glad you could join me today, Geri." Tillie sat her fork down and wiped her mouth with the thick white napkin. "Edwina told me about the downturn in your living situation, and I wanted to see if there was anything I could do to help."

"I'm sure Edwina is gloating over our misfortune. She doesn't have a single kind bone in her body and wouldn't offer assistance even if her life depended on it." Geri speared a piece of lettuce. "I've heard some nice things about you, though. Why *did* you make the trip all the way out here?"

"My visit has nothing to do with Edwina. I truly am concerned about you."

"That's very kind of you, Matilda." Geri edged a piece of garlic bread away from her salad, but didn't eat it. "You're the first person I've heard from since we left the club."

Tillie forked another dainty bite of salad then leaned in toward Geri. "You've probably heard about the untimely demise of Ian Hesser?"

"Ha! That snake got what was coming to him." She reached for the wine bottle and tried to pour more into her empty wineglass. Nothing but a dribble fell into the goblet. She turned her glazed eyes in my direction. "Order us another bottle, will ya?"

"You've probably had enough to drink for now." Tillie gently pried the wine bottle from her hands. "Our meal will be here soon, and I'd like to talk about Ian."

"All you need to know about him is that he's a snake. When he's in the ground, I'm gonna go dance on his grave." Geri tilted her wineglass and swallowed the dribble of wine.

I tried to keep my expression neutral, but this woman sounded unhinged. Did she have the wherewithal to plan and execute Ian's murder? Neither Gabe nor Brad had answered the text I'd sent them that morning. I still knew nothing about the poison Ian had ingested or what the delivery method had been.

"Can you tell me how Ian talked William into making such a foolish investment? They were business partners for a while, weren't they?" Tillie kept her voice low, as if to soothe Geri.

"They started Consolidated Investments, a financial consulting firm, together a couple of years ago. William put a lot of money into getting it going, but until a year ago, it seemed like it was doing well, and they had a lot of clients." Geri eyed the wine bottle then gulped down the water Tillie had poured for her.

The server brought the heaped platters of lasagna and tortellini, along with another basket of garlic bread. He offered to serve us, but I told him I could manage. We needed to keep Geri talking, and I was afraid she'd come to her senses and stop sharing such personal things. I quickly added pieces of lasagna to their plates, along with a scoop of tortellini.

Tillie nodded her thanks then went back to prompting Geri into answering. "But then six or eight months ago, things didn't go so well?"

"That's right, although it was closer to ten months ago. William never said what the problem was, but clients dried up, and then Ian got the bright idea of leveraging their company to buy a similar consulting firm and expanding." She toyed with the mound of pasta on her plate and pushed it around, without taking even a single bite. "It was a scam. Ian claims he lost just as much money as we did, but I have a feeling he was behind the con and cheated us. When our money was transferred to the owners of the other firm for purchase, it turns out the property didn't even belong to them, and all the employees and assets we were gaining were nothing but meaningless numbers on paper. And our money vanished with the purported owners."

"How is that possible? Didn't your husband and Ian do due diligence and inspect the building and talk to the employees? What about their attorneys? If they'd done their job, they would have spotted the scam." I couldn't help but jump into the conversation. In my former life, I'd been an accountant in the auditing division of a large national firm. I'd gone over more than my fair share of corporate documents and financial documents to substantiate balance sheets for mergers and outright purchases of other companies.

Geri put her fork down and began wringing her hands. "I have no idea. It was William's company, and he always took care of our finances and stuff like that. I've never seen a bill or even had to pay one in all the thirty years we've been married."

"Why do you think Ian was behind the scam?" I asked.

"That's what William told me." She guzzled the water sitting in the glass by Tillie's plate. I refilled it. "He has no reason to lie to me."

Maybe, maybe not. "Would you mind if we speak with your husband when we take you home? I'm a former auditor, and I might be able to help find a forensic accountant to track down your money."

Geri froze, and the water glass she'd picked up slid from her fingers and tipped over. "He's not at home."

I piled napkins onto the spreading water, and a server rushed over with towels to clean the table.

"I'll bring you more water and clean glasses," he said. He picked up the bread basket and peered inside. "And some more garlic bread too."

"Thank you." Tillie pressed some cash into his free hand. "We appreciate it."

He mumbled his thanks, shoved the money into his pocket, and left, carrying the detritus away.

Geri seemed fidgety and had perched on the edge of her seat like she was ready to flee.

"Mrs. Dalton, do you know when your husband will return or where we can find him? I think it's important we speak with him right away."

"I don't know." She wrung her hands together.

Had something happened to Mr. Dalton, or had he killed Ian and then taken off to hide from the police? "When was the last time you saw him?"

"It's been at least a week, maybe closer to two weeks." She waved a hand around, as if batting away an insect, and narrowly missed knocking the empty wine bottle over. "We had a fight, and he said he needed some space. I thought he'd be gone a few hours, maybe overnight, but he hasn't called or texted, nor will he answer my calls. His phone just drops me into voice mail, which is now full."

Tillie and I exchanged a worried glance. Either William was in deep trouble, or he'd killed Ian and gone into hiding.

"I'm so sorry, Geri. You must be distraught." Tillie kept her voice in a low, soothing murmur. "Have you tried to track him down?"

"No." She rubbed her face, smearing her eye makeup. "If you want my honest opinion, I think he dumped me and has moved in with his mistress."

Oh. I hadn't considered that possibility. "Do you know her name or where we can find her?"

"Don't you think I would have tried tracking him down if I knew who she was?" She choked out a mirthless laugh. "Not only did he leave me dead broke, without my own home, and shunned by all our former friends, but he's saddled me with his terminally ill mother. She needs constant care. Except she can't afford it and refuses to go to a government-run facility, so guess who's been working nonstop since moving into that hovel five months ago? Me. It's been only me, and I'm so darn exhausted."

Tillie put her arm around the now-sobbing woman and led her toward the exit while I directed the waiter to box up the meal we hadn't eaten. I paid the bill, including the cocktails and wine consumed before we'd joined her.

Arriving just as Tillie settled Geri into the back seat of the car, I leaned over and pointed at Geri's purse. "If you give me your car keys, I'll drive your car home."

She fished around her designer bag and, after a long minute, dumped the contents out. Lipsticks, scraps of receipts, two combs and one brush, bobby pins, gum, tissues, and several unprofitable scratch-off lottery tickets littered her lap and the car seat. Geri shook the upside-down bag, and a lone key tumbled out. The top was boxy black plastic while the key part was slender, ribbed metal. She clumsily picked it up and handed it to me.

"It's my mother-in-law's car. That old Corolla parked over there on the corner." She hitched her thumb over her shoulder.

My gaze followed the direction of her thumb until it landed on the battered faded-burgundy car. I couldn't help but wonder where Geri's own car was, but perhaps they had sold all but one vehicle, and then her husband had taken it when he disappeared and left her with only his mother's ancient vehicle for transportation. Southern California had only nominal public transportation, and it wasn't out of the ordinary for everyone of drivable age to own a vehicle. Especially amongst those in Geri and Tillie's country-club set.

"I'll follow you home," I said, nodding at Andrew. He'd keep an eye on me to make sure I didn't get stuck at a red light and lose him.

"Thanks for taking care of her car." Tillie reached out and

patted my hand. "I'll contact a medical employment agency and have them send a nurse out to the house as soon as possible. I think we need to get an ombudsman involved as well, so I'm hoping they can provide a recommendation."

"Please don't do that." Geri's words slurred together even more. "I can't afford it, and neither can my mother-in-law."

"You don't have to worry about a thing." Tillie waved me away. "We need to get going, and Emory will follow us. Just relax, and I'll take care of it all."

I knew for certain Tillie would pay all the fees associated with the in-home care for the sick woman. She was generous that way. If anyone could help straighten out the wreckage of Geri's life, it would be Tillie.

## Chapter 17

By the time we settled Geri in at her home and offered to check on her sick mother-in-law—Geri declined, stating the woman was sleeping and shouldn't be disturbed—we hit bumper-to-bumper traffic all the way back to Newport Beach. The stress from the last few days had hit hard, so I leaned back into the luxurious leather seat and closed my eyes, hoping my headache would subside.

"Do you need a nap, or should we talk about the next steps?" Tillie placed her hand on my forehead. "You feel warm. You're not sick, are you?"

I couldn't help but smile at her concern. "I'm sitting in the sun is all, plus I have a headache."

"We can trade places if that'll be more comfortable for you." She dug around her capacious handbag and pulled out a travel-sized bottle of ibuprofen, a sleeve of crackers, and a small bottle of unopened water and handed them to me. "We didn't get to eat lunch, so it's no wonder you have a headache."

"I think it's more from stress. I've had a horrible few days between Detective Reece and the poisoned cupcakes."

"We don't know if your cupcakes were tampered with, so don't go borrowing trouble yet."

"It's a bit late for that." I opened the crackers and offered them to Tillie, who declined. After nibbling on a couple, I washed two ibuprofen tablets down with the tepid water.

"Andrew, please go through the drive-through at the next McD's you spot. I think Emory will feel better with something more than crackers for lunch."

"Yes, Mrs. Skyler." Andrew gave a brief salute then slowly merged several lanes over until we'd reached the far-right lane, which was supposed to be the slow lane. Except all five lanes were so jammed, traffic had almost come to a complete stop.

"Feel free to get yourself something as well. My treat, of course."

"Thanks, but you know me. I'll pass."

Over the time that I'd gotten to know Andrew, I'd found out that he had severe food allergies. He never ate anything that he hadn't fixed himself. I felt bad that I could never thank him for all the care he showed toward Tillie and me by baking cupcakes or cookies for him. Instead, I made an effort to keep my ears open for new thriller and suspense releases that I thought he might enjoy and bought the hardcover edition to gift him with.

Tillie had been right about needing to eat, so by the time we returned home, my headache had vanished and my mood had improved. That is, until I saw Detective Reece standing by the gate with a thunderous scowl covering his face.

"Uh-oh. Looks like you've got company." Andrew slowed the car to a crawl. "If you duck down, Emory, I can keep driving, and he'll never know you were here."

The idea sorely tempted me because with the back seat windows tinted limousine dark, the detective couldn't have noticed me yet. Andrew could take me to Carrie's house—it'd been at least a couple weeks since I'd seen my nieces and nephew—but deep down, I knew I needed to face whatever reason the detective was here, right now. If I didn't, I'd be stewing with the not-knowing. Besides, if he couldn't talk to me, he might set his sights on Tillie and Vannie, which wasn't fair to either of them.

"What'll it be?" Andrew asked, still puttering along at a snail's pace.

"I might as well get this over with, so go ahead and park."

Tillie had her cell phone out and was already punching in numbers before Andrew had applied the brakes. "I'm calling my attorney's office again. They'd better have figured out something, and if they don't send someone over immediately, I'll be finding a new firm."

"Don't be too hard on them. Your attorney should be allowed to have a relaxing vacation without having to deal with an irate client." I went to open the door when Andrew put the car in park mode. Tillie reached across my lap and slapped my hand away from the door handle. She held up her index finger, which I took to show she wanted me to wait. Even though Detective Reece's face turned redder by the second, and his hands had clenched into tight fists, I did as she wanted. There would probably be consequences later with the detective, but I'd deal with it then.

Tillie's sharply raised voice filled the interior of the car. She'd donned her full society-maven persona. "This is Mrs. Matilda Skyler. I left a message with your service two—let me clearly repeat that—*two* days ago, and I have yet to receive an acknowledgment from the attorney taking over for Ms. Cumberland."

Tillie fell silent for a moment while the personnel who'd had the misfortune of answering the call responded.

"Let me finish speaking, young lady. I don't want to be shoved into some voice mail hinterland with the vague promise someone will get back to me. As I stated in my conversation with your service, I wasn't in an emergency situation at that exact moment, but I was heading in that direction, and here we are. I need an immediate attorney presence at my home, or I'll be finding a new firm."

Tillie waited until the other person stopped talking. "Your answering service isn't my concern. If they aren't reliable, then it's your company's responsibility to correct the problem instead of leaving your clients in a lurch. Now please, connect me to an attorney immediately."

Tillie grinned at me and flashed a thumbs-up. Muzak faintly played from her phone while we waited… impatiently, I might add. I kept a close watch on Detective Reece, but he hadn't strayed from my gate despite what appeared to be his growing annoyance.

A male voice sounded over the phone, and Tillie pressed it back to her ear.

"Yes, Charles, is it? I'm Matilda Skyler, and I'm in desperate need of an attorney at my residence immediately."

She waited a moment while he spoke then began talking over him. "An odious detective is standing by my gate, waiting to interrogate my granddaughter-in-law about a murder victim. He's already threatened her twice, without provocation, and he appears to be going against his superiors' instructions where it pertains to my family member. Now, can you or someone from your firm be here in a reasonable amount of time? If not, it'll be time for my son and me to move on to a new firm."

This was the first time I'd seen Tillie throw her family's wealth and position in the community around. It made me uneasy, yet I couldn't deny I was grateful she was on my side. I had to remind myself that she never used it for her own benefit and instead did everything she could to help the less fortunate, whether or not she knew them.

"Fine. We'll see you in thirty minutes. I'm sure you have my address on record. Or do you need me to provide it?"

Tillie's voice softened, and she winked at me. "Wonderful. We'll see you then."

She disconnected the call and placed her cell into her handbag. "It's all set. Now let's go declaw that nasty detective."

# Chapter 18

Detective Reece headed our way when Andrew and I emerged from the car. He froze when Tillie popped out and held her hand up in the stop position.

"Our attorney is on the way and should be here in thirty minutes. We will not talk to you until he arrives, so don't take another step closer unless you have a warrant."

His face went from dark red to almost purple, and I worried he might have a stroke or something. He probably needed to get his blood pressure checked, at the least. "Now see here, you have no right to interfere with a police investigation. I could arrest you right this minute for obstruction."

Andrew held his cell phone up, and from my vantage, I could see he'd been recording the entire exchange. "I think you'd better wait for the attorney, or this video with your threats just might go viral."

My mouth dropped open, but then I snapped it shut. Andrew was on social media? I'd done a cursory search for him a while ago—I was curious to see if he'd been a model in his younger days—but couldn't find a single profile for him on any of the sites. Maybe he used an alias?

By this time, Piper and Missy must've heard our voices

because they were on the other side of the gate, barking for all they were worth.

Detective Reece backed away from the gate and glared at us. "Have it your way. I'll be back in an hour."

After he'd stomped to his car, which he'd parked in front of our neighbor's garage, blocking them in, I opened the gate to let Piper and Missy join us. They helicoptered their tails around with pure happiness at seeing us, and they were even more excited when Andrew pulled treats from the glove box and had them go through their short repertoire of tricks.

"Thank you for sticking up for me, Andrew." I tucked in a strand of my curly hair that had come loose from the gold clip behind my ear.

"It felt good to put a bully like him in his place." Andrew seemed to gaze in the distance, as if recalling a memory. I wish I knew more about his past. "Mrs. Skyler, would you like me to stay until your attorney arrives?"

"There's no need, but I appreciate your offer."

We said our goodbyes, and Andrew drove off, but not before he made sure we were securely inside Tillie's house with the door locked.

Exactly twenty-six minutes after the call—Tillie had set a timer on her phone—the attorney arrived. Charles Thierry was young, perhaps in his very early thirties. He wore his sandy-blond hair in a sideswept crew cut style, and instead of a suit and tie, he wore jeans and a vivid-orange polo shirt that matched the shade of running shoes on his feet. A sports emblem sat on the left chest side.

Personally, I liked he wasn't a staid, elderly attorney. He looked like a contemporary and would, hopefully, be more in tune with protecting victims and those wrongly accused rather than thinking those in authority had the law on their side.

"Mrs. Skyler, I can't apologize enough for the miscommunication. I'll do everything in my power to rebuild your trust in our firm." He thrust out his hand, and when she offered hers, he pumped it twice then released it. "And you must be the granddaughter-in-law?"

I threw a furtive glance at Tillie—she'd sidestepped my questions about why she'd lied about my relationship to her—then stuck out my hand. "I'm Emory. It's nice to meet you, Mr. Thierry."

"Please, call me Charles. And you're Emory Skyler?" he asked as he shook my hand.

"No, I still use my name. Emory Martinez." Which was actually my ex's last name, but I'd never followed through to legally change it.

"All righty, Ms. Martinez. Shall we take this inside and you can fill me in on what's going on?"

"Oh, please, just call me Emory. There's no need for formalities."

He nodded and then his face turned a bright shade of pink when he caught Tillie looking over his attire. "I'm so sorry for my casual wear. I'd been getting ready to head to the airport to meet up with friends for a Phoenix Suns game in Houston."

Did this mean he was abandoning us as soon as he could? Tillie must've been thinking the same thing because she pursed her lips and narrowed her eyes.

Charles's face suddenly paled. "But of course, your situation takes priority, and I'm at your disposal as long as you require. What I meant to say is that I didn't take the time to change into my suit before coming since I understand you're in a dire situation. My assistant is canceling the trip for the time being."

"I'm so sorry for the imposition, but Detective Reece has given us no recourse." Tillie ushered him into the long hallway that had museum-quality art lining the walls.

Charles's gaze darted from the artwork to the far side of the great room that featured a view of the bay through the wall of glass doors that led to the patio.

Both the art and the view were impressive, in my opinion.

We followed Tillie to one of the cozy seating arrangements in the great room, and she motioned for Charles to take the love seat facing the bay. It might have not been the best option, since the boats puttering by or the formation of pelicans soaring through the air could be quite distracting. But maybe Charles had better concentration and self-control than I did.

Once Tillie sat across from Charles on a cushy sofa, I asked, "Can I get you some tea or coffee before we begin?"

"Why don't you bring us a carafe of coffee and some of Vannie's butterscotch cookies." Tillie leaned forward and placed marble coasters on the glass coffee table that sat between the sofa and love seat. "I'll chat with Charles and find out about him and his credentials."

"Sure. I'll be right back." I hurried from the room, trying to hide my chuckle at Charles's look of discomfort at being the object of Tillie's questioning.

By the time I returned with a tray containing the coffee, with all the fixings, and cookies, the attorney looked relaxed and seemed to be sharing a humorous anecdote with Tillie. He took the mug of coffee I held out, and I indicated he should add cream and-or sugar to his liking. After adding a liberal dollop of cream to my mug, I sat next to Tillie.

"I gave Charles a quick overview of what's been going on with the murder and Detective Reece aggressively threatening to arrest you." Tillie added cream and sugar to her mug. She lifted the cup, shook her head with a minute movement—I knew she preferred her teacup—then took a sip.

"I don't know why he's so set upon me being the guilty party. They haven't even determined what killed the victim, as far as I know, so how can he jump to conclusions like that?" I shuddered as I remembered the gleam the detective had in his eyes as he dangled his handcuffs in front of me. It had been creepy.

"Correct me if I'm misunderstanding, but what you're saying is they don't know what killed the victim, Ian Hesser, nor were you found anywhere near him when he expired, yet you're being treated as their primary suspect?"

"That's exactly it." I wasn't hungry, but I plucked a cookie from the plate and nibbled. The creamy sweetness of butterscotch coated my tongue.

"You can't overlook the fact that Detective Gabe O'Neill stated that the captain had told Detective Reece to back off, and Gabe told him the same thing when he barged in here Saturday night."

My phone dinged with an incoming text. I'd left Brad a voice mail telling him about Detective Reece showing up, while we waited for the attorney. Even though it was rude, I picked my phone up to read the text. It was brief, and full of abbreviations, but the message made my heart skip a beat.

**Sry I missed yr call. In mtg. Found out Reece's exwif is a redhead, lk u. Prob why he so angry and wants 2 arrest u. Ill call ltr.**

## Chapter 19

I replied with a thumbs-up emoji then showed the message to Charles and Tillie.

Charles immediately jumped onto his phone and called the Newport Beach Police Department and demanded to speak to the captain. While he waited to be connected, he turned to me. "I won't allow this Detective Reece to interview you, unless his supervisor or the captain is in the same room. And under no circumstances should you have any type of dialogue or contact with him without me being present. If he continues to harass you, we'll sue the NBPD and the city."

I nodded and wrapped my arms around my middle.

It took less than a minute for Charles to explain the situation to the captain. I'd expected some pushback, with the police department standing behind Detective Reece's right to question me, but it didn't happen. Instead, Charles ended the call after profusely thanking the captain.

"Well, what did he say, young man?" Tillie leaned forward and rolled her hand in a circle, as if she could hurry his answer.

"Reece had already been taken out of the field and placed on desk duty for the time being. There's no reason he should have been on your property, threatening you, and he'll receive disciplinary actions." Charles eyed the cookies and took two. "If you could have your driver forward the video to me, and Emory, please forward the text from your friend. I'll add them to your file in case we need them for any future actions."

"Thank you. I can't tell you how relieved I am." My limbs and stomach still felt shaky, but this was the best news I could have received. "Can you find out what killed Ian and how the poison was delivered?"

Charles eyed me speculatively. "With Reece out of the picture, why do you want to know?"

"I'm a cupcake caterer, and my cupcakes were found in the office where Ian died." I shuddered at the thought of my cupcake lying by his side. "He was actually in the middle of eating one of them. And now, all my customers are canceling orders, and I'm going to lose my business if the case isn't solved soon. I need to prove that my cupcakes weren't poisoned."

"I have full confidence that the investigating detective will find the perpetrator, and you should leave it up to them to do so. It won't do anyone any good if you try to get involved." He stood and handed us each a business card. "My cell number is listed on the back, so if there's an emergency, call it. Otherwise, call my office, and my assistant can take a message if I'm not immediately available."

"Thank you, again, for putting your plans on hold and coming today." Tillie rose and walked toward the door. "I'll be sure to put in a good word with Irene."

He turned to us when we'd reached the front door. "If Reece shows up, don't open the door. Instead, call 911 immediately. He might become dangerous after being thwarted."

When Charles was gone, Tillie and I made our way to the kitchen. The dogs must've sensed my sour mood because they nudged my legs and wouldn't let up until I'd given them attention. Even after I sat at the table, they stayed close to me, their heads resting on my legs and their toffee-brown eyes gazing up.

"On one hand, I feel relieved that Reece was taken off the case, but I can't help but feel like we're not any closer to solving the murder." I rested my forehead on the table and dropped my hands into my lap. The dogs took that opportunity to nudge my hands into giving them caresses.

"You know, it always takes time to solve a case." Tillie set the plate of cookies in front of me and poured coffee into fresh mugs for us. "Send Brad a text and tell him he can come over for dinner as long as he finds out if the toxicology report is available yet."

Pulling my cell from my pocket, I plopped it onto the table. "At this point, I don't even care what kind of poison killed Ian. I just need to know if my cupcakes were the delivery method, or if they were an accidental pastry bystander."

"Text Brad and tell him that. The worst that can happen is Gabe tells him there's nothing new to report, and then we can sit around this evening drinking gimlets or wine." Tillie poured kibble into the dogs' bowls, and they abandoned me to check out the food. Not content with kibble alone, they lay down, heads on their front paws, and rolled their eyes up to beg for something better.

It was just the cute levity I needed. "You dogs are so spoiled!"

"What shall I feed you today? Chicken?" Tillie waited for a response, but when none came, she continued. "Beef?" Their ears perked up, but they remained in the same position. "Salmon?"

They jumped up and pawed her leg. "Salmon it is, then."

I retrieved flaked cooked salmon filets from the freezer and defrosted a couple of tablespoons in the microwave. Tillie immediately sprinkled it over their kibble, which they gobbled up almost before it hit the bowl.

"How did we get to this point where the dogs eat almost better than we do?" I returned the remaining salmon to the freezer.

"Look how happy they are." Tillie made kissy noises. "Aren't you girls just the cutest?"

I washed my hands then sent Brad a text begging him to find out if my cupcakes had been poisoned, promising him dinner in exchange for information.

Brad responded almost immediately.

**I'll c what I can do. Whats 4 dnr?**

"He's coming for dinner, but wants to know what we're having." I opened the refrigerator but saw nothing that tempted my taste buds.

"Have Vannie stop at the fish market and pick up swordfish or halibut. It'll be quick to prepare, and you can make a nice lemon caper sauce to go with it." Tillie went to her wine fridge and pulled out a couple of bottles. "I think this French Chablis should go well with the sauce."

"Perfect." I texted the request to Vannie, who said she'd be home in less than an hour with the fish.

"There are some lemon cupcakes in the freezer over at my place. We can have those for dessert." I called for the dogs. "Let me take the girls for a walk, and I'll collect the cupcakes and be back before Vannie makes it home."

"Do you think it's safe?" Tillie, not usually a worrier, sounded concerned. Her brows drew together, and her mouth turned down at the corners.

"Reece would be an idiot to harass me again. Don't you think the captain or Gabe would have contacted him to warn him off?" The dogs pranced beside me, eager for their walk.

"That's kind of what I'm worried about. If they warned him off again, he may be looking for payback."

I chewed my lower lip. The dogs pawed at my feet. "I'll take pepper spray with me, and I promise I'll stick to the main thoroughfare. There should be enough traffic, and I'll avoid all the dark alleys where he could ambush me."

"If you think it's safe enough."

"It should be." I took Tillie's hands into my own. "I can't live shut up in the house because I'm afraid. Now that I know Reece doesn't have the authority of the law behind him, I can be more assertive."

"Keep your cell on you, and promise me you'll carry the pepper spray and not stick it in your pocket."

I kissed her cheek. "I promise."

The walk proved uneventful, aside from Missy lunging for a teasing squirrel and almost ripping the leash from my grip. We were back at Tillie's, frozen lemon cupcakes in hand, within forty-five minutes. The dogs collapsed into their cozy beds nestled into the far corner of the kitchen while I went to work on the lemon caper sauce, and Tillie worked on a cross-word puzzle.

"Hey, guys, I'm home," Vannie called from the hallway, and the dogs scampered to meet her. She came into the kitchen and placed the sack containing the fresh fish into the refrigerator. "Did you know that detective is staking out our house?"

I nearly dropped the sauté pan I'd been holding. "You mean Reece?"

"Yeah. He's parked in front of your garage, Em, with a pair of binoculars looking over here. It's pretty creepy, if you ask me."

# Chapter 20

My fingers shook so hard I could barely pull up Gabe's contact information. The call went straight to voice mail. "It's Em. Reece is parked in front of our house using binoculars. What should I do?"

Disconnecting, I called Brad, who answered on the first ring. I started talking before he'd even said hello.

"Whoa, Em. Slow down. I can't understand a word you're saying." There was a rustling sound, and then he was back. "Gabe's right here. Should I put you on speaker?"

"Yes!" I practically shouted into the phone.

"Are you in danger? If so, hang up and call 911." Gabe's no-nonsense manner calmed me a bit.

"It's that Detective Reece. He's parked in front of my garage and is using binoculars to look at Tillie's house." I switched the phone to my other ear. "He hasn't been out there for very long, maybe less than ten or fifteen minutes. What should I do?"

Gabe swore, something he rarely did. "I'll have dispatch send a couple patrol cars out and talk to the captain, see if he wants to arrest Reece for stalking. What vehicle is he driving?"

"Hang on, let me ask Vannie. She's the one who saw him." I put my phone on speaker. "You're on speaker now."

"Ask me what?" Vannie's face was practically glued to her phone. She looked up and showed me the screen. It was the app for our security cameras. Reece climbed out of his car and started taking photos of Tillie's house, a huge telephoto lens attached to his camera.

Tillie leaned over my arm, trying to get a better view.

"He's out of the car taking photos of the house now," I practically screamed into the phone. "Vannie, set the alarm system. Tillie, get the baseball bats out of the pantry."

They both jumped into action.

My screech brought them right back to the scene unfolding on the phone. "He's trying to climb over the security gate! Did you lock the front door, Vannie?"

"I think so? I can't remember." She darted for the hallway to check. The dogs ran after her, barking and growling, as if it were a fun game of chase.

"Emory, don't panic." Gabe's voice was louder than usual, and not at all like his normally calm manner. "The patrol cars are on their way and know that this is turning into a potential emergency. Start listening for sirens. They'll be there soon."

Vannie rushed back into the kitchen. "The door is locked, and I set the alarm."

She joined Tillie and me, and we watched Reece's progress from the small phone screen. The camera dangled from around his neck as he slung a leg over the top of the gate. He must've heard the sirens a second or two before we did. Dropping back onto the street side of the gate, he ran to his car, tossed his camera into the front seat, jumped in, and roared off.

About a minute later, two patrol cars stopped in front of Tillie's gate, lights flashing and sirens blaring. I felt sorry for our neighbors. There was never a dull moment around here, thanks to me.

"Reece took off before the police got here." I took the phone off of the speaker setting.

"Can you tell me the make and model of his car? If you have his license plate number, that would be even better," Gabe said.

"The best I can do is show you, or the officers, the security footage recording." I motioned for Vannie to pull it up. "We'll take it out to the officers right now. Can you let them know we're coming out?"

"Will do. Brad and I are on our way over. We'll be there in about twenty." Without saying goodbye, he disconnected.

Disarming the alarm system from yet another app on my phone, I tugged Vannie along with me as I went to meet the two police officers. Tillie stayed behind with the dogs, setting up the gate to block them in the kitchen with her so they wouldn't get underfoot.

"I appreciate you responding so quickly," I hollered. Hurrying down the steps, with Vannie on my heels, I opened the gate. "We have security footage recorded, so maybe you can figure out his vehicle and get a license plate number."

Vannie handed over her phone and pressed Play for them.

"Hey, isn't that Detective Reece?" the younger officer asked. "Dispatch didn't tell us law enforcement was involved."

I froze, unsure how to respond. Why hadn't Gabe told them who the stalker-turned-almost-intruder was? Would these two men automatically stick up for a fellow officer, or would they do the right thing? "Yes, it is Detective Reece. He's been, uh, stalking me. It's gotten worse since he's been taken off a case I'm involved in."

The older, steel-gray-haired officer scratched his head. "He's an odd one, that's for sure. Phelps, go through the footage and see if you can get a license plate number, then forward the footage to Detective O'Neill. I'll call in a BOLO on his black Ford Explorer just in case someone spots him before we've got all the info."

Phelps snorted. "Officer Campbell, don't you think they'll be stopping dozens of black Explorers in the next five minutes if we don't give them a better description?"

"Good point. Well, see what you come up with and call it in." The older officer lumbered to his vehicle and plopped into the front seat.

Officer Phelps closed his eyes a moment then caught me staring. He lowered his voice to barely a whisper. "Officer Campbell is retiring next week and is doing the bare minimum until then. They should have put him on parking-violation duty instead of saddling us with his lack of effort."

"Sorry about that. It probably makes your job even harder." Vannie reached for her phone, her fingers trembling, then pulled her hand back when the officer waggled his index finger at her. "I want to check and see if he's been hanging around here prior to this."

"He was here Saturday evening, but Detective O'Neill came with him. And then a couple hours ago, he showed up again, demanding to interview me, but we told him he had to wait until my attorney came, so he left." I wasn't sure how much I should share or how much needed to remain confidential with what I'd learned from Brad and Gabe. Thankfully, they both arrived and saved me from having to decide.

"Detective O'Neill." Officer Phelps reached out and shook Gabe's hand then handed him Vannie's phone. "I trust you know what this is all about. We reviewed the security footage of the incident, but aside from determining the make and model of the vehicle, the license plates were obscured. I'll call in a BOLO with the car and Reece's description."

"Thanks. It's appreciated." Gabe jerked a thumb over his shoulder toward the older officer, who was slouched in the front seat of his patrol car. "Retirement-itis?"

Officer Phelps huffed. "You got it." He walked back toward his own patrol car, still shaking his head.

Brad had hung back while Gabe conducted official business, but now that the officer had left, he slung an arm around my shoulder and pulled me in for a hug. He released me and did the same with Vannie. She clung to Brad longer than usual, and when she stepped away, I thought I saw her lips quivering. Maybe she still had a surge of adrenaline going through her after the harrowing ordeal.

"Hey, you're safe, Vannie." Gabe gave her a hug. "We'll find the guy and, in the meantime, I'll have patrols drive by regularly."

"Okay. I trust you." She stepped toward the house. "We'd better go in and see how Gram is doing."

I followed behind, all the while trying to convince myself that we'd never really been in danger. Tillie had sturdy locks on all her doors and windows, and the alarm had been activated. Still, if Reece had been determined enough, he could have broken a window and gained entry that way. But… he carried at least one gun, if not more. We could have been at his mercy had Gabe and the police not responded when they did. I gave myself a mental shake and told myself to stop worrying about the "what ifs." It had worked out fine, and it wouldn't take long for Reece to be captured.

Brian tried to comfort me when I called him and then promised he'd get one of the sous-chefs to fill in for him that evening. He'd come home to be with us, just as soon as he could, but it probably wouldn't be until nine or later. Vannie and I weren't hungry, but we grilled the swordfish she'd brought home and had dinner with Brad and Gabe. Even the wine didn't taste good to me as I fretted. Reece had evaded capture, and no one knew where he could have disappeared to.

By the time Brian showed up, Brad and Gabe were long gone—and still no word on Reece. We decided it would be best if we all slept at Tillie's for the security. As I tumbled into the downy soft bed and snuggled in, I hoped the morning would bring better news. It didn't.

## Chapter 21

A shrill siren pulled me from the depths of my dreams. Had the noise been a part of those dreams? I didn't hear it again, so I decided I didn't need to dart out of bed just yet. Daylight streamed through the blind slats, and the aroma of bacon and coffee wafted from the kitchen. Fumbling around in the tangle of sheets, I found my phone and squinted at the screen. It was already eight. How had I slept so long? I hadn't even noticed Brian getting up when he took the dogs out.

The siren coming from my phone sounded again. I jumped and nearly dropped it back into the sheets. Who had loaded that annoying ring tone? I checked the caller ID. It was Brad and most likely the culprit behind the new sound. I'd get even with him one of these days.

"Good morning, brat."

He giggled like a little kid. "You weren't still sleeping, were you?"

"Ha. As if anyone could sleep through the racket you loaded onto my phone," I grumbled. "Thanks. Thanks a lot."

"Sorry, cupcake. Actually, I was going to call over an hour

ago, but thought I'd have pity on you and wait for a decent time."

"You could have had pity on me by never loading such a heart-stopping sound for my ringtone." I threw myself back onto the pillows and closed my eyes.

"It's only for my calls. You know how important they are." Brad giggled again.

"Yes, we all know you can be a little diva at times." I yawned. "What's so important you needed to call at the crack of dawn?"

There was a slight hesitation, a sharp intake of breath. Something had happened, or he had bad news. I sat straight up. "Spill it, Brad. I know whatever it is, I'm not going to like it, so just tell me."

"Some of the lab results came back on the poison used. Your cupcakes contained the solution that killed Ian. I'm so sorry, Em."

"Even though I'd hoped for better news, I'm glad you told me." I plopped back down. "What was the poison?"

"Someone got creative and brewed up quite the concoction of botanicals. There was belladonna, hemlock, tansy, lily of the valley, and oleander." He coughed. "Any of those alone could cause death. Together, there was no chance Ian would have survived."

I'd seen someone who'd been murdered with oleander. It wasn't something I ever wanted to witness again. But here we were. "That's horrific. What made him foam at the mouth?"

"The hemlock and tansy would both cause that effect. They also found antinausea medication in his system, which explains why his stomach didn't reject it."

Shuddering, I massaged my temples. What other guests had gotten ahold of the tainted cupcakes? "Do they know how the poison was added to the cupcakes? I didn't notice any leaves or stems or anything."

"From the remaining cupcakes they inspected, it appears

whoever did this probably boiled the botanicals together in water, then reduced the water so the poison was concentrated. It would have been easy enough to add the mixture to the cupcakes using a syringe, without disturbing the frosting. Ian probably thought your cupcakes were very moist."

"But wouldn't it have tasted bitter?" I couldn't wrap my head around the premeditation and preparation to commit the murder.

"The poisoned cupcakes contained agave syrup, so they're working with the assumption that the killer used the sweetener to mask the taste. Gabe will probably contact you later today to give you this information…. which you didn't hear from me. Right?"

Agave syrup is made from the blue agave plant, native to the southwestern United States and Latin America. What makes it so unique is that it's about one and a half times sweeter than regular granulated sugar and, since it's a syrup, doesn't need to be dissolved. It would be the perfect ingredient to use in the poisonous solution.

"I don't know anything about who might have poisoned my cupcakes. I'll keep wringing my hands, worrying about it, until they're caught."

Brad's deep laughter filled my ear. "Don't overdo the dramatics. It'll make him suspicious, no matter what you say."

"Got it. It's a good thing Reece is off the investigation. He'd probably get a search warrant and tear my kitchen apart looking for a bottle of the stuff instead of just talking to me."

"Or plant it if he couldn't find any."

"Please don't remind me." I rolled over to my side and propped my head up on my arm. "We've got to find out why he acted like he did toward me. Isn't there something really weird about that? I don't recall meeting him before or double-crossing him or anything."

"Look, I've got to go." It sounded like Brad covered his phone with his hand, then he came back. "As soon as I'm done with this meeting, I'll come over, and we can brainstorm. You gonna be at Tillie's all day?"

"There's nowhere else I need to be unless Gabe drags me down to the station for interrogation."

"We'll figure it out, Em."

After disconnecting, I rolled out of bed and headed down to breakfast and several cups of coffee.

Tillie and Brian sat huddled over her iPad.

"What are you two looking at?"

They were startled and looked guilty. Tillie swiped the screen closed and placed her iPad face down.

"Let me pour you a cup of coffee, and then I'll cook some eggs and reheat the bacon for you." Brian hopped up from the table and gave me a quick kiss. "I'm glad you could sleep in."

"Me too. I'm exhausted emotionally and physically after dealing with Reece." I accepted the mug of coffee that Brian fixed just the way I liked it. "Have you heard if he's been found yet?"

"No, we haven't heard anything new." Tillie held her teacup up to Brian. "Give me a refill, doll."

He complied and placed a kiss on the top of his grand-mother's head. I sat next to Tillie and tried to inch her iPad toward me. She pulled it back and tucked it beneath the chair she sat on.

"You should call Gabe after breakfast and see if he has an update." Tillie took a sip of coffee then grimaced. "This has been sitting on the burner too long. I'll make another pot."

"Let me take care of it, Gram." Brian got busy tending to the eggs and making coffee.

I pulled my gaze from his toned backside and looked at Tillie. "He's supposed to contact me this afternoon. Brad called and woke me up to give me an update."

"Did they find that horrible man?" Tillie asked.

"He didn't say they did, so I'm guessing not."

"Then what did Brad want?"

"Some of the toxicology reports came back, and my cupcakes were definitely the method to deliver the poison."

"Oh, Em. I'm so sorry." Tillie shot a side-eye at Brian and gave a brief shake of her head.

"What kind of poison did the murderer use?" Brian placed scrambled eggs in front of me, with a couple slices of bacon.

My appetite vanished. I should have waited to talk about the poisonous cupcakes after breakfast. "It was a concoction of several poisonous plants. They surmise they boiled the plants together, mixed it with agave syrup, then used a syringe to inject the liquid into my cupcakes."

"That's terrible. Poor Ian." Tillie pulled a basket of muffins toward me. "Help yourself. Vannie made lemon poppyseed muffins before work. She couldn't sleep, so she decided to bake."

Without a doubt, Tillie was trying to distract me from what she and Brian had been looking at on her iPad.

"Okay, you two. What is it you don't want me to see online?" I tried to reach down to snatch the iPad, but Tillie batted my hand away.

"Nothing you need to concern yourself with, my dear." Tillie took a muffin and broke it in half. She placed a piece on my plate. "Eat before your food gets cold. I'm going to go get ready for the day."

Before I could ask what she was getting ready for, Tillie scooped up the iPad and scurried out the door. Brian sat beside me, coffee mug in hand.

"Well? What is it you both are trying to protect me from?"

"Eat first, then we'll talk." At the look of what was probably terror that crossed my face, he leaned over and kissed me. "It's nothing that's life or death, so don't worry."

Telling someone "don't worry" never worked. I'd never eaten as quickly as I did then, and I was surprised I didn't choke on the bacon as I barely chewed and swallowed. After washing it all down with several large gulps of coffee, I put the mug down.

"Tell me, please." I crossed my arms. "Otherwise, I'm going to think of the worst-case scenarios and give myself a heart attack."

"We were scrolling through social media which led us to some Yelp reviews…" Brian scrubbed his face and wouldn't meet my gaze. "You know trolls and how brutal they can be…"

"Are you trying to say that someone or several someones are leaving bad reviews for my Sprinkles and Spice Cupcakery?"

He scrunched up his face. "They're not just bad. The comments are vicious. Not only that, they're mentioning Carrie's company, Pacific Palates, and Oceana as a connection to you."

My stomach churned, and I wished I hadn't eaten. It was one thing to ruin my fledgling business. I had other skills I could draw on to support myself. But to attack my sister and Brian's companies was unforgiveable.

"Don't pass out, Em. We'll get through this." He stood and brought me a glass of water. "I know Gram would pour some tea and brandy for you, but this is probably better for you."

The thought of Tillie and her tea with brandy for every malaise made me laugh, which turned into a sob. Brian gathered me in his arms and offered soothing sounds as he stroked my back. The dogs nudged my legs and placed warm kisses on my hands. When I'd cried myself out, he handed me clean tissues then pulled his phone out and made a call.

"Hey, Brad. I need some trolls buried, and I'll pay whatever it costs to get it done."

He waited for my best friend's reply then continued, "I'll send you the links and can pay your guy in cash or reimburse you. Whichever way is fine."

I could hear Brad answering but couldn't discern the words.

"Thanks, bro. We'll see you soon." Brian put his phone back into the pocket of his cargo shorts. "Done. The reviews should disappear in a matter of minutes, and his guy will ferret out the trolls and make their lives miserable."

"I just want the reviews taken down. You don't have to make them miserable."

"Cupcake, these trolls aren't only going after you. They're probably targeting a lot of different people and business simply because they like being malicious." He put his finger beneath my chin so he could gaze directly into my eyes. "Not everyone has hacker resources like you via Brad, so let's take the opportunity to save other innocent people the heartache and financial distress caused by these trolls."

"Okay, that makes sense. Is it Ethan who'll do the work?" Ethan was an expert hacker who had helped us find the stalker who had intended to disrupt Brad and Gabe's wedding.

"Yeah. He's a good kid and very talented."

"You don't have to pay him. I can do it." Maybe. I didn't have a lot in my savings because I'd been paying off the debt my ex had saddled me with. But it wasn't fair that Brian foot the bill when my poisoned cupcakes started the whole mess.

"You should know Brad well enough to realize he won't let either of us pay even a single cent." He nudged my shoulder. "Are you feeling better yet?"

I held my index finger and thumb up, with barely half an inch space between the two digits. "I feel like I should get out of the catering business and go back to being a boring old accountant. There've been too many murders."

"First off, you were a boring old accountant when you found Tori, right?"

I nodded. I hated thinking about the heartache my ex-best

friend had caused me by cheating with my then husband. Still, she hadn't deserved to be killed.

"Crunching numbers never gave you joy, nor did your job give others joy."

He was right about that. My audits probably caused people a lot of heartburn and anxiety.

"People, and especially kids, love your cupcake creations. You're spreading happiness and sprinkles, both in your life and in theirs." He kissed my cheek. "We'll get those trolls shut down, find the monster who poisoned your cupcakes, and then live happily ever after. Deal?"

I couldn't help but smile. "Thanks for the pep talk. And you're right. I'd die if I had to go back to a cubicle and stare at numbers all day long."

Tillie peeked around the corner. "Can I barge in now?"

"Of course. And thanks for trying to protect me." Brian vacated the seat next to me, and Tillie took his place. I gave her a hug. "But I'd rather be aware of what's going on than ignorantly blissful."

"You can't blame an old lady for trying to shelter you." She returned my hug and held on extra tight.

# Chapter 22

Brad and Gabe showed up at lunchtime, with takeout pizzas in hand. Brian scarfed down a slice before running out the door to get to Oceana and dinner prep.

"Hey cupcake, the trolls are taken care of," Brad whispered to me. I'd known better than to bring up the hacking job when the guys first got there. Gabe didn't approve of using illegal methods but decided what he didn't know he wouldn't worry about, so he never pried.

"Thanks. I owe you."

"Owe you what?" Tillie asked as she reached around us and pulled another slice of pizza from the box.

"For putting a siren ringtone on my phone." I elbowed Brad in the ribs. "It just about gave me a heart attack when this guy called me this morning."

"Too bad you didn't get that on video. It probably would've gone viral." Tillie laughed. "Lemme hear it."

"I already deleted it and put a normal, calm ringtone back on."

"Spoilsport." He leaned toward me once Tillie moved away. "Nice save."

"I thought so, but trust me, there'll be paybacks when you least suspect it."

"Emory. Would you mind if we go over to your house and chat?" Gabe flashed a pointed look at his husband. "I think my beloved already shared some confidential information with you this morning, but we need to talk further."

"Of course. Let me grab my keys, and we can head over there."

The dogs, thinking they were going for a walk, tore themselves away from Tillie and her pieces of pepperoni and pizza crusts.

"Sorry girls, you're going to have to stay here." I rummaged through the junk drawer and plucked my house key out.

"I don't mind if they come with us. We can even take them around the block, if you'd like."

"Oh, they'd like, all right." We headed toward the front door, the dogs hot on our heels. We snapped on the leashes and went for a walk around the block—which probably took twice as long as Gabe had expected—before ending up at my pool house.

We sat on cushioned chairs beneath the patio cover. Piper and Missy guzzled water then plopped down in the sun to rest. It hadn't been a strenuous walk, but perhaps they wanted to relax and soak up the sunlight after being cooped up at Tillie's house.

"I think you have all the details, and more, about the poison and how it was delivered." Gabe rested his elbows on the tops of his knees. He waited for my affirmation, so I nodded. "I'd like to look at your ingredients. Specifically, I'm looking for agave syrup, and any plant material, live or dried. I haven't requested a search warrant, but I can get one if you'd rather not give me your permission."

Gabe would be fair and would do his utmost to respect my property and ingredients. "You have my permission. As far as plant material, I have a lot of dried herbs for cooking. Are you going to take all of my jars?"

"Unfortunately, yes." He grimaced. "My supervisor also thinks we need to push to examine Tillie's kitchen as well, but for now, I've put them off. She didn't bake the cupcakes, nor did she deliver them. Besides, accusing someone like *the* Mrs. Matilda Skyler of poisoning someone with ingredients from her kitchen would open up the NBPD to a lawsuit and public condemnation."

"Do you want to examine my ingredients now?"

"I think it's best. We can't have anyone—like Reece—claiming I gave you preferential treatment." He let out a long sigh. "I'm going to need to record the entire search, but first I'd like to get you on video, allowing me to search without a warrant and agreeing to it without your attorney present."

Panic momentarily seized me. I should have called my attorney and asked him to come. What if the murderer planted poisonous matter in my pantry? Had anything seemed out of place over the last week? I couldn't remember. It had been too hectic with Valentine's Day orders and the Dying for Chocolate party.

"Em, is something wrong?" Gabe looked concerned and touched my shoulder for a moment.

"As a friend, not a detective, would you advise me to get my attorney first?" I chewed the inside of my cheek. "While I don't want to make your job harder, I worry someone might have snuck in and left something to implicate me. Not that I've noticed anything out of the ordinary recently, but you've seen my kitchen. It's stuffed to the rafters with ingredients and baking pans. If there's something hidden, I wouldn't know."

Gabe ran his fingers through his hair, making it stand on end. "As a friend? Yes, by all means, you should have your attorney here. But you didn't get that advice from me, okay?"

I thought for a moment. Time was of the essence, and if I

waited for Charles, it would only delay Gabe in investigating other aspects of the case. "Can we compromise?"

"What do you have in mind?"

"Video me giving permission to search my home, but skip asking me about the attorney. If you find something concerning, allow me to call my attorney before you proceed further."

Gabe's face pinched together. "I don't know, Em. That's really skirting the edges of procedure."

"Here's why I think it'll be okay…" I honestly had no idea what I was talking about, but it was worth a shot. "If someone hid poisonous plant matter in my house, they probably put it in one of my dried herb jars. You won't immediately know and will have to wait until the lab tests it. It'll take a few days, so it won't matter if my attorney was here or not right now."

"You and Brad are going to torpedo my career one of these days, you know?"

"Nah. It won't happen. You're too smart for that." I fake punched his shoulder. "Will my plan work?"

"Lead the way, and I'll don the disposable gloves."

Gabe was methodical and extremely respectful as he examined my cupboards and pantry. He'd brought a collapsable tripod for his cell phone so he'd have both hands free to search. I waited on the patio and almost fell asleep, lulled by Gabe's droning voice as he narrated each and every item he examined in my kitchen.

"I think I'm done here," Gabe said as he strode back onto the patio. He clutched a medium-size paper bag. "I took seven jars of dried herbs for testing. If you've been cautious about keeping your doors locked and your alarm set when you're not home, I'm sure we have nothing to worry about."

Locking the doors when I left home, even if only for a few minutes, had become second nature to me. Setting the alarm each time, not so much. "I'll hope for the best."

Gabe tapped his phone a few times then smiled at me. "I emailed the video to my work email address for backup. I don't want anyone questioning whether I edited the video to protect you."

"With Reece out of the picture, I doubt there'll be any issues."

He'd just returned the phone to his trouser pocket when it rang. He pulled it out and looked at the screen. Frowning, he answered. "O'Neill here."

The caller spoke for several minutes while Gabe grunted occasionally. Still holding the phone to his ear, he sank onto one of the patio chairs and pulled a small notebook and pen from a pocket. "Give me the address again."

He scribbled in the notebook. "Who's there now?"

Gabe added more notes. "Tell them it'll take me an hour or so to get there."

Disconnecting the call, Gabe searched my face. "I understand you had lunch with Mrs. Dalton yesterday."

It was a statement and not a question, so I merely dipped my head in response.

"Did she say anything about her husband?"

"Only that he took off over a week ago and left her to care for her ill mother-in-law."

"And she hadn't heard from him in all that time?" Gabe tapped the tabletop with his pen.

"No, and she is quite upset about it." I wished I could read upside down, and then I would have known what Gabe had scribbled in the notepad. "Why? Has he shown up?"

"You could say that." He let out a long breath of air. "A hiker found his body beneath some rocks off of one of the trails in Red Rock Canyon. He's been there a while, and the cause of death is definitely murder. There was a gunshot wound in the middle of his forehead."

# Chapter 23

Gabe attached a portable light and siren to the roof of his vehicle and roared out of our alleyway, heading to the crime scene. I promised Brad that I'd drive him home later since the guys had come together for lunch.

"Emory, I think you should bake some cookies to take to Geri tomorrow morning. We'll pick up flowers on the way and pay a condolence call on her and her mother-in-law." Tillie blinked her eyes quickly, as if chasing off tears.

"Do you think she'll have any ideas about who might have killed William?" I asked. "It can't be a coincidence that both Ian and William were murdered."

"There's no way it's a coincidence." Brad rummaged around in the cookie jar and pulled two cookies out. "While you're baking cookies, make extra. I'm taking the last two."

After pulling the mixing bowl out, I added cubes of butter I'd chopped into it. Letting the small pieces of butter soften at room temperature, I gathered the rest of the ingredients I'd need for raspberry lemon cookies. To be honest, I was tired of chocolate, which shocked me. I didn't think I could ever have too much chocolate.

I measured out the sugar then whisked flour together with baking powder, baking soda, and salt. Next, I zested a large lemon then juiced it. The tart lemon would complement the zingy tang of frozen raspberries folded into the vanilla-based cookie dough.

"You might want to double the batch, Em." Vannie came into the kitchen, her messenger bag loaded down with books and papers to grade. "Theresa is coming over in a while. We're going to grade papers together then go out to dinner."

"We haven't seen her lately. Has she been traveling or just busy?" I quickly added more butter to the bowl and remeasured the ingredients. Theresa was Vannie's close friend. While they both admitted a strong attraction to each other, they'd decided to take their relationship slowly since they worked at the same school. I had a feeling Vannie was holding back on the relationship because of her past trauma, but she refused to talk about it and shut down at the barest hint of a question.

"She's been in Texas for the past week. Her grandma turned ninety, and her grandpa had to undergo surgery the day after the birthday party." Vannie dumped the messenger bag onto a chair. It dropped with a loud thud. "Theresa thought she should extend her trip and help her grandma out until her grandpa transferred to the rehabilitation center."

"I hope her grandpa is recovering quickly." I started the oven preheating. Usually, I liked allowing the cookie dough to rest in the refrigerator for at least an hour. It allowed the flour to absorb the moisture and the flavors to meld together a bit more. The cookies still needed a bit of refrigeration to firm up the dough, but they would still be yummy even without the extended refrigeration. "I'll have the first batch of cookies done in about forty-five minutes, since the dough needs to chill a bit. Shall I make a pot of coffee to go with them?"

"That would be great." Vannie bent over and gave Tillie a kiss on her temple. "You okay, Gram? You seem kind of sad."

"We just heard that William Dalton has been located. Someone murdered him. I feel for his poor wife and mother." Tillie shifted in her seat and reached an arm out and hugged her granddaughter's waist. "And then Gabe searched Emory's place and confiscated some of her ingredients."

"No! How could he?" Vannie scowled at Brad. "Why'd you let him do that?"

He raised both hands up in the air, palms facing toward her. "I knew nothing about it. I swear."

"It's true, Vannie. Gabe asked to speak privately to me and told me what he needed to do."

"You made him show you a search warrant and then called the attorney, didn't you?" When I didn't answer, Vannie threw up her hands. "You were foolish. Anything could happen, and you won't be able to do a darn thing about it now."

"Vannie, Gabe isn't like that. He recorded the entire thing and narrated every move he made. There's solid proof he did nothing untoward and didn't find anything."

"I thought he confiscated some of your ingredients." Vannie didn't look convinced that I'd done the right thing.

"Just my jars of store-bought dried herbs. The lab will need to confirm that they don't contain any botanical poisons that matched what killed Ian."

"Ian was poisoned with a plant? Are they sure it was your cupcakes that delivered the poison?" Vannie held her hand over her heart, her mouth held halfway open.

I slapped my hand on my forehead. "I forgot you were already at school when Brad told me. We should have texted you."

"No, it's best you didn't. I would've wanted to leave work, and that wouldn't have gone over well with the principal." Crease lines appeared on her forehead.

"Is something wrong at school?" I asked.

"Phew. Politics and egos are the crux of the trouble. It'll

blow over… eventually." Vannie began filling the coffee carafe with water. "I'll get the coffee going, and then I'm going to change into some yoga pants and a sweater before Theresa shows up."

"Would you girls like to use my office to work?" Tillie leaned over and stroked Piper's ears. "I can move the papers off my desk, so there'll be plenty of room for you both."

"I think we'll sit out on the back patio. Fresh air will do us good after being cooped up in the classrooms with those stinky teen boys." Vannie cracked a smile and waved her hand in front of her nose.

"Hey, I was a teen boy once." Brad stuck out his lower lip. "I wasn't that bad, was I, Em?"

"You were better than most of the boys, but you had your moments." I scooped cookie dough out onto a parchment-lined baking sheet.

He stuck his tongue out at me then swiped one of the cookie doughballs and popped it in his mouth.

"That's not exactly healthy, Brad." Vannie tsked. "Raw eggs can be dangerous."

"He's safe…this time around." I stuck my tongue out at him then tried to slyly sneak a bit of dough to nibble on. Of course, they both caught me. "I substituted aquafaba for the egg. I'm going to try it with vegan butter and gluten-free flour next time, so I have a nonchocolate allergen-free cookie to offer at future events."

"Ooh. Maybe you should make a triple batch." Vannie plucked a package each of vegan chocolate chips and vegan white chocolate chips from the pantry and handed them to me. "Or try adding some of each flavor to a portion of the dough."

"Those both sound like great additions. Let's try it." After pulling two small mixing bowls from beneath the counter, I added a cup of dough to each. I cut the packages open, sprinkled a healthy amount into each bowl, then handed one of the bowls and a spoon to Vannie while I took the other. "Stir the chips in, and then I'll bake the cookies."

She did as directed, as did I, and then I used a large tablespoon-sized scoop to place doughballs onto the baking sheet. "If we go through the double batch within a day or two, I'll mix more up. There are some lemon crinkle and ginger crackle cookie doughballs in my freezer. I can bake some of those to take to Geri as well."

"I think a selection of three kinds of cookies will be appreciated." Tillie stood. "Is the coffee ready? Or have you been too busy swiping the cookie dough and chips?"

I didn't think Tillie had been paying close attention, but apparently she'd noticed Vannie and me sneaking chocolate chips to pop into our mouths.

"Give it a couple minutes, Gram, and there'll be enough for a cup." Vannie hastily added coffee grounds to the filter, inserted it into the machine, and pressed Start. "If Theresa comes before I'm back down here, offer her cookies and coffee. And be nice."

Brad and I exchanged a puzzled look. What did she mean by telling us to be nice? We all loved Theresa. She was easy-going but could joke and kid around with us like a sibling or any family member would do.

"We're always nice, Vannie." Brad sounded like a whiny child.

"Yeah, like swap out salt for the sugar bowl when you serve her coffee nice." Vannie headed for the door.

"She laughed just as much as we did," Brad protested. "You have to admit, the face she made when she tasted her salty coffee was pretty funny."

Vannie huffed. "Neither of us is in the mood for a jokester today, is all I'm saying."

Before my sister could leave the kitchen, I hurried over to her and gave her a tight squeeze. "I'm sorry you're having a bad day. We'll be extra nice and do whatever we can to help you relax."

"It sounds like you need some tea and brandy." Tillie popped up and rushed to put the teakettle on. "That always helps."

Vannie and I started laughing, and soon Brad and Tillie joined in.

"Well, maybe it doesn't always help, but it can't hurt either."

"We'll pass, Gram. We have dinner reservations at seven and need to be able to drive." She yawned. "A cup of coffee and a couple of cookies will be perfect."

## Chapter 24

Traffic wasn't nearly so bad the following morning as Andrew drove us back to Chino Hills for another visit with Geri and her mother-in-law. Resting my head against the seatback, I contemplated the questions I was desperate to find answers to, including how to help Vannie get through whatever was bothering her. She'd settled down and seemed cheerful enough when Theresa arrived, but her earlier outburst had me worried.

"Do you need more ibuprofen?" Tillie shook the bottle at me.

"No, thanks. I'm thinking about Vannie. There's more going on with her than it being the anniversary of her parents' death, except she won't talk about what's bothering her."

Tillie's face fell. "My heart aches for that poor girl. Well, young woman."

"There's got to be something we can do to help her." I scrubbed my face with my hands then belatedly remembered I'd applied mascara. Using the side of my index fingers, I swept beneath my eyes to remove any smeared traces of black.

"She's determined to keep it to herself for now." Tillie handed me a tissue and pointed to a spot on my upper cheek.

"If we pry too aggressively, she's only going to shut down more. We need to give her hugs and show her support in other ways. Hopefully, she'll follow through and book an appointment with the therapist."

"You're right, as always." I flashed her a wry smile then tapped my chest. "But I feel like *I* should do more to help her."

"Give her some time and as much space as she needs, and it'll work out." It worried me that Tillie didn't sound nearly as confident as her statement. She was just as worried as I was, so I changed the subject.

"What questions should we should ask Geri without seeming insensitive? We need a plan before we see her, but I'm not coming up with…."

Andrew slammed on his brakes and swerved to miss the pickup truck that darted right in front of us, missing us by mere inches. Tillie reflexively reached out her hand to steady the platter of cookies sitting between us before they slid to the floor, and my grip tightened on the vase of flowers I held on my lap. My heart jackhammered in my chest, and I resisted the urge to roll my window down and yell at the truck as it careened down the freeway.

"I apologize for the sudden maneuver, but I was afraid he would have hit us if I didn't take evasive action." Andrew put his blinker on and merged back into the lane we'd been blissfully traveling in before the truck kicked us out.

"No need to worry about it. I saved the cookies, and we're all intact." Tillie looked at her watch.

"Are we late? What time did you tell Geri we'd be there?"

"I didn't tell her we were coming. If we want an honest reaction from her, I thought it best we show up unannounced."

"What if she's making funeral arrangements or has family or friends visiting? How long do you plan on hanging around waiting for her?" I didn't like this plan in the least. The widow was probably overcome with deep grief on top of the stress of their financial difficulties. Springing our visit on her seemed, well, tactless.

"First off, the police won't have released the body yet. It could take a long time unless it was easy to determine the manner of death."

A gunshot in the middle of his forehead should make it easy to confirm the manner of death. But I kept my promise to Gabe and said nothing.

"That's true. But I'd be surprised if she didn't have family visiting her or at least some close friends."

"You can rule out the friends. She said it herself over lunch that they've all shunned her since William's financial ruin." Tillie thought a moment. "I doubt she, or William for that matter, has family to gather around her. If they did, why would she have been left alone to care for her mother-in-law all this time, with no one stepping in to provide help with the ill woman or aid in finding William after his disappearance?"

"Another good point." I looked at the cookies and wished I'd packed some extras for a snack. "Don't you feel bad ambushing her like this? It seems like she's had enough shocks lately."

"We're doing this with her best interests in mind. It may be painful for her to talk about her husband, but that'll be the only way to figure out who killed him and Ian. The two deaths have to be connected."

"I agree with you on that." The homes and businesses whizzed by once we exited the freeway and made our way to the small bungalow-style home. I recognized where we were when Andrew turned down Geri's street and remembered her house was five up from the corner, on the right-hand side.

Two houses down from Geri's, a black Ford Explorer had parked catawampus alongside the curb. My heart jolted. It was the same make and model that Detective Reece had been driving. Had he tracked Geri down? Could he be lying in wait for us? Andrew slowed as we approached the house, and I twisted in my seat to get a better look. No one sat in the vehicle, and there wasn't a license plate on the front bumper.

"Is something wrong?" Tillie asked.

"That car back there is very similar to Detective Reece's vehicle." I turned back to face the front of the car. "He couldn't have known we were coming to visit Geri, could he?"

"Not a chance." Tillie twisted to look behind us. "Besides, there are a gazillion black Fords in California. I'm sure it's nothing to worry about. He's gotta be long gone, running from the law."

"That sounds like a bad country western song." As soon as Andrew placed the car in park, I opened the door, picked up the flowers, and slid out.

Tillie joined me, and we walked toward the front door. The shingled gable roof had seen better days, while the garish-yellow paint on the stucco siding was an eyesore amongst the subdued-toned houses in the neighborhood. Chunky square columns supported the overhead beams of the porch. Four narrow windows were on each side of the front door, lining the front of the house. The screens covering the windows were dusty, with several cobwebs draping from the edges. They looked authentic and not left over from Halloween.

After climbing the four steps to the porch, Tillie rang the doorbell. When no one answered, she rang it again and knocked on the paint-deprived door. A moment later, Geri finally opened the door, just wide enough to peer out. "Matilda. What brings you all the way out here this morning?"

Geri's makeup looked fresh and expertly applied, and her hair styled. She didn't look nearly as gaunt as the last time we'd seen her. There was nary a red-rimmed eye, nor an irritated nose from tissues mopping up tears. Dressed in a navy pantsuit with a cream-colored silk blouse, Geri hadn't put shoes on yet, but it appeared she'd applied a fresh coat of red polish on her toes.

"We're here to pay our condolences." Tillie thrust the platter of cookies toward the widow. And, as had happened with Rebecca, Geri reached out to take them, giving her an opportunity to enter the house.

"Matilda, wait." Geri looked back over her shoulder then back at us. "While I appreciate you making the trip out here, now isn't a good time for a visit. I'm, um, on my way out. There are things that need to be taken care of now that William has been found."

"We'll only take a moment of your time, dear." Tillie didn't stop but continued into the family room and sat down on the sagging sofa. "I want to make sure the nurse showed up to care for your mother-in-law. I'd like to talk to the nurse after we chat first with you, of course."

Geri looked taken aback, but plastered a smile on her face anyway. "That's very kind of you, but my mother-in-law sent the nurse away."

Tillie gasped and placed a hand over her mouth. "Did something happen? Was the nurse not professional?"

"It's nothing like that."

I was curious why the nurse had been dismissed, but before Geri could elaborate, Tillie turned to me and the vase of flowers I still held. "Dear, go to the kitchen and add water to the flowers. While you're at it, you might as well fix some tea for us and Geri's mother-in-law. What's her name? I don't recall what you'd said."

"No! Um, what I mean is there's no need to trouble yourself with the flowers." She rushed over to me and took the vase. "I'll put them on the coffee table and tend to them later."

"Let Emory take care of them and get us the tea. It's no trouble at all." Tillie pulled on Geri's hand in an attempt to get her to sit. She had no choice but to comply.

I took the vase back from her but couldn't help but notice the way she kept furtively glancing toward the kitchen. "It won't take me long."

"You'll find the tea bags and mugs in the cupboard above the dishwasher." Geri's voice was unnaturally high and abnormally loud.

Just when I wondered if someone could be hiding out in the kitchen, I heard the creak of a door being opened and then the slam of it shutting. Not caring if it was rude of me, I raced to the kitchen, placed the flowers on the kitchen table, and headed out the door, into the backyard.

Bright sunlight nearly blinded me, so I shaded my eyes with my hands. The overgrown yard desperately needed a lawn mower and some pruning shears. No one was in sight. A gate at the side of the yard was slightly ajar, so I jogged over to see if the person was hiding there. The concrete sidewalk leading toward the front of the house was empty, and there wasn't a single item anyone could have hidden behind. I followed it to the front yard and opened the door to Tillie's car.

Andrew's head shot up, and he snapped his book shut.

"Sorry for startling you. Did you notice anyone running by a minute or so ago?"

"No, I'm sorry I didn't see anyone." He looked sheepish. "I was at an exciting part of the story and got kind of sucked in."

"It okay." I glanced down the street. The black Ford was gone.

# Chapter 25

After returning to the kitchen from the same route I'd left it, I heated water, found the tea bags and mugs, and added water to the flowers. Delivering the mugs of hot tea, I studied Geri's face. She looked pensive and had eaten off half the lipstick on her lips. From what I'd overheard, she'd only answered Tillie in monosyllables.

"Should I make some tea for your mother-in-law?" I asked. I still didn't know her name.

"She's napping, so there's no need to bother." Geri wrung her hands together. "But thank you for thinking of her."

I retrieved a mug of tea for myself then perched on the edge of an armchair opposite the two women sitting on the sofa.

"Geri was just telling me about Nora firing the nurse." Tillie took a delicate sip of tea.

"What happened?" I asked.

"Nora is set in her ways and didn't want a stranger in her house." Geri sniffed. "She insists I'm capable of looking after her, preparing all our meals, and doing all the housework. She even wanted me to fire the gardener and have William take over his duties, but William—God rest his soul—flat out refused."

"But he was okay with you taking on all the responsibilities?" I eyed the platter of cookies sitting on the coffee table in front of me. Would it be rude of me to remove the plastic wrap and pass them around? My rumbling stomach decided for me.

"He'd say anything to appease his mother, and my objections meant nothing." Geri declined the cookies I'd offered, as did Tillie.

I covered the cookies back up and forlornly set the platter back onto the table. My stomach protested.

"Did you tell your mother-in-law that the nurse wouldn't cost her anything?" I couldn't quite understand why someone so seriously ill wouldn't want to have a trained medical professional look after them.

Geri seemed to look into her mug of tea, as if in deep thought. "William would never acknowledge it, but his mother is, in my opinion, an agoraphobic, on top of having scelerophobia."

"I know what agoraphobia is, but what is scel, uh, phobia?" I was sure I'd mangled the word.

"It's the fear of being burgled or robbed. She thinks any strangers coming to the house are coming to harm her." Geri's sigh filled the room. "It's a challenge, and it's getting worse as she ages."

"Oh dear. We're not causing her distress, are we?" Tillie looked contrite. She was probably regretting pushing herself into the house.

"She's on some pretty strong pain medication right now, which makes her sleep a lot. She doesn't know you're here, otherwise she'd be yelling for you to get out."

Which meant Nora hadn't known there had been someone with Geri before we showed up. Had Geri drugged her mother-in-law before that someone showed up?

Geri swallowed the rest of her tea and pointedly looked at her watch. "I really do have some appointments to get to, ladies. Thank you for the flowers and cookies. It means a lot that you've thought of me in this trying time."

Tillie lifted her mug and didn't budge an inch. "Just a few more minutes of your time, if you please."

The widow sank back into the limp cushions. "What questions do you need to ask me about my husband's murder, Matilda? I guess that's why you're paying a condolence call?"

It was nice that she got straight to the point instead of making us dance around to get answers. I jumped when Tillie spoke my name.

"What?"

"Emory, what is it you needed to know?" Tillie practically purred, and I glared at her. She should be the one asking questions.

"Mrs. Dalton, do you have any idea—even a wild guess—of who might have wanted to kill your husband?"

"No, and I told that detective the same thing. William didn't have any enemies." Geri twisted her fingers together.

"Detective? What detective?" I crossed my fingers, hoping it was Gabe and not Reece.

"I forget his name, but he's quite handsome and tall. Strawberry-blond hair, amber-colored eyes."

"Was his name Detective Gabe O'Neill?" Gabe's hair was golden, but perhaps in the lighting it looked redder.

"Yes, that's it." She fiddled with the thin gold chain she wore around her neck.

I didn't want to step on any toes, and I knew she would not like my next question, but it had to be asked. "Is it possible that one of your husband's clients was angry about the financial difficulty he and Ian found themselves in? Did someone else invest in the expansion with them?"

"Don't be ridiculous. That was all on Ian. William had

nothing to do with it except investing our hard-earned money and getting swindled."

"So there's no other silent business partner who invested with them?"

"How would I know?" she snapped. "It was William and Ian's company, which I had nothing to do with."

"I don't mean to cause you distress, but these questions need to be answered to rule out possible suspects." Even though Geri hadn't provided me with any useful information in the least, I still needed to pry.

"Shouldn't the police be investigating? I don't know why you think you should get involved. My husband's death has nothing to do with you."

Indirectly, it did because of Ian's poisoning. I wouldn't get into that with her though, so I ignored her comment. "Did Mr. Dalton and Mr. Hesser have office staff, like an administrative assistant?"

"They shared a secretary. I don't know what happened to her when the company folded, so don't ask me." She looked at her watch again. "Really, I can't delay leaving any longer. If you don't mind, I need to go."

Acquiescing, Tillie stood. I collected the tea mugs to take them to the kitchen.

Geri waved me off and moved to the front door, which she opened. "You can leave them. I don't mind cleaning them up later."

"Again, please accept our condolences and sympathy for your loss." Tillie reached out to touch Geri's arm, but the woman backed away. Tillie dropped her hand. "And please let your mother-in-law know we're so sorry for her loss as well."

Geri nodded, but I highly doubted our message would be passed along. She firmly shut the door the second we stepped outside.

"That didn't go too badly." Tillie looked up and down the street. "The black Ford Explorer has left."

"I know. It seems to have disappeared right around the same time the person in Geri's kitchen ran away." I didn't want to alarm Tillie but thought it better to voice my concerns. Leading her to the car, I waited until we were buckled up and driving out of the neighborhood. "What's the possibility of Detective Reece having something to do with Mrs. Dalton and her husband's murder?"

Tillie's head whipped around. "Do you mean to ask if he's investigating William's murder?"

"No…" I paused as I collected my thoughts. "What if he's personally involved with Mrs. Dalton, and he killed her husband?"

"That makes no sense if we agree Ian and William's deaths are connected."

"You make a good point, although I'm desperate to know who was hiding in the kitchen and why Mrs. Dalton didn't want us finding out." I watched as a car full of teen girls drove by, their windows down, music blasting. They all looked care-free, without a worry in the world. Had I ever been like that?

"Let's determine who stands to benefit from both Ian and William's deaths." Tillie's voice pulled me back from my musings.

"Presumably, Geri inherits whatever wasn't lost in the collapse of her husband's portion of the company and what-ever other assets they might have." I tapped a finger on my lips. "Did Ian change his beneficiary while going through the divorce, or will Rebecca stand to inherit any assets that weren't lost? Or is Frances his new beneficiary?"

"Maybe we need to be looking at this from another angle since everyone agrees both men lost just about everything with the collapse of their ill-advised venture. Who would be angry enough to kill both men? It could be for revenge if that person lost a lot of money too."

"Maybe Rebecca and Geri killed each other's spouse, or ex-spouse, as Rebecca's case may be. Kind of like a *Stranger on a Train* scenario." I racked my brain on how to prove or disprove any of our scenarios.

"Mrs. Skyler, might I interject a theory?" Andrew kept his eyes forward on the road, his gaze intent on the traffic.

"Please, go right ahead, Andrew. We need all the help we can get."

"If I recall correctly, Mrs. Allain's great-niece, Paris is her name, I believe?"

Tillie affirmed it was indeed Paris.

"She seemed overly dramatic upon Mr. Hesser's demise, on top of being quite—what's the word I'm looking for?— quite entitled, even more so than Mrs. Allain herself."

"You're not wrong, Andrew." I clapped him on his broad shoulder and felt nothing but hard muscles.

"It might behoove you to find out if Paris is the beneficiary of Mrs. Allain's estate. She seems the sort of person who would not take kindly to someone interjecting themselves into her aunt's affections and risk losing an inheritance to someone she clearly thought was a buffoon."

"And you know this how?" I asked.

"While serving the champagne, I happened to overhear a conversation she was having on the phone. She was quite livid about the engagement announcement, from what I gathered."

"But that wouldn't explain how or why she killed William. I don't see the connection there."

"I realize it would be a tremendous coincidence that both men were killed around the same time after both suffered enormous financial losses." Andrew turned the turn signal on, looked over his right shoulder, then merged into the lane that would take us to the 91 Freeway.

Once safely over, he continued. "But it's more probable that they were killed for different reasons by two different people. Paris, for one, is likely thrilled that Mr. Hesser is out of the picture. It puts her in a stronger position with her great-aunt. There's also his ex-wife. She's absolutely livid over his betrayal, both for the marital vows and for the financial support."

"It sounds like you picked up a lot of information at the reception." Tillie beamed like a proud parent. "What's your opinion about William's death?"

"From all accounts, he was the driving force behind the expansion of the company. Dig deep, and you'll probably find a silent investor."

Tillie and I looked at each other and exclaimed, at the same time, "Brad!"

"That would be a safe place to start." Andrew cleared his throat. "There's also the newly widowed Mrs. Dalton. By precipitating their destitution, dumping her with his sick mother, and expecting her to take over all the domestic duties, he may have pushed her over the edge."

## Chapter 26

Calling Brad was the second thing I did when we returned to Tillie's house. The dogs demanded a walk as soon as I opened the door. Worried about Reece returning, we'd left Piper and Missy locked tight at Tillie's instead of letting them have free access to my pool house and the accompanying yard. Once enough of their energy had been burned up on our brisk walk, I filled their bowls with fresh water and grabbed a glass of iced tea for myself.

"What's up, cupcake?" Brad sounded happy, so I hoped he wasn't on a deadline for anything.

"I have desperate need of Ethan's services. May I come down and talk to you both?" The ice tinkled in the glass as I tipped it to get the last swallow. Instead of the mouthful of tea slipping into my mouth, the ice cubes jetted out of the glass, ricocheted off my face, and clattered to the table and onto the floor.

"Em? You okay? What's that racket?"

I sputtered and used the sleeve of my dress—at least it was black—to wipe my face and neck off. "I'm okay. Sorry about that."

"What happened?"

Brad barely gave me time to explain before he guffawed into the phone. I held my cell away from my ear and waited for him to quiet down.

"I'm glad you found that entertaining," I said dryly.

"Emory. Why are there ice cubes melting all over the floor?" Tillie pointed beneath the table and around the chair I sat in.

This brought another outburst of laughter from Brad. I held a finger up to Tillie, indicating I needed a moment.

"Brad, unless you tell me otherwise, I'm coming to your office in about thirty minutes." Without giving him time to respond, I disconnected.

Once I'd grabbed a wad of paper towels, I told Tillie about my mishap while I cleaned up the mess. While she laughed alongside me, she wasn't quite as tickled as my best friend.

"I'm heading to Brad's office to detail what information we need Ethan to track down." I threw the paper towels away and wet a rag to mop the area of the spill. "Once I'm done there, I'll pick something up for dinner. Can you let Vannie know?"

"I'm texting her as we speak. I'll ask her if there's anything in particular she's craving for dinner."

"Good. She does so much cooking for us, I feel like I need to reciprocate more often." I rinsed out the rag and remopped the area.

"She's happy to do it and has told me frequently that it's her way of saying thank you for giving her a place to live— rent-free, she always says—and for embracing her as an integral part of the family."

For some reason, those words caused my eyes to prick with tears. "We're the lucky ones."

"Yes, we are, in so many ways." Tillie sniffed then went to

the dogs' cookie jar. "You girls have been so good today, yes you have."

She tossed them each a soft, chewy treat. Piper daintily chewed hers while Missy swallowed it whole then looked expectantly for another one. Tillie happily obliged, while I bit my tongue about spoiling them too much.

My messy mishap cleaned up, I kissed Tillie on the cheek, scratched the dogs behind their ears, and drove to Brad's office in Irvine, close to the airport. With no traffic, it might take twenty minutes. But late afternoon meant too many cars were out and about. It took forty minutes to pull into the crowded parking lot. Brad, having pity on me, had coned off one of the visitor parking spaces, so I didn't have to cruise around the neighborhood hunting for parking. It wasn't unusual to have to hike a quarter mile or more to the office after finding a curbside spot.

Brad must've been monitoring my progress on our shared location app because the door had been unlocked and he stood at the front counter. "I'm starving. Please tell me you brought cookies or cupcakes or something."

I rummaged in my handbag and brought out a gallon-sized plastic bag stuffed with cookies. When baking cookies the evening before, I'd baked up most of the frozen cookie dough in my freezer and had packaged them up just for this purpose.

Before I handed the bag to Brad, I shook my finger at him. "These are to share with your entire staff. Do not. Let me repeat that: do not eat these by yourself."

"Where's the fun in that?"

"Yeah, boss. You heard the cupcake lady. You gotta share with us lowly worker bees." Sylvia, her long black hair swinging over her shoulders, sauntered into the reception area. She took the bag from Brad's hands. "I'll go divide these into containers. You can have one and the rest of us will share."

"I want at least a dozen cookies in my container." Brad watched Sylvia amble away. "Do you hear me?"

"Yeah, yeah, boss. Don't worry. We won't let you waste away."

"I get no respect around here." Brad flicked the collar of my dress. "It's still wet from your tea. Why didn't you change?"

"I'm in too much of a hurry to find out a bunch of information." I pulled two small sandwich-sized plastic baggies filled with cookies from my purse. "For you and Ethan. I thought you both deserved extra treats."

"Not above bribing us, are you, cupcake?" Brad waggled his eyebrows then led me to Ethan's office.

"Thanks for the cookies," Ethan said when Brad tossed the plastic bag to him. He motioned for me to take a seat on the comfortable chair situated to the side of his desk, then pushed his black-framed glasses back up his nose. He looked like he could still be in high school, even though I knew he was already twenty-five. "I've gotten all the troll comments taken down from the review sites and your website. I'm still working on disrupting their systems so they'll be too busy trying to fix their computers to spread more malicious content. But the less you know about that, the better."

"I appreciate all you've done. Please let me know how much I owe you for the work."

"Boss man's already taken care of it." Ethan swooped his hand through his curly dark-brown hair, and his coal-black eyes glittered. "Besides, it's fun messin' with trolls like that."

"I know you're busy with that, along with your own company work, but I have some additional information I need pertaining to a couple of murders." I bit my lower lip, worried Ethan might be too busy.

"What kind of information?" The hacker opened the baggie and took out a few cookies. He popped an entire cookie into his mouth, chewed a few times, then swallowed. It was a good thing I'd packed him a dozen cookies. At this rate, they wouldn't last long.

"Do you mind, Brad, if I give Ethan details about the cases?" I waited, holding my breath, to hear his answer. If he worried Gabe would be upset about another civilian getting involved and wouldn't approve Ethan's involvement, I wasn't sure where I'd find the information I needed.

"As long as you're comfortable with it, Ethan, by all means, you're free to take on the work."

"With overtime pay?" He popped another cookie in his mouth.

"Naturally." Brad fist-bumped his employee. "And if you help solve the case, I'll throw in a bonus as well."

"Cool, dude." Ethan threaded his fingers together, flexed them backward until they popped, then pulled his keyboard toward him. "Hit me with the deets."

I gave him a quick overview of Ian's murder and the relationship between Frances Allain and Paris. "We need to find out if Paris stood to inherit a substantial portion of Frances's estate before Ian became involved with Frances. And if so, did Frances change her will to leave less to Paris so that Ian received her portion? It would be an excellent motive for Paris to have poisoned him."

"What's the name of the attorney and the law firm who drew up the will?" Ethan held his long, slender fingers over the keyboard, ready to type.

"Oh. I don't know." I frowned. "Can't you log in to some government site to find that out?"

"It's only available for public perusal after the person is deceased and the will has been submitted for probate with the proper authorities. While that person is alive, it's a confidential document between them and the attorney." Ethan clicked a few keys. "If you find out the name of the attorney and the law firm, I can probably get the information for you. Err, illegally, of course. Or, if you get me Mrs. Allain's email address,

I might be able to see if the attorney attached the will to an email for her review."

I seemed to recall Tillie complaining that Frances was a complete Luddite, which made working with her on a committee so difficult. I highly doubted she'd have asked her attorney to communicate and send sensitive documents along that route.

"Let me check with Tillie on that, and I'll get back to you." Disappointment made my shoulders sag. If we couldn't find out who benefited after Frances's death, we'd be at a dead end. Neither Frances nor Paris would give us the time of day, let alone answer sensitive questions.

"You said there had been a couple of murders. Is there any other information you need to find?" Ethan gazed at me expectantly.

"Both of the victims were joint owners of a business called Consolidated Investments. People we spoke with claim the first victim, Ian Hesser, is the one who pushed to expand their company and for the takeover by some other company, although I don't know the name. There are even rumors that Ian stole the money and defrauded the second victim, William Dalton."

A crease appeared between Ethan's eyebrows.

"Am I making this too complicated?" I asked.

"Not at all. I'm just envisioning the company setup." He waved his hand. "Please, continue."

"I'm wondering if there was a silent third party who invested in Consolidated Investments. When the company collapsed after the supposed takeover, this unknown person probably lost everything he'd invested. What if he, or she, decided retribution was called for and killed both Ian and William? Is it possible to locate any loan records between Ian, William, and a possible third person?"

"That's quite a challenging scenario you've just painted." Ethan pursed his lips and rested his chin on his palms, elbows propped up on the desk. "If this alleged third silent investor exists, I'm guessing the paperwork wasn't filed with the city or state government. At best, it was handled by attorneys between the three of them—I'll need their names and firms—or they may have even gone the route of a simple promissory note without involving attorneys."

I blew out a raspberry. "So this is a bust."

"Can't hack into everything, cupcake." Brad put his hand on my shoulder. "We'll have to resort to the old-fashion gumshoe method of investigating."

"You mean you'll interrogate Gabe and drag the answers out of him?" I winked at Ethan.

"Gah! You're determined to make this hard on me." He gave my shoulder a quick squeeze then sat down beside me. "No. You bake some swoon-worthy cupcakes—filled with booze—and get Tillie to shmooze those society ladies into spilling secrets with you by her side."

"Guess that'll have to do, except Frances and Paris Allain hate Tillie, and me by association, and they'll never agree to speak with us."

"What's the story between those two?" Brad asked.

"I dunno. Tillie won't say, and Frances is so awful, I don't dare ask her."

Ethan's gaze darted back and forth between us as he listened to our discussion. "I wouldn't mind some of those booze-filled cupcakes."

"Is he even twenty-one yet?" I whispered to Brad.

"I'm not sure," he answered from the side of his mouth.

"Dude, you know I am." Ethan stood, pulled his wallet from the side pocket of his tangerine-hued board shorts, extracted his driver's license, and handed it to me. "See? I turned twenty-five last month, so I'm legal."

"Just kidding. I bought your birthday cake with the twenty-five candles on it, remember?" Brad took the license from me and gave it back to Ethan. "Tell you what. Next time we have a company party, I'll have Em make some boozy cupcakes, as long as people who consume them have a safe ride home."

Brad had frequent nonmandatory fun events for his staff but never allowed alcohol except for his holiday bash. For the holiday party, he provided limos for everyone to ensure people could indulge without worrying about getting home.

"Sounds awesome. How about a margarita cupcake? Can you make those?" Ethan's eyes went wide.

"Sure. I'll keep on top of Brad to schedule something fun this spring that'll go with margaritas and margarita cupcakes." Brad might not appreciate my meddling, but Ethan had come through for me a few times, and it seemed the least I could do to pay him back—and maybe I'd inspire him to help us find a way to track down a killer.

# Chapter 27

Returning to Tillie's house, I toted in sacks of Thai takeout, enough for ten people. I wasn't sure who all would be around to eat, so I wanted to be prepared. Brad said he'd try to drop by later unless Gabe got off work at a decent hour, Vannie said she'd invite Theresa, and Brian said he'd eat leftovers when he came to my house after work.

Vannie sat at the kitchen table, with Theresa on one side and Tillie on the other. Their heads were bent together to look at the screen of a laptop. Piper and Missy finally noticed my arrival—or more likely smelled the food—and bolted from beneath the table to greet me.

"What are you studying?" I placed the takeout on the counter and pulled plates and flatware from their cupboard and drawer.

"You know how Gabe told Brad who told you that Detective Reece's ex-wife was a redhead just like you and that's his problem with you?" Vannie swiveled to look at me. "We got curious and decided to see if we could track her down on social media to find out if there are other similarities."

"I'm hoping if we find her, we'll be able to find him and

sic Gabe on him." Tillie's lips were pressed together in a firm, straight line. "Every second he's out there is another second I worry he's going to do something to you."

"I'm sure Gabe has thought of contacting his ex-wife. She might be in as much danger as me." I hated the thought of Reece jeopardizing the life of the mother of his children. But things like that happened. Unfortunately. "Are you having any luck finding her on social media?"

"Her name is fairly common, so we're trying to narrow down the parameters," Theresa said.

"Wait a minute. How do you know her name?" I didn't recall Brad or Gabe ever giving that information to me.

"I called that handsome detective and charmed it out of him." Tillie batted her realistic-looking fake eyelashes. "Her name is Ashley Greene."

"If anyone can do it, you're the one." I smiled fondly at her, enjoying her flirtatious nature. The Skyler family had hired me to care for Tillie and watch over her after she'd fallen down the stairs and broken her arm two years prior. They'd thought the accident had happened because she'd become feeble in her advanced age. In actuality, it was because she'd been sexting a silver fox while walking downstairs. I'd kept her secret the same as she'd kept my confidences.

"Something smells amazing." Brian walked into the kitchen. Both dogs danced around his feet, blocking me from getting a hug and kiss.

"You're here early!" I beamed, grateful I'd get more time to spend with him.

"I called in a favor, so here I am." He opened his arms wide, and I sidestepped the dogs and snuggled in for a quick hug.

"You just made my day a whole lot better. The Thai food is hot, and we're talking about the murder investigation." I handed him a plate then gave the dogs a bully stick each—

safely tethered to a device so they couldn't swallow the piece whole, which Missy was prone to do. I passed out the remaining plates and poured iced water for everyone.

"Let me know what I can do to help with the investigation." Brian piled his plate high with jasmine rice, red curried chicken, shrimp pad Thai, and lemon fish.

Vannie nudged her half brother. "Hungry a bit?"

"I haven't eaten since eight this morning." Brian grinned at her to let her know he didn't mind that she teased him.

Tillie gasped. "Brian, you know that's not healthy."

"Trust me, Gram. It wasn't intentional." He balanced a summer roll on top of his food before taking a seat. "Lunch service got insane… in a good way, and then I decided I needed to spend time with Em and the family. After practically coercing my replacement into covering for me, I had to scramble to do everything else I would have done between dinner prep and cleanup."

I sat beside Brian, my plate filled with Thai delicacies, and hugged him. "I'm so glad you're here."

"While we're eating, catch me up on your investigation. Have they caught that Reece guy yet?"

"Regrettably, no. Vannie, Theresa, and Tillie are hunting online for the ex-wife. According to Gabe, she recently moved to Southern California with their two teen kids, which is why he followed them out here." I forked a large bite of spicy red chicken curry into my mouth. My eyes watered from the spicy heat while my cheeks flushed hot.

Brian noticed and jumped up. He returned to the table with a large glass of milk and a carton of sour cream. "Drink the milk. It'll tone down the capsaicin."

I did as he suggested, and it didn't take long for the burning to be soothed. Before Brian and I had become a couple, he'd saved me from an errant jalapeño by sharing some cheese with me. I'd been mortified then, given my uncontrollable coughing fit and the mascara running down my cheeks, but also grateful that he knew what to do.

"Thanks. I'm sure I told them mild curry, but they must've gotten the order wrong."

Theresa had practically finished her red curry and rice. "I'm glad they goofed. This is delicious."

Brian handed the sour cream to me. "Mix some into the rest of your curry and you should be okay."

I did as instructed then shared the sour cream with Tillie. Vannie apparently had a tongue of steel because she had no trouble eating the spicy dish.

"Back to tracking down the ex-wife. You found her on social media?" Brian asked, inhaling another large bite of the curry. The spiciness didn't affect him at all.

"We've narrowed her name down to about forty Facebook profiles. Who knew there'd be so many Ashley Greenes out there? We'd just started clicking through them when you got here." Vannie pulled her laptop over, woke up the screen, and started scrolling. "A lot of the profiles have privacy controls in place, and their profile pics are avatars or nature scenes."

"I'll bet she has the max security and privacy controls in place after being married to a law enforcement officer." Brian picked up the carton and scraped the remaining curry onto his plate. It was a good thing there was another container of it left in case Brad joined us.

"Is that because she doesn't want him to find her, or she doesn't want other people to find her?"

"Now that they're divorced, it might be for both reasons."

"Do any of the profile photos show someone with red hair?" I thought it would be the easiest way to narrow down the profiles.

"I already thought of that, and unfortunately, no one has red hair." Vannie began clicking on the tiny profile photos then scrolling through news feeds. It astounded me how many people put all their posts out for the entire world to see, without a care for security.

The rest of us returned to our meal while Vannie clicked away. She'd occasionally take a bite of food or a sip of water but then would go straight back to hunting for the elusive redheaded woman. I was beginning to think she must not have a Facebook account when Vannie lifted her finger into the air.

"Hold on. I think I might have found her." She swiveled her laptop to face us. "This Ashley used a flower for her profile pic, and her cover photo is more flowers."

She continued to scroll down the newsfeed until she came to a group of about ten people posing for the photo in front of a lake. "Someone, using the public security setting, tagged her three years ago. They also tagged the location as Mohonk Resort in the Hudson Valley. Didn't you say she moved here from back East a while ago with her two kids?"

"Yes. It's why Reece followed her." I got up and stood behind Vannie, wanting to get a closer look at the woman. There was only one redheaded woman, and she had her arms draped over the shoulders of a boy and a girl, perhaps eleven or twelve years old. The woman's hair was similar to my color, but our similarities ended there. Her hair was long, and she wore it in a braid that cascaded over her shoulder. She was tall and slender, with long, long legs that were tanned. The halter top she wore showcased well-toned muscles. It made little sense that Reece would fixate on me simply because of my hair color. Nothing else about me was remotely similar to his ex-wife.

"I don't suppose her page indicates where she's now living?" I asked my sister, even though I knew the answer.

"No."

"Em, call Brad and have his guy track her down now that we know her name." Tillie rubbed her hands together. "I feel like we're closing in on that horrible Reece, and we can't waste any time."

"If you got Ashley's name from Gabe, don't you think he's already contacted her to see if she knew where Reece was? He is a good detective, and it's probably one of the first things he did when Reece got away."

"Humor an old lady, please?" Tillie flashed a duck-face pose at me. "Gabe is probably tied up with William's murder out in the wilderness. We need to give him a helping hand however we can, and tracking down the ex-wife is the place to start."

"Okay, but just giving Ethan a name with no other information aside from the facts that she has red hair, is about thirty-five or forty years old, used to be married to Reece, and has two kids probably isn't going to be enough."

Brian picked up my phone and handed it to me. "The fact that she is Reece's ex-wife should be enough for him to track her down. She's probably listed as his emergency contact, and Ethan can take it from there."

"Good point." I quickly thumbed a text to Brad, hoping he hadn't left the office yet. I promised cupcakes would be forthcoming within the next day or two.

The message swooshed off into cyberspace, and we waited for a reply. It came in the form of a thumbs-up emoji less than a minute later. A minute after that, he sent another text. Tillie and Vannie crowded around me to read it. Disappointment swept over me when it didn't contain any information about Ashley.

**Something came up at work. Can't make it over tonite. I'll call u tomorrow.**

"There's nothing more we can do this evening, so you lovebirds should take the dogs for a walk and call it a night." Tillie practically pushed us from the kitchen. The dogs, hearing the word "walk," scrambled to their feet and galloped toward the front door.

"We'll clean up dinner dishes first." I tried picking up the dirty plates, but with Vannie, Theresa, and Tillie insisting they'd do it, Brian and I left.

Nothing untoward happened during our walk, and in fact, it was quite peaceful. We went back to the pool house, watched some TV, and didn't talk once about murder before settling in for slumber.

## Chapter 28

When I hadn't heard from Brad by ten the next morning, I boxed up the raspberry lemon cupcakes I'd baked since I had extra raspberries on hand and headed to his office. Brian had taken the opportunity to get some early morning surfing in, Tillie had a hair appointment, and Vannie was at work. I felt at loose ends having so many clients cancel their cupcake orders, and the rest of my people were busy with their own lives.

Besides catering cupcakes and desserts, I worked part-time for David Skyler, Tillie's son, doing some administrative and accounting work at his home. He allowed me to come and go from his house as I pleased, which gave me the flexibility needed for my cupcake business. Since David had been traveling in Europe for the past two weeks and wouldn't be home for another week, I hadn't stopped by his house in quite a while. It was past time I tended to those admin responsibilities after checking in with Brad.

The office door to Brad's company was locked when I arrived—which wasn't abnormal since most of their clients did business with his company virtually—so I called the office phone number. A young woman answered, identifying herself as Star. I'd never spoken to or met her before. She seemed hesitant to come let me in, but she promised to check with one of the other employees. I shifted the cupcake box to my other arm and started to call Brad when the snick of the door lock made me look up from my screen.

"Emory. You should have let us know you were coming." Sylvia held the door wide open and, once I'd stepped inside the office, locked it behind me. "Ooh, what goodies did you bring today?"

"Raspberry lemon cupcakes. Should I put them in the break room?"

"Nope. You should hand them over to me." Brad held his hands out, palms up, fingers curling in and out.

"There's no need to be greedy. I brought enough for everyone unless you have a bunch of new employees I don't know about." I handed the box over to Sylvia and ignored Brad's pout.

"Only Star. She started today, so maybe she should be the first to get a cupcake." Sylvia pulled the box away from Brad and started down the hall.

"Make sure Ethan gets one," I yelled at her retreating figure.

"There'd better be at least one, if not two, cupcakes left for me." Brad followed down the hall, and I fell into step beside him.

"Has Ethan found any information for us?"

"Not yet. One of the games we're slated to release in a couple of weeks had a major programming glitch, so it's been all hands on deck to find the bug." Brad tugged at the ends of his wavy hair. "I didn't get much sleep last night, and I've got a splitting headache."

"I'm sorry I'm intruding this morning. Maybe I should have called first."

"No prob. Besides, your cupcakes are just what we needed to rally the troops. That, and a few gallons of coffee."

"Would you like me to make some fresh coffee while I'm here?" I'd spent enough time in Brad's office to know where everything was.

"I just hit the brew button when Star told me you were at the front door." Brad led the way to the open room that contained several cubicles.

There were seven employees sitting in their gray-fabric cubicles. Most had headphones on, and all were glued to the large monitors sitting in front of them. Sylvia went to each person, added a cupcake to one of the paper plates she'd picked up from the break room, and set it on their desk. Almost none of the employees looked up from their work. Those who looked up acknowledged her with a dip of their head or a quick wave of a hand.

"You're busy, so I'm going to get out of your hair." I turned and went back to the front office, with Brad beside me. "It's been over a week since I've worked at David's, and it'd be my luck he decides to come home early, without warning."

"Is Hannah there?" Brad asked.

He knew I had a difficult time being at David's house without his trusted housekeeper there. I'd found a body in the pool before, and ever since, I felt uneasy being alone in the house.

"No, she's on vacation this week."

"If I didn't have this nightmare of a deadline, I'd come keep you company." He stroked his chin, his unshaven skin rasping beneath his fingers. "Take Piper and Missy with you. They're good company and watchdogs."

I almost snorted. "Yeah, they're great watchdogs until someone offers them a treat, and then they become their new best friend. Don't worry. I'll be all right."

Brad slung an arm around my shoulder and gave me a tight squeeze before he unlocked the front door for me. "I'll let you know the second Ethan can track down that info for you."

•  •  •

WORKING QUICKLY to sort through the mail, pay bills, and respond to gala and charity event invitations, it only took me a couple of hours to finish at David's. Still feeling at loose ends, I decided to pick up a burger and fries and drive back to Chino Hills to question Geri. Tillie wouldn't be happy about me going on my own, but she was busy, and I had nothing better to do.

With Reece out of the picture, my imminent arrest wasn't nearly as dire. Still, with the lack of cupcake orders and all but a small handful of customers canceling their current orders, if I didn't clear my name, I might as well trade in my apron for a calculator and spreadsheet.

Traffic was light, and I arrived on Geri's street just before two. I parked at the curb in front of her house, careful to not scrape my tires on the concrete berm. Tossing the empty burger sack onto the passenger-side floorboard, I tidied up my hair and reapplied some lipstick. I'd just opened my door when I spotted the black Explorer parked three houses up, on the opposite side of the street… several houses away from where it had been parked on our previous visit.

Could it be the same vehicle? Was that person visiting Geri? Or did I just have an overactive imagination? There was only one way to find out. Taking a deep breath, I threw my SUV's door open and made my way to ring the doorbell. Faint chimes could be heard from inside the house, but no one came to answer. I rang again, and after opening the screen door, pounded on the door using my fist. Still, no one came. Had something happened to Geri's mother-in-law? Surely she wouldn't have been left on her own. I wished I was tall enough to peek in through the garage windows that lined the top edge of the door, but I wasn't. If a vehicle were parked in the garage, I'd hang around longer and try ringing the doorbell again.

Giving up, I returned to my vehicle. The black Explorer still sat parked down the block, and not a single person could be seen. I climbed into my vehicle, shut the door, then glanced back at the house. A curtain twitched at the far-left window, from a bedroom was my guess.

I pretended not to notice and drove off down the street. Turning the corner, I did a U-turn and pulled back onto Geri's street and parked several car lengths back from the Explorer. Sorry I had ever chosen the brightly colored cherry-red paint for my vehicle, I slunk down into my seat. I'm sure I wasn't fooling anyone, as conspicuous as I was, but hopefully, whoever owned the Explorer would have their minds on other things and not on keeping a watchful eye out for an inquisitive cupcake baker.

An hour later and with an overly full bladder, I gave up on the stakeout. Tillie had texted me three times, asking me to call—I didn't, not wanting a lecture on my foolhardiness of visiting Geri alone. Vannie texted me once saying she wouldn't be home for dinner and a second time telling me to call Tillie. I thought I'd knock on Geri's door one more time—after hitting a fast-food establishment for their restroom facilities and a Coke—before heading home.

It had only taken me fifteen minutes to take care of my pressing needs, but in that time, the Explorer had left. Had they been watching me and departed once I was out of the area? Or was I being paranoid?

This time, I parked curbside in front of the house and practically stomped up to the front door. I pressed on the doorbell several times and knocked, using my fists. No one answered. Giving up, I stomped back to my car and sent Tillie a text.

**Sorry for delay. On way hm. C u in about an hr.**

Little dots appeared, so I waited for her reply. I almost started driving when the dots disappeared, then decided—wisely, if I say so myself—to wait a bit longer. I didn't need a ticket for reading a text while driving, and if I reached the freeway before it came, there wouldn't be anywhere to safely pull over.

After what felt like an hour—but was likely only three minutes—Tillie's text appeared.

**Frances and Paris will be at club for an event tonight. Hurry home and dress nice. We need to leave at six. It'll be the perfect cover to interrogate them.**

I mulled over the part about dressing nicely. Nice as in business casual or nice as in formal wear? Or somewhere in between?

**What shd I wear?**

While waiting for her reply, I examined my ragged nails and wished I had an emery board in the car. My mind wandered to other items I wished I had available in my car for times like this, and I made a mental list to put together a small tote.

**Your black cocktail dress. The one you wore to Brad and Gabe's wedding.**

Whoa. She was talking formal. I wasn't sure I was up for something like that tonight.

**What's the event? It sounds 2 formal.**

She instantly replied.

**I'll tell you on the way. Don't be late.**

And with that admonishment, I put the car into drive and headed into the traffic to fight my way home.

Chapter 29

S eated beside Tillie in the back seat of the town car, I fidgeted with the neckline of my dress. The sweetheart style had just enough ruching to complement my minimal assets, but it felt like it was gaping at the side. Had I lost some weight? The wrap-style dress still clung to all the good curves while the black silk skirt fabric floated around the curves I'd prefer to be minimized. Still, it felt looser than when I'd last worn it at Brad and Gabe's wedding.

"Tell me about the event and why you think it's a good place to question Frances and Paris?" In my mind, the best-case scenario would be the snooty pair would simply ignore us. The worst would be Frances and Paris would cause a big scene and place the blame on us. I would've placed money on the latter, yet Tillie didn't seem concerned.

"It's a cocktail reception for some famous retired New York baseball personality who wants to join the club. I wasn't planning on attending, but then I heard they're bringing in his favorite band, FS Reimagined—well, I guess it's really a cover band playing Frank Sinatra's top hits—to play during the cocktail hour." Tillie smoothed down her platinum hair cut in a chin-length bob. "The music will be loud enough to cover our questions, and the band is popular enough that most people will have their attention on them instead of on us."

"Do you really think Frances will allow herself to be cornered by us?" I took the lipstick Tillie handed to me and swiped the familiar pink onto my lips.

She took the lipstick back and tucked it into her black velvet clutch. "She's not wily enough to evade me. You'll be in charge of cornering Paris and questioning her."

"You have a lot of faith in my abilities. Paris is going to take off running as soon as she sees me."

"I highly doubt that, Emory. People like her never notice the 'help.'" Tillie curled her index fingers over and bounced them a few times. "Trust me. She won't remember seeing you at Frances's house on Saturday."

"Let me get this straight. I should simply walk up to her and start a conversation then ask some pointed questions about the murder?" It was much easier to do when I offered cupcakes first.

"You'd be better off bringing an extra glass of champagne to offer her. She's not much younger than you, so I'm sure she'll be bored being surrounded by all us old geezers listening to old-time music. You can bond over that or over her having to work for her great-aunt and you having to work for your grandmother."

"I guess we'll never know if it'll work if we don't give it a try." I gave Tillie a side-eye. "And how are you planning on getting Frances alone to question her? She'll see you coming and will avoid you like the plague."

Tillie's eyes held a wicked gleam. "My secret weapon is meeting us there and will have her corralled and waiting for my interrogation."

"Who's your secret weapon?" I wrinkled my nose. "She'll never fall for it."

"Frances is mighty interested in claiming a certain English

baron for herself." Tillie rubbed her hands together with glee. "And he's agreed to sacrifice his dignity to trap her for me."

"I didn't know John was in town!" John was Tillie's significant other when he came to town every couple of months. While Tillie was petite and elegant, John was a bit on the roly-poly side. Until you heard him speak, most people would assume he was unsophisticated. But as soon as his posh baritone words hit the air, I always felt like I was listening to some BBC royalty drama.

"He flew in yesterday but has been caught up in meetings in LA. We were planning on getting together this evening anyway when this opportunity to investigate came up." Tillie's face turned rosy. "John's always game for intrigue just as much as I am."

"That's great, but isn't Frances in mourning or something? Her fiancé just died."

Tillie snorted. "I doubt that biddy has given Ian an iota of a thought except to be annoyed by the inconvenience his murder may have caused her."

"Harsh…"

"But true. Trust me, she'll be latching on to John the second she sees him walk through the door and me nowhere in sight." She used a compact mirror to double-check her makeup. It was flawless, as usual.

"If she's not upset over Ian's death, why was she engaged to him in the first place?"

"He made for good arm candy at all the functions she attends—a younger man paying court to an older woman and all that nonsense. I also heard that one of the younger divorcees at the club had been seen flirting with Ian, and Frances most likely wanted to snatch him up before anyone else did."

"I almost feel sorry for the guy." Almost, but not quite. He'd treated his ex-wife horribly in front of all their contemporaries.

Andrew pulled up in front of the clubhouse and came to a stop. He had Tillie's door open before I'd even unlatched my seat belt.

"Ladies, text me when you're ready to depart, and it'll take but a moment to meet you right here." He shut the door, offered Tillie his arm, and walked her to the front door. I followed behind.

The strains of jazz music drifted to the foyer before a male voice began singing familiar lyrics. The hum of conversation and clinking crystal joined the sibilation. Tillie and I left Andrew behind and climbed the stairs to the main ballroom. Before we reached the sumptuously decorated large room, Tillie pulled me into an alcove and took her phone out.

"I need to text John and find out where they are." She thumbed the text then closed the phone. "He's supposed to keep an eye out for Paris, if at all possible. We don't need you wandering all over the place, hunting for her, and giving Frances an opportunity to see you."

A server walked by, carrying a tray filled with bubbling crystal flutes of champagne. Tillie waved him over and took two glasses.

Before she'd taken a sip, her phone chimed with a text. She handed her glass to me and read the screen.

"Paris is parked at the bar, chatting up Vince. John has Frances out on the balcony overlooking the golf course and says to come rescue him." Tillie chuckled. "We have our marching orders, so let's do this."

She clinked her flute to mine, took a sip, then hustled to track down her prey. I took a healthy gulp from my flute and went to find Paris.

As John had said, Paris was indeed at the bar, practically draped over the counter as she flirted with Vince. She wore a black halter dress that hugged her curves. The skirt of the dress barely covered her slender tanned thighs, catching the attention of most of the men waiting in line for a cocktail.

There were plenty of waitstaff circling around to fetch cocktails and hors d'oeuvres, so I had a feeling it was Paris who'd lured them over to the bar. I tugged at my dress again, making sure it was straight.

Vince spied me before I sidled up beside Paris. "Hey, Emory, what can I get you?"

A few of the men waiting to be served glowered at me. I didn't blame them. Paris remained facing Vince and never glanced in my direction.

"I'm good for now," I said, holding up the champagne flute.

"Just let me know when you need a refill." Vince returned to the cocktail he was crafting then handed the pink concoction to Paris with a flourish. "And I'll be happy to make another when you're ready."

This time, none of the men glowered. Instead, their gaze seemed to follow every movement Paris made. Vince winked at Paris and started pouring three glasses of wine and two old-fashioned glasses of whiskey. I sat on the barstool next to Paris and took another sip of champagne.

"Why are you behind the bar tonight? Shouldn't you be managing the party?" I asked Vince.

"One of the scheduled bartenders called in sick, and we couldn't get anyone to fill in, so here I am." He handed off the glasses of wine to a server. "The club's special event manager is in charge tonight anyway, and the second bartender is holding down the fort out on the patio."

I held up my champagne flute in a toast and tilted my head toward the growing line. "Good luck."

Paris didn't exactly guzzle her cocktail, but neither did she sip it slow enough to make it last more than ten minutes. She seemed to have ignored my conversation with Vince, and I'd hoped she'd join in to give me an opening to chat with her. I gritted my teeth, forced myself to relax, then pasted a smile on my lips.

"What kind of cocktail is that?" I placed my still half-full flute of champagne on the counter. The small red dots floating in the pink mixture intrigued me.

"A pink pomegranate margarita. It's good. You should try one." She braced her stilettos on the barstool rung and lifted herself to drape halfway over the bar. "Hey, Vince. Make another couple of these and give one to her."

Paris slurred just a bit and seemed unsteady on her feet. I raised an arm behind her to catch her should she fall. It seemed like most of the men in line were prepared to do the same.

"You got it, Paris." Vince plucked a bottle of tequila, one I wasn't familiar with, and started making the pink margarita.

"Uh, don't rush it on my account." I nodded toward the line. "These gentlemen were here before me."

Paris plopped back onto her seat and playfully slapped my hand. "You silly. They don't mind at all. Ladies first. Am I right?"

Two guys seemed to want to disagree with her, but the rest appeared content to wait.

"Thanks. That's such a pretty shade of pink."

She finally turned to take a good look at me. "It doesn't go with your hair color very well. Maybe Vince should make you something else."

"No. I'm good with the pomegranate margarita. It looks very refreshing."

"Oh, it is." She finished the inch of cocktail left and set the empty glass on the bar top. "Oh, Vince. I'm ready when you are."

Paris's singsong voice seemed to throw out inappropriate meaning to her words.

Vince's smile caused his dimple to appear. He set the two glasses, filled to the brim, in front of us. "Let me know when you're ready for another."

Paris picked her glass up and tapped it against mine. "Here's to getting through this mind-numbing night."

My cocktail sloshed over the top when Paris tapped it, and I hastily grabbed a napkin and blotted up the liquid. Taking a tentative sip, I almost choked. Vince had gone extra heavy on the tequila and extra light on pomegranate juice. I struggled to keep a smile on my face as I swallowed.

"Wow."

"Vince is an amazing mixologist, isn't he?" She took another healthy swig. My eyes watered just watching her drink the stuff.

"Uh, yes, he is." I pretended to take another drink. "How'd you end up at this thing?"

"Gah. My great-aunt made me come. She said it was a good place to find a suitable husband." Paris whipped her head around to gaze behind her, hair flying. "As if there's anyone here worth looking at. Well, besides Vince."

It was good to know she wasn't snobby when it came to men who had to work for a living.

"Of course he's gorgeous and would be fun to slum around with, but he could never support me in the way I deserve."

I'd been too gracious with my thoughts on her snobbishness. It was time to change the subject to crime before Vince overheard Paris insulting him. I'd hate for there to be another murder that evening.

"Who's your great-aunt?"

"Frances Allain. I'm sure you've heard of her. She's high society and all that." Paris pulled a red tube from the tiny purse sitting on the bar. She slowly twisted the lipstick tube until the vivid red appeared over the barrel. She swiveled her stool until she faced the line of men, crossed her legs, then slowly glided the lipstick over her lips.

I took a healthy gulp of margarita and managed to not

cough. We'd only been at the event for twenty minutes, and I was ready to throttle the young woman.

When she finally turned her attention back to her drink, I decided it was time to plunge in before she got plastered or wandered off with a man willing to support her in the way she deserved.

"Oh-em-gee. Didn't her fiancé just die?" I widened my eyes and tried to act shocked. It didn't really matter because she wasn't paying me much attention.

"Yeah. The caterer poisoned him with a cupcake." Paris looked bored by the conversation.

I bit my tongue and cautioned myself to stay calm. "Wow. Was the caterer arrested?"

She shrugged. "I dunno. Probably?"

"Why is your aunt here this evening? I'd think she'd want to be at home grieving. I know I would if I just lost my fiancé to a murderer."

Paris turned her gaze to me. Her eyes were becoming bloodshot, and they seemed to have a hard time focusing. "Just between us girls, and because I'm bored out of my mind, I'll tell you."

I leaned in to hear her slurring words better.

"Promise you won't tell anyone I told you?"

I quickly agreed while crossing my fingers behind my back.

"She's here looking for another husband to prop up her finances." Paris took a cautious look around us, as if to make sure no one was listening in. "Her fiancé, Ian, invested most of her money and lost it all. She didn't find out until he'd been murdered."

# Chapter 30

It was a good thing I hadn't consumed the entire margarita because I would've fallen off the barstool. "No! How did that happen?"

Paris turned back to her drink, took a long sip, and shrugged. I guess sharing time was over.

I looked up just in time to see Vince's eyes go wide. His gaze darted to me, and he mouthed the word "run" while pointing to the side of the bar that led to the kitchen. I didn't bother looking over my shoulder and took Vince at his word. Trotting the best I could in the high heels I wore, I scurried from the bar.

I'd just stepped around the corner of the hallway leading to the kitchen when I heard Frances Allain berating Paris. Beads of sweat popped out on my forehead, thinking about what would have happened had she caught me.

Not knowing what to do, I stayed put, waiting until I was certain Frances was no longer in the vicinity. Several of the waitstaff gave me quizzical looks, but none stopped to ask if I needed help or told me to leave.

A few minutes later, Vince appeared. "Girl, you're playing with fire."

"Don't I know it." I swiped the back of my hand across my forehead in a dramatic gesture. "Are they gone yet?"

"Yep. Mrs. Allain practically pulled Paris out of the ballroom by her ear."

"Yikes." I kind of felt sorry for Paris, but then I remembered her condescending attitude about those she deemed inferior.

"No kidding." Vince swept his arm toward the ballroom. "Would you like a fresh pomegranate margarita or something else?"

"No thanks. I think it's time to find Tillie."

"If you change your mind, let me know." He saluted. "And I hope you got the information you were hunting for."

I meandered through the ballroom, searching for Tillie and John. Tillie was close to five and a half feet tall when wearing heels, but John was a couple of inches shorter than her. It made it difficult trying to find them, since most of the men in the room were closer to six feet. When I didn't see them, I checked the various balconies with no success. Next, I checked the ladies' lounge. Tillie wasn't there, although I spotted two of her bridge cohorts touching up their makeup. Neither of them had seen Tillie recently.

Flummoxed, I retrieved my cell phone from my less-than-glamourous purse, intending to text her. When it powered on —the country club had a no-cell policy, although I was probably the only one who adhered to the rules—I found a text from Tillie.

**I'm leaving with John. Frances is on the warpath, so if you're with Paris, get out. I'll let Andrew know you'll need a ride home.**

Tillie should have warned me to leave my phone on. I shuddered, thinking about what could have happened had Frances caught me, especially after Tillie thwarted her attempt at wooing John.

A text from Andrew appeared, letting me know he'd wait for me to contact him whenever I wanted to leave.

Now was as good a time as any. My stomach rumbled, and I was sorry I'd missed the hors d'oeuvres since I'd been intent on questioning Paris. I replied to Andrew, letting him know I'd be heading out within a couple of minutes.

No one paid me any attention as I wound my way through the throngs of people standing in clusters, sipping on cocktails. Passing by a group of four men, all dressed in black suits and red power ties, I heard one of them mention Ian. I paused and tried to listen in while I pretended to search my purse for something.

"If you ask me, Ian got what he deserved." The baritone's voice practically growled. "First, he bankrupts the Daltons and the Mitchells, then he leaves Rebecca high and dry. She's going to lose her house, from what I hear."

"I heard he left Frances Allain a lot poorer too," another man said.

The men all chuckled before the same man continued. "You'd better watch out for her, though. From the looks of things this evening, she's back on the hunt for another husband."

"You couldn't pay me enough to date her," the baritone answered.

"Has anyone set up a betting pool on who killed Ian?" The speaker's voice was tinny, and from the corner of my eye, I could see he was extremely skinny, with a pencil-thin mustache. "If not, we need to start one."

The baritone guffawed. "That's too easy. It was William Dalton for sure."

Apparently, word hadn't gotten out that William had been murdered as well. I desperately hoped they threw out a few more suspects' names.

"Miss, can I help you?" An older man with a nameplate of

Adam Sutton pinned to his lapel stood next to me. He looked like a manager.

"Uh, no thanks. I'm looking for my car keys before I head out." I held up my purse.

"May I ask which member you're here with?"

"Matilda Skyler." I looked around the ballroom, as if searching for her.

"She's already departed, so I recommend you follow suit." He held his arm out, toward the exit, as if to escort me.

Heat flooded my face and grew even hotter when the four men turned to look at me. I hoped they hadn't noticed me eavesdropping on their conversation. Nodding, I followed the manager. He walked with me all the way to the front door and made sure I was outside and crossing the parking lot before he returned to the clubhouse.

The parking lot was filled with row after row of luxury cars. Not knowing where Andrew had parked, I sent him a text telling him to meet me by the entrance of the parking lot. I didn't want to be seen anywhere close to the clubhouse in case the manager was waiting to kick me off the property.

I scurried behind the cars parked in the furthest row from the clubhouse entrance, bent over at the waist to keep from being easily seen. I found Andrew behind the wheel of the town car, the engine running, prepared to flee the parking lot as soon as I slid into the back seat. The second I slammed the car door closed, he put the car into drive and headed toward my home. Once I was safely buckled in, I sent Tillie a text about the conversation I'd eavesdropped on.

**I overheard someone mention Mitchells in rela-tion to Ian and being bankrupt. Do u know them? Maybe new suspects?**

I felt like we'd done nothing but spin our wheels so far, going nowhere in solving the crimes. Were we overlooking information, or had some unknown person killed both men and the cases might never be solved?

Tillie texted back right away.

**Come to my house. We'll brainstorm then.**

My mind felt like I was on a Tilt-A-Whirl ride, and I didn't want to wait another minute to talk about what I'd discovered. But, since I had no choice, I tried to relax my shoulders and played Candy Crush to distract myself.

Chapter 31

Piper and Missy greeted me like a long-lost relative when I walked in. I gave them some extra attention then followed them to the kitchen. Gabe had settled in at the table, with Vannie and Tillie flanking him. An enormous platter piled high with nachos sat in the middle of the table, along with a pitcher of what I assumed was margaritas. Smaller bowls of sour cream and guacamole were beside the platter.

"Where's Brad?" I asked.

Gabe wrinkled his nose and drew his eyebrows downward. "Working. It's going on two days since he's been home."

"You poor dear." Tillie patted his hand. "You know you're welcome here anytime you need family to hang out with. Even when you don't have a case to discuss with us."

Vannie pushed a clean plate toward Gabe. "Help yourself to the nachos. If you don't want a margarita, we have beer, soda, or water."

"I think I deserve a margarita, but make it a small one." Gabe used the spatula to pile nachos onto his plate.

A stray tortilla chip flew from the spatula across the table and landed on the floor. Missy snatched it up before Piper even knew something had been there. I felt sorry for Piper, so I dropped another chip for her to scoop up. Missy's toffee-brown eyes gazed at me sorrowfully, so I gave them both a half chip each.

"Now who's spoiling the dogs?" Vannie shook her index finger at me. "At least Gram usually gives them dog-appropriate food, like meat or dog treats."

"You're right." I shook my finger at the dogs. "You got me in trouble. No more swiping from either of you."

Once we all had plates filled with nachos and drinks of our choosing, Tillie tapped my arm. "Tell us about the event this evening. I didn't quite understand all that you were texting about."

More likely, John had kept her distracted. Which made me realize he wasn't here. "Where did John go? I didn't even have a chance to say hello to him at the event."

"He had another meeting at the crack of dawn up in LA, so he left already."

"How long is he in town for?" Vannie asked.

"At least another two weeks. He'll be here this weekend, so we'll need to plan a family dinner."

Tillie, Vannie, and I hosted a family—with friends included—Sunday dinner at least once or twice a month. We'd started out with a weekly dinner but, with everyone's schedules, found it to be too much. Plus, with my twin nieces busy with school and activities, staying out on a Sunday evening made it more difficult for my sister to get them out the door Monday morning.

"Back to the murder investigation." I put my margarita down. "I, ah, overheard a conversation about Ian. Not only did the Daltons go bankrupt, but the Mitchells did as well. They also thought Rebecca would lose her house soon because of Ian's financial disaster. And, get this, Ian invested Frances's money and lost that too! According to Paris, she didn't find out until he'd already been killed."

"It's a good thing he was already dead, otherwise Frances would have done the deed herself." Tillie pursed her lips. "Maybe she found out about his faulty investment before they made the announcement and went ahead with the engagement scene to cover her tracks?"

"Could be, but I don't see her shooting William and dragging him out into the wilderness. Unless there are two murderers, or she had an accomplice, I think we need to look elsewhere." I took a sip of the margarita. It was a lot milder than what Vince had made at the country club and much more to my liking. It reminded me we hadn't talked about Frances's niece as a suspect. "Gabe, have you looked into Paris Allain yet? Is it possible she wanted Ian out of the way so she'd inherit Frances's estate?"

"But why would she kill William?" Tillie shook her head. "I'm not a fan of the young woman, but I don't see her doing in either of those men."

"It could be she found out Ian lost Frances's investment, and she blamed both him and William for it. They were business partners, after all." Out of everyone we'd talked to, Paris had the most access to poisoning the cupcakes, and she was young enough, and probably devious enough, to have lured William to his death.

"We've looked into Ms. Allain's background, but there's no evidence that proves she killed anyone." Gabe's mouth pressed into a thin line.

"What I'm hearing you say is there is no evidence, but that doesn't rule her out. Am I right?" I almost laughed at Gabe's annoyed expression. "At any rate, Tillie, do you know the Mitchells and if they could have been involved in either Ian's or William's death?"

"Yes, I know them. Lovely people, although it's quite tragic what happened to them." Tillie blotted her lips with a linen napkin.

"What happened?" Vannie and I both said at the same

time. I glanced over at Gabe. He was busy shoveling food into his mouth.

"Oh, it must've been three or four months ago. Frank Mitchell had a stroke, which incapacitated him, even though he was only in his early sixties. Last I heard, he was in a nursing home."

"What about his wife?" Not that I thought an elderly woman could drag a man through the wilderness to hide his body.

"Even sadder yet." Tillie shuddered. "Evie apparently had, or I guess still has, early onset dementia. Frank did a good job of covering for her, but once he had his stroke, it became apparent. She's in the same facility he is."

We could safely cross their names off our suspect list. "I wonder why those men at the club didn't know that about the Mitchells?"

Tillie scoffed. "If the Mitchells weren't part of their inner circle or weekly golf buddies, they wouldn't have paid attention to what happened to them."

"But those men knew the Mitchells and Daltons lost a lot of money because of Ian."

"And I bet they were gloating?" Tillie swirled her drink.

"Well, it seemed like they wanted to set up some type of betting pool on who killed Ian. I guess when it comes to money, they pay attention." I studied Gabe to see if he'd been following our conversation. He acted like he was more interested in the food, but I could tell by the muscles clenching in his jaws that he'd been soaking up every single word. It was time for him to reciprocate.

"Gabe, is there any word on locating Reece?" I took another helping of nachos and topped it with sour cream and guacamole.

"So far, we have been unable to locate him. But it's not for lack of trying."

"How about his ex-wife? Does she know where he is, or

could she be hiding him?" I bit my tongue when I almost blurted out that we were waiting for Ethan to provide her address and any other information he could dig up on her.

"She hasn't seen him." Gabe set his margarita down. "And she's not hiding him. When she heard what he'd done and how he's on the run, she packed up and took her kids to stay with her sister in Phoenix. She wants nothing to do with the guy, so you don't need to get the hacker involved in tracking her down."

Tillie and I exchanged a guilty look.

"We'd never break the law like that." Tillie patted Gabe's muscular forearm. "Are you ready for dessert?"

"Sure." Gabe popped the last bite of nacho into his mouth.

"Do you think Reece could have followed his ex to Phoenix, and that's why you're not finding him?" Vannie asked.

He shrugged. "Hard to say. The department has reached out to the Phoenix PD and asked them to be on the lookout, just in case."

"Does he have any other friends or family in the area that might hide him?" I stood and started clearing the dirty dishes. "Or maybe he hightailed it back east, where he came from."

"Since it's impossible to know, I suggest you continue keeping your eyes open for anything suspicious and not run off by yourself. There's no need to continue your investigation." Gabe directed his laser focus toward me. "We'll find out who killed the two men."

# Chapter 32

The next morning found Tillie and me driving back to Chino Hills. After Gabe had departed the previous evening, Tillie expressed her worry over Geri and thought we should check in on her. I jumped at the chance. Even though I hadn't told Gabe about the black Explorer, something about it bugged me, and I wanted to find out who owned it, even if it was inconsequential.

"I told Geri to choose a restaurant and make reservations." Tillie held up her phone and checked the traffic app. We'd come to a complete standstill on the freeway. "If we don't start moving soon, I'll have to call her to let her know we'll be late picking her up."

We inched forward for about ten seconds before we came to another halt. "Can you tell if there's been an accident?"

"So far, the app isn't saying. Just red stop and go for the next"—Tillie used her thumb and forefinger to zoom in on the screen—"three exits. So probably a mile and a half?"

"I can try to get off at the next exit and take surface streets to get around this mess." Putting my blinker on, I tried merging to the next lane over, not that it did any good since no one was moving. I turned the blinker off and stayed right where we were.

"I doubt that will be any better. Everyone else will try it, and it'll be gridlocked too."

We sat in the same position for ten minutes—I timed it—when suddenly traffic started moving. Within a minute, we were back at full speed. It didn't take long before we passed two tow trucks loaded with a smashed car each, a fire truck, and several highway patrol cars parked along the side of the freeway.

I shivered. It looked like it had been a nasty accident. I sent good thoughts toward the victims. "How are we doing on time?"

"We'll probably be a couple minutes later than I'd told Geri we'd be, but we'll be fine for making the reservations." Tillie tapped her screen and examined the map. "We'll be just fine."

We chatted little for the rest of the trip. My mind was on driving cautiously after seeing the accident—something I always did until I'd forgotten about it. Not that I'm a bad or distracted driver. But coming across a devastating accident made me more aware.

Parking in front of Geri's house, I scanned both sides of the street, as far as I could see. There weren't any black vehicles parked on the block. We'd barely emerged from my SUV when Geri opened the front door and hustled down the walkway to meet us.

"I appreciate you picking me up." Geri patted her hair, and I couldn't help but notice her freshly manicured nails and the enormous diamond ring sitting on her right middle finger. Her left ring finger was bare. She seemed happier and more put together than the last time I'd seen her.

"We wanted to check on you. It's been such a trying time, and we thought you could use a friendly face." Tillie pointed at my SUV. "Emory will chauffeur us today, so give her the address of where we'll be having lunch."

Geri gave me the name, the Blooming Tea Room, but didn't have an address. I quickly located it on my map app, opened the rear door for Geri, then jogged around the other side of the vehicle and did the same for Tillie. The two women were silent as I drove, and I was too busy following the navigation instructions to create conversation.

Once we arrived at the restaurant, I used the valet service. While the valet was opening the door for Geri, I did the same for Tillie. Geri didn't wait until I'd turned the keys over to the valet. Instead, she hurried inside the charming cottage. The creamy painted exterior was merely a canvas for the riotous colorful flowers blooming in the window boxes and in flower beds bordering the shop. Tillie raised her eyebrows but followed at a more sedate pace.

By the time I entered the restaurant, Geri and Tillie were being seated across the room. It was a table for two only. Geri put her hand on the waitress's arm and gestured at a four-top table, then held up three fingers. Geri smiled as they moved to a larger table. Tillie waved me over, and I joined them, relieved that Geri didn't seem snobbish like the other country club ladies I'd encountered in the past.

After giving the waitress our order, Tillie leaned over and placed her hand over Geri's. "Now, dear, how are you faring?"

Geri dabbed at nonexistent tears and crooked her mouth downward. "It's been such a struggle. William's mother has been going downhill ever since he left. I had no choice and had to place her in a nursing home. She's so unhappy and blames me."

"Is she close by so you can visit her often?" I asked, trying to keep my voice gentle.

"With the financial mess William left us in, she had to take whatever facility the government could fit her in. She's in

Riverside. It's difficult to go see her, especially when all she does is complain when I do."

Tillie visibly cringed. Some nursing homes could be awful, especially when the patient wasn't financially sound and didn't have family to be their advocate. "Your poor mother-in-law. Perhaps Emory and I can visit her after we drop you off. We'd love to take her some flowers to brighten her room."

Geri waved off our suggestion. "That's unnecessary. They keep her loaded up on pain medication, so she sleeps almost all the time."

I felt like she was giving us conflicting information and didn't know why she'd do that. Had she merely tired of caring for her mother-in-law and dumped her onto the government's shoulders, or was the woman so ill she needed round-the-clock care? Tillie must've had the same thoughts.

"It's absolutely no trouble at all. I insist on going." Tillie placed her hand over her heart. "If I were in the same position, especially after losing my son, I'd want to see a kind face no matter how medicated I was."

Geri pursed her lips as if in thought, but before she could respond, our food arrived. By the time we'd settled in and chosen from the sandwiches, scones, mini quiches, and desserts displayed on the floral china three-tiered stand, Geri's face had smoothed over.

Tillie waited until we'd begun eating to ask for the nursing home facility information again.

Geri took her time, blotting her lips with the white cloth napkin, before answering. "You've given me a great idea since you're so gracious to be concerned about my mother-in-law. I know the staff at the facility is overworked and underappreciated, so I'd like to order five dozen cupcakes—Emory, you can choose whatever flavors you'd like—and deliver them when you go to visit."

"That's a lovely idea," Tillie said. "Emory can deliver one

to your mother-in-law as well. Does she have a favorite flavor?"

Geri thought for a moment. "I think it's red velvet with cream cheese frosting. But any flavor will be fine. Do you think you can deliver them tomorrow?"

Aside from needing to deliver cupcakes to Brian for Oceana before dinner, I didn't have anything on my calendar. "That will work fine."

"I'll have to text the office to let them know when to expect you. They don't like drop-in visitors. It's by appointment only."

"As long as traffic isn't horrendous, we can be there by eleven." I glanced at Tillie. "Does that work for you?"

"I'll make it work." Tillie picked up the delicate floral teacup, which matched the tiered stand and the teapot, and took a sip of jasmine tea.

Geri slowly tapped into her notes app, using only her right index finger. It seemed to take forever, but she finally set her phone down. "I wrote myself a reminder. These days, I seem to forget so much with all the stress of what's been going on. You'd better remind me to write you a check when you drop me off back home."

I nodded my agreement.

"Have you arranged for a funeral or memorial service yet?" Tillie asked. "We'd like to come to support you."

"I'm waiting for the police to release his body." Geri dabbed at her eyes again, which looked clear and bright to me. "But honestly, with his mother in the facility and his friends having already shunned him, I don't think I'll have a service."

"If you decide otherwise, let us know, and we'll attend."

"There's no changing my mind, but thank you."

Tillie poured more tea into our teacups. "Will you be staying in your mother-in-law's house or moving now that she's at the facility?"

A brief flash of what seemed like irritation passed over Geri's face, but it disappeared so quickly I thought I might have imagined it.

"It's too soon to make a decision. I need to come to terms with William being gone before deciding."

What was implied, although not spoken aloud, is that without money, she probably didn't have anywhere else to go.

We ate the miniature desserts but didn't linger over tea for more conversation. Instead, Tillie picked up the check for our meal, then we went to Geri's house. She quickly wrote out the check for the cupcakes—I only charged her for ingredients instead of my usual markup.

"I'll text the address to you once I confirm where they'll want the cupcakes delivered." Before I could answer, she stood and herded us to the door. "Now, if you'll excuse me, I have an appointment I'm running late for."

We'd barely stepped onto the front porch when she firmly shut and locked the door.

"Well, that was an awkward ending." I took Tillie's arm and led her to my vehicle. Not once did Geri thank us for her generosity in taking her to lunch, and I voiced my complaint to Tillie on the way home.

"She's got a lot of grievous things going on. I'm glad we could do something nice to help take her mind off all those awful situations, at least for a while."

"But don't you think it's odd she didn't want us to visit her mother-in-law?" Something felt hinky about Geri's response to Tillie's offer.

"You're seeing trouble where trouble doesn't exist, Emory." Tillie huffed. "Think about it. Her husband's been murdered, her friends have abandoned her, and she's broke. Being saddled with a sick mother-in-law—and it sounds like they were never close—is likely the straw that broke the camel's back. Geri probably jumped at the chance to let someone else take care of William's mother and didn't look closely at the quality of the facility. And she's probably embarrassed. She took the woman out of her home and forced her into a nursing home."

"You make a good point." I merged into the left lane to get around a slow-moving car billowing smoke from its exhaust pipe. "I imagine her mother-in-law is angry about the move and would have a lot to say about it to anyone who came to visit."

"We'll find out tomorrow." Tillie grimaced. "And if there's anything nefarious going on with Geri dumping her mother-in-law, we might find out about that too."

# Chapter 33

Upon returning to Tillie's house, I called Brian while I walked the dogs. One of his sous-chefs had quit, so he'd needed to work longer hours to prep for dinner. I filled him in on the investigation and the cupcakes I needed to deliver to Riverside the following day.

"Geri said to make whatever flavors I wanted. I'll just double the batches of whatever flavors you want for Oceana." I tugged the leashes to pull the dogs away from a pile of dropped French fries.

"Swordfish piccata is my special for the weekend, so maybe a lemon cupcake? And vanilla for those who want something milder." Brian raised his voice to speak over the clashing of pots and pans. "Sorry. Let me get to my office."

The noise retreated, and Brian came back on the phone. "I have a new dishwasher being trained. He's a bit clumsy with the larger pots."

"Geri mentioned her mother-in-law liked red velvet cupcakes. I thought it would be nice to include some just for her. Shall I make a dozen for you as well?" Piper and Missy tried to pull me toward the beach, but I diverted them with a couple of treats. I didn't have time to bathe them and try to remove all the sand out of their Velcro fur.

"Sure. I have a few reservations from people who couldn't get seating on Valentine's weekend, so they're celebrating this weekend. Maybe I'll pair the red velvet cupcake with some heart-shaped chocolate truffles for an extended Valentine's dessert." The cell phone was muffled, and then Brian was back. "I need to run. If I can make it over late tonight, I'll send you a text. Love you."

He disconnected without waiting for a reply. I knew he was busy, so I tried not to take it personally. Running a successful restaurant took long, never-ending hours. As hard as Brian tried to hire additional chefs and sous-chefs, when it came down to it, he needed to be there as much as humanly possible. His business and his reputation depended on it.

"Okay, doggies, it's time for me to get home and get baking."


I SPENT the afternoon baking at Tillie's. The sweet fragrance of vanilla and chocolate filled the air, along with the earthy scent of baked beets. Since Brian would add the red velvet cupcakes to his menu, I needed to make these as natural as possible and avoid the chemical taste of food dyes. Using beet puree would not only lend the quintessential red color to the tiny cakes but would also add a nice moistness. Topped with a rich cream cheese buttercream, no one would be able to resist the delectable dessert, nor would they be able to guess that the humble beetroot had been used.

By early evening, the counters were filled with cooling cupcakes, frosted cupcakes, and bowls of buttercream. Vannie was out for the evening with Theresa, and I eyed the refrigerator, wondering what I could easily whip up for dinner for Tillie. I wasn't hungry, having sampled the cupcakes and frosting to make sure they were acceptable for Oceana and the nursing home. They were.

While I stood at the refrigerator, door wide-open, staring at the contents, Tillie breezed into the kitchen. The dogs whined from the other side of the dog gate that kept them from entering the kitchen while I baked.

"What sounds good for dinner?" I looked up and found Tillie dressed in her favorite vintage Chanel skirt suit, with its jeweled flower-shaped buttons twinkling in the light. She had high heels on, flawless makeup, and freshly coiffed hair. "Oh, never mind. You're going out tonight. Is John done with his meetings?"

"Not quite. He's taking his clients out for a late dinner tonight and wants me to join them." She plucked a couple of dog treats from their cookie jar and tossed them to Piper and Missy. Tillie cleared her throat. "He's sending a car to pick me up and asked me to stay over in LA with him so we could fly his clients up to the wine country tomorrow for a day of wine tasting. I know I promised to go with you to visit Geri's mother-in-law."

"Don't even worry about it. Go. Have fun." I closed the refrigerator. "Just be sure to drink a glass or two of wine for me."

"You can count on that, kiddo." Tillie kissed my cheek. "By the way, I finally heard from Geri with the address you're supposed to deliver the cupcakes to. I told her you'd be going solo. I'll forward it to you."

Tillie tapped on her messaging app, and within a moment, my phone chimed. I double-checked to make sure the address came through. It had.

"Send me a text tomorrow and let me know how your visit goes. You have me curious if William's mother has anything of value to say about Geri or what the situation is at the nursing home."

"I'm sure I'm falling down a conspiracy rabbit hole… and you were right about Geri only being overwhelmed." I'd walked with Tillie to the front door when she received a text that the car service had arrived. Her suitcase stood next to the door, and the dogs hurried to sniff it. "Let me carry that to the car for you."

"There's no need. I can manage." Tillie held up her arm in a muscle pose.

"The dogs and I need a break anyway." I snapped the leashes onto the dogs then picked up the large suitcase. "Are you sure you're only going for one night? It looks like you packed for a week."

"No sense in not going prepared." Tillie winked at me. "Who knows… maybe John and I will stay in Napa for a few extra days."

"Let me know, so I don't worry about you." I gave the leashes to Tillie and trudged down the steps toward the car. I handed over the suitcase to the driver and took the leashes back from her. "Have fun, and give John my love."

The dogs and I watched Tillie drive away, and then we walked around the block to stretch our legs. Back at Tillie's, I worked on the cupcakes until nine, and once the kitchen was spick-and-span, I took the dogs back to my pool house. I was disappointed Vannie hadn't made it home yet. With Tillie gone, I thought it might be the perfect opportunity to have a heart-to-heart talk about what was bothering her. Perhaps she'd known that's what I'd do, and that's why she'd stayed out so late.

Brian crawled into bed sometime after one in the morning. Over a quick breakfast, I couldn't help but notice the dark circles beneath his eyes. He seemed to lack his usual energy, and he drank more coffee than normal.

"I'm sorry I can't take the dogs for a run, but I need to get to the fish market this morning." He ran long fingers through his hair and hunched his shoulders over. "I feel like I'm running on fumes and can't catch a break."

"Is there anything I can do to help?" Not that I knew a thing about running a restaurant or cooking a ton of different dishes for a large number of people.

"Thanks, but there's really nothing anyone can do." Brian straightened and caught my hand between his. "As soon as I can get enough kitchen staff hired and keep them, it'll be easier."

"You're right. I can't help you there." I squeezed his hand then leaned over and kissed him. "If you think of anything, though, just let me know."

"Thanks, Em. You're the best." He raised his coffee cup in a salute then took a long drink. "It's all my fault."

"What's your fault?"

"Oceana was, or still is, doing so great. We're slammed with reservations and getting great reviews." He sighed. "But I jumped the gun in extending our business hours to include lunch six days a week on top of Sunday brunch. I didn't have the infrastructure in place to keep up with the demand."

"Can you cut back on the days you offer lunch?" When Brian first mentioned opening the restaurant for lunch, I'd been concerned about the hours he'd need to work to keep up. I hadn't been wrong. Brian's last days off had been when we'd taken our trip at the first of the year.

"I'm considering it, but I'll wait another three or four weeks to make a decision." He gazed at me. "I'm afraid the public will think I've cut back because business is poor and not because of staffing. It wouldn't be a good look for Oceana."

"Hopefully, you'll find the right people for your kitchen." I retrieved the coffeepot to refill his mug.

He held up his hand. "As much as I need more caffeine, I really have to go."

"I'll fix a to-go mug while you get ready." I rummaged in the cupboard and pulled out a twenty-ounce travel mug and filled it. Brian kissed my cheek and headed to the bathroom. I refilled my ceramic mug, added a splash of milk, and cleaned up the breakfast dishes. As usual, Brian had cooked for us—scrambled eggs and toast—and I did the dishes.

My phone pinged with a text. It was from Brad.

**Emerging from dungeon ltr tody... hopefully. Can we get dinr aftr I tak shwr?**

I thumbed a reply.

**Yep. Keep me psted. Is Gabe bzy?**

While waiting for Brad's reply, I gave my boyfriend a long kiss and hug goodbye then helped him carry the cupcakes out to his car. It would be one less thing I needed to do.

"I'll call you later to let you know if I can make it back here tonight." He kissed me again then ruffled Piper and Missy's ears.

As he drove off, they whined, disappointed they didn't get a morning run.

"I'll take you for a walk." They pranced around and ran to their leashes. "In a while. I have to get dressed first."

They ignored me, so I closed the garage door and went back inside. They followed me in and ran to the French doors, tails wagging. I opened the doors wide and let the dogs out into the yard. They'd have to keep themselves entertained until I was ready. My phone pinged again.

**If not wrking, he has fam dinr. Im NOT going.**

I laughed at the skull and crossbones emoji he inserted. Gabe was one of the nicest guys—a little uptight sometimes—but definitely nice. His family, though. Almost obscenely wealthy, they didn't like that Gabe was a detective. They didn't like that Brad was in computer games. They didn't like the small house Brad and Gabe lived in, even though it was in a perfectly lovely neighborhood. And the list went on. Actually, Gabe's parents weren't so terrible unless his grandparents were around. And then the litany of complaints came out in full force.

**Come to my hs. I'll cook.**

He sent a thumbs up and a cryptic message.

**Mite hv important info for you then. Bye.**

I sent several texts demanding to know what information he was talking about, but Brad remained silent.

# Chapter 34

By the time I returned home after a long walk with the dogs and showered, I was almost late leaving for Riverside. Close to fifty miles inland, Riverside was so named because of its proximity to the Santa Ana River. Founded in the 1870s, Riverside was the birthplace of California's citrus industry, but because of the scarcity of water over the years, orchards and productivity had declined. Instead, manufacturing had taken over in providing jobs and supporting the economic growth of the area.

At least traffic complied, so it was only a few minutes after eleven when I parked. I'd packed the boxes of cupcakes into a tote bag with a single-cupcake box, containing a red velvet cupcake, sitting on top. Riverside, being a semiarid desert climate, was considerably hotter than Newport Beach, even in February. I hoped they'd be able to refrigerate the cupcakes topped with cream cheese frosting if they weren't consumed right away.

The facility was a square boxy building, reminiscent of an older industrial site. With its dusty concrete gray walls, its appearance was on the bleak side. As the electric double-glass doors whooshed open, the scent of disinfectant and perfumed air freshener greeted me. It wasn't the most pleasant combination. A reception desk with a built-in counter ran halfway across the small room. Uncomfortable-looking plastic chairs had been placed in front of the floor-to-ceiling windows that faced the parking lot. To the left side of the desk, heavy-duty double steel doors, painted an institutional beige color, sat closed. The metal push bars on the doors were scuffed and dingy. The place was unusually quiet. Could everyone be taking naps?

A woman, probably in her early sixties, given her sallow skin that showed deep grooves around her eyes and mouth, sat at the reception desk. She eyed my tote bag.

"Hi. Geri Dalton said she notified someone that I'd deliver cupcakes today for the staff. Should I give them to you?" I held up the light-pink tote with the logo Brad had created for me. A hot-pink cupcake wrapper piled high with buttercream piped on top had multicolored sprinkles scattered across the frosting. My business name—it had taken me a long time to finally come up with one and get it registered with the city—Sprinkles and Spice Cupcakery had been stenciled in hot-pink swirly font above the cupcake. I'd wanted to put catering in the business name, but both Carrie and Brad had talked me out of it. Their opinion was that if I ever wanted to open a storefront, I wouldn't want to have to change the business's name.

"Sure. I'll make sure they get to the break room." She stood, her shoulders rounded into a dowager's hump. I bumped her age up to somewhere in the seventies. She appeared frail, and I worried the five dozen cupcakes would be too much.

"The tote is heavy. I'm happy to take them for you, if you'll point me in the right direction."

"Sorry. We can't allow unescorted visitors to roam around." She pushed a piece of paper attached to a metal clipboard over to me. "Sign in. I'll need to take a copy of your driver's license or another form of government-issued ID."

I fished my wallet out of my purse, extracted my license, and handed it to her. The pen attached to the clipboard looked as if it had been chewed on. Digging back into my purse, I found my own pen and wrote my name. After making a photocopy, the woman handed back my license. This place felt more like a prison than a care facility.

Once I'd replaced my wallet back into my purse, she hobbled toward the double doors. "Bring the cupcakes and follow me."

The second she pushed one of the double doors open, sound assaulted me. There were several overly loud television programs blaring for attention. I picked out at least four women crying. My heart broke for them. A man was hollering from somewhere down the corridor. It sounded like someone was hitting a wall with a stick. A telephone jangled for attention. The squeak of rubber-soled shoes, worn by employees walking quickly down linoleum hallways, filled the air. It was utter chaos.

As I followed the woman, who hobbled painfully slowly, we passed rooms where residents stared into space or gazed at us with bleary eyes. A few were settled onto sagging couches, but for the majority, they were strapped into wheelchairs. When we made the first left turn, we must've entered the residents' living quarters. It got more depressing when I realized they were nothing more than hospital rooms. There were few personal touches, maybe a crocheted afghan here or a colorful blanket or throw pillow there. Most had two hospital-style beds, but a few had three beds in a room.

We made two more turns down corridors containing bedrooms until we came to another set of double steel doors. As I followed her into the large, open room, the heavy door shut behind me. Immediately, the cacophony died out. There were a slew of round tables spread across the room, with a handful of employees sitting around, eating while staring at their phone screens. Countertops and cabinets lined two of the walls. Three refrigerators, a sink, dishwasher, toaster oven, and microwave took up another wall. An opening led to a hallway at the back of the room, which probably led to lockers and restrooms.

"You can put the cupcakes on the counter." The woman pointed at the far wall then side eyed the few people sitting at the tables.

Ambling over to a drawer closest to the refrigerators, she pulled out a marker and a blank piece of paper. After scrawling something, she found some tape then ambled over to my cupcake boxes. She taped the note on the cabinet above the boxes.

I squinted to make out what it said, but finally figured out it was to warn employees it was one cupcake per person.

"The employees will descend on them like locusts once word gets around. Not that anyone will pay attention to my note, but at least I can say I tried when the afternoon shift arrives and finds out there aren't any left."

Before we'd even reached the doors to head back to the residents' area, every person in the break room had gathered around the cupcakes.

"How many employees do you have here?" From what I'd seen walking to the break room, there had to be at least fifty rooms on this floor alone. Since the building had six floors, I wondered if that meant there were three hundred rooms with around six hundred residents? It boggled my mind.

"Too many to count, that's for sure." She eyed me speculatively. "Why do you want to know?"

"I'm just curious. This facility is much larger than I'd expected."

"Hmm."

I followed her back to the front office. She settled behind the desk and picked up the handset to the phone. I waited, impatiently to be honest, for her to request another employee to come take me to see Mrs. Dalton. Instead, she called one of her friends and started chatting about a church social coming up. When I began tapping my foot, she glared at me then asked her friend to hold for a moment.

"Yes?"

"I'd like to visit Mrs. Dalton while I'm here."

She heaved a sigh and went back to her friend. They chatted another minute before disconnecting. "Did you make an appointment?"

"Mrs. Dalton's daughter-in-law, Geri Dalton, said she called in my visit."

Her lips pursed together while she powered on the computer. The computer, like the building, seemed to be a dinosaur. It wheezed, and from my vantage, I could see the screen flickering off and on, like it was on its last legs. Finally, a password screen appeared. I looked away, afraid she'd think I was trying to snoop.

"Can you spell the last name of the resident?"

"D-a-l-t-o-n." I looked back at the monitor. The curser sat there, blinking.

"And her first name?"

"Nora. Or maybe it's a nickname for Elenora?"

She typed again and then again. "Sorry. I don't have any residents here by that name."

"Do you know who Geri Dalton spoke with yesterday evening about me delivering the cupcakes today?"

She rolled her eyes, x'd out the screen, and went to the menu. What seemed like minutes later, a spreadsheet came up. "What time did she call? We log all incoming calls."

Guess it was a good thing they didn't have to log outgoing calls considering how much time she spent talking to her friend. "It was before six, but that's all I know."

She scrolled through the log then reverse scrolled. "Nope. No Geri Dalton called in."

"What?" I swiped my phone open and double-checked the address forwarded from Tillie. I showed her the screen. "Am I at the right place?"

"Yep. That's us."

"If you weren't expecting the cupcakes, why did you let me take them to the break room?"

Her deep guffaw belied her petite size. "No one's going to pass up the chance to get some fancy bakery cupcakes for free."

Not wanting to disabuse her belief that my cupcakes were from a fancy bakery, I didn't correct her. Instead, I placed the single red velvet cupcake protected in its own small box on the counter. "Since Mrs. Dalton doesn't reside here, you might as well take this cupcake."

"Thank you kindly. I'll certainly enjoy it." She picked up the phone receiver. "Is there anything else you need?"

"That's it. Thanks for your help." Heading to my car, I sent Tillie a text.

**There is NO Mrs. Dalton at this facility. Could she be under a different name?**

Why had Geri lied? I had a sick feeling in the pit of my stomach that something had happened to William's mother. We'd never seen the woman but had taken Geri's word for it that the elder Mrs. Dalton was critically ill and had been in the home before being admitted recently to the facility. Was it all a lie? And why would she lie about something like that?

No dots appeared, so I slipped my phone back into the purse slung across my shoulders. I felt at a loss. Should I swing by Geri's house on the way home and see if I could get answers? Or report it to the police? I immediately discarded that idea since I had zero proof that the elderly Mrs. Dalton existed.

I'd parked beneath a tree at the far end of the parking lot, wanting to get some extra steps in while toting the cupcakes to the office. The parking lot was filled with cars, but not so crowded that a delivery van from some office products store I'd never heard of would have needed to park so close to my SUV. Maybe they wanted some shade from the tree too. As the sun traversed overhead, it was heating up, and I guessed it was probably in the high seventies already. I pushed up the sleeves of my sweater and wished I'd worn a short-sleeved lightweight blouse. It was warm enough to feel like summer already, and I couldn't imagine being there in the full heat of summer when it easily hit triple digits consistently.

I eyed the front door of my SUV and thought I might be able to open it wide enough for me to squeeze through. Otherwise, I'd have to enter from the opposite side and crawl over the gearshift and console to reach the driver's seat. Sucking in my stomach, I turned sideways and sidestepped between the two vehicles. As I reached the back seat passenger door, a rolling sound echoed from behind me.

Rough hands gripped my shoulders and yanked me backward. I landed on my back, and my head hit the floor with a hard thud. Everything went black.

## Chapter 35

My screaming back pain woke me, and I found myself in darkness. There weren't any windows in the back of the van, and not a speck of light filtered in from the door. The floor of the van beneath me was hard metal, and my spine whacked on a hard ridge with every bump in the road. My hands had been tied in front of my body, so I was able to use them to roll over onto my side. From there, I pushed myself to a sitting position and used my feet to find the side of the van.

Carefully inching over, I found the side, scooted around in a half circle, then rested my back against the smooth surface. The jolts from hitting potholes or bumps made my bones ache. I had no idea how long I'd been unconscious or what direction the van was taking me. I berated myself for not paying attention to my surroundings and allowing someone to put me in this situation. Who had snatched me? I hadn't seen even a glimpse of their face when they pulled me into the vehicle.

Had my purse and phone made it into the van with me? It had been slung across my body when I'd been taken. Turning onto my hands and knees, I slowly crept around, feeling for the familiar soft leather purse Tillie had gifted me last Christmas. I found nothing but dirt, a few scraps of paper that felt like labels, and some pieces of netting. A pungent smell drifted up from the paper when I moved it around, but I couldn't place the odor.

Wanting to loosen the bonds that held my hands together, I brought the ties to my mouth. I wrinkled my nose at the smell and tentatively bit into the tie around my wrist. I immediately yanked my hand away and spat the bitterness out. The texture of the tie was plastic, but I couldn't figure out what caused it to taste so bitter. Had he—I was certain my captor was a man because of his strength in pulling me into the van —soaked the ties in something poisonous? I recalled the poisonous botanicals used to kill Ian. I spit again and hoped I hadn't ingested enough to kill me.

I pulled my wrists apart as hard as I could. The tie didn't do anything except create pain around my wrists. If the tie had been poisoned, could it seep inside me if I broke the skin while trying to loosen the tie? Not wanting to risk it, I stopped tugging. Recalling the time I'd been zip-tied before, I wondered if I could use the same method to get out of this bond. I tried standing, but every time I got halfway up, the van jolted and threw me against the side. After a few tries, and several bruises later, I sat back down.

I propped myself up against the van's wall, stretched out my left leg to give me balance, and bent my right knee at a forty-five-degree angle. I raised my arms over my head and, as hard as I could, snapped my arms down over the shin of my right leg. The pain in my wrists and my shin made me shriek, and stars danced in front of my eyes... but my hands were free!

A wet warmth dripped onto my leg. I used my now-free hands to inspect my wrists. Both had broken skin, and both were bleeding. As much as the pain made me want to cry and bind up the wounds with the tank top I wore beneath my sweater, I decided if the tie had been poisonous, it was better to flush it off my skin with the blood.

Tearing my focus away from the potentially deadly tie, I inched around the sides of the van, hunting for a door handle or a way to exit. Where there should have been handles, nothing could be found but some screws and jagged metal, which punctured my left index finger. If I made it out alive, I'd probably need an updated tetanus shot. My kidnapping had been well planned, from where I'd been snatched—Geri had to have been in on the plot—to a van that had no means of escape.

Geri. Who was she colluding with? Was it a romantic interest who killed her husband so they could be together? But why kill Ian? And, more importantly, how did they poison my cupcakes and kill him? Tillie was certain Geri hadn't attended Frances's event.

Tillie. Oh-em-gee. What would have happened had Tillie come with me to deliver the cupcakes? I shuddered, thinking of all the things that could have injured my beloved almost-grandmother had she been kidnapped alongside me. Did Geri know that Tillie had made other plans and wouldn't be with me? I strained my memory, trying to remember if Tillie had mentioned anything about it. My mind was blank. I blamed it on the stress.

If my imagination wasn't playing tricks on me, the van slowed down. It made a sudden sharp turn, and I went flying against the wall. Gasping for air when my breath was knocked from my lungs, I crumpled into a ball on the hard floor. We slowed again, and I tried bracing myself for another sharp turn. Instead, we came to a stop. The *click-click-click* of a turn signal sounded faintly. Slowly, very slowly, the van turned right again. Instead of speeding up, we crept along then made a gentle turn upward. I envisioned a driveway of sorts. It was a very bumpy driveway. We drove a short way, and then we stopped again.

When the engine turned off, I began shivering. This was it. This is when I'd come face-to-face with my captor. I either had to spring out the door and run as fast as I could to escape or accept the fact that I probably would be killed.

Refusing to accept that fate without a fight, or at least a flight, I braced myself against the side of the van, crouched in a runner's position. I was more than ready to bolt the second the door slid open.

Except the door slid open behind me, and I tumbled sideways, off-balance.

A face loomed over me, and the barrel of a big black gun was thrust into my face.

Chapter 36

The gun filled my vision, and then I lifted my gaze to look at the face behind the gun.

Detective Reece.

He grinned, like he'd won a goldfish at the county fair, his crooked eyeteeth catching the afternoon sun. "Well, well, well. Looks like I caught Miss Marple herself. Or you probably think you're more like Nancy Drew and your nosy friend is Miss Marple. It's a shame she couldn't join us today. It would have made what I have in mind for you so much better."

I tried not to show how much his mention of Tillie rattled me. Instead, I scooted along the floor of the van when he used his gun to motion me out. Once my legs dangled over the edge, I stood on wobbly legs.

"Why are you doing this? Wasn't it enough trying to prove I killed Ian?" I raised my voice, not quite yelling, but not quiet either. Maybe someone close by would hear me and call the police.

"Shut up." He waved his gun at me. "Let's take this inside, where we can have a more *private* chat."

I didn't like the sound of that, and I definitely did not like the way he raised his eyebrows.

"I think I'd rather stay…" My words were cut off when he sprang at me and clamped his hand over my mouth.

"No back talk from you, do you hear me? Let's take this inside." His meaty hand squeezed my face until tears blurred my eyes from the pain. "Nod if you understand, and I'll release my hand."

I carefully nodded, wanting to get away from his vicelike grip. He let go of my face but grabbed my arm and pulled me toward the house. The color looked familiar, as did the style. Then it hit me. We were in the backyard of Geri's mother-in-law's house. How were Geri and Reece connected?

At least ten years separated the pair, with Geri being older. Not that age should matter one way or another in romance when you're older, but they didn't seem to have anything else in common. Plus, Reece had just moved from the East Coast. How had they met and connected so quickly? It didn't seem plausible.

I slowed, reluctant to enter the house. Reece twisted my arm up behind my back. Pain shot through me, and I continued walking, whether or not I wanted to. And I did not. No one knew I was here. Only Tillie, who was incommunicado for the time being, knew I'd planned on visiting the nursing home. With my phone left behind with my vehicle, Tillie and, eventually, the police would only find a dead end at the facility.

This was it. I was no match for a former detective. Why did I have to procrastinate on the self-defense courses I'd promised to take? The screaming pain in the arm that had recently been broken gave me permission to not be too hard on myself for postponing the classes. The way Reece had twisted it made me worry he'd damage my arm even more.

I stumbled when he pushed me through the doorway. More pain shot through my arm when he yanked to keep me upright. We'd entered the house through a small laundry room that led to the kitchen. Dirty dishes and uneaten food littered the counter and tabletop. It hadn't been in this state of array when I'd made tea just a few days before. Reece must've been hiding out here all that time. Where was Geri, and why hadn't she cleaned up the mess?

He led me to the living room, where Tillie and I had done our best to offer sympathy and support to Geri. And she'd done nothing but repay us with betrayal. The heavy damask curtains were drawn and, with no lamps on, the room was dim. I almost didn't see Geri when we entered the room. But as my eyes adjusted to the darkness, there she was, slumped over in the corner love seat with her head propped up by the armrest. He had tied her hands in front of her with zip ties and secured her ankles to the base of the love seat with ropes.

She was a victim just as much as I'd become. Reece had forced her to lure me to my abduction.

"Sit on the sofa," Reece commanded. "Don't move a muscle, or I'll shoot."

He was going to kill me at some point, but I did as he requested. Instead of using zip ties on me, he retrieved a roll of duct tape from a side table. "Hold out your hands."

I complied. Trying not to gasp when he taped my wrists together tight enough that it felt like the tape was digging into my already injured extremities, I sucked in my breath. He finished taping my hands together and then did the same to my ankles.

"If you make any loud noises or yell to get someone's attention, I'll tape your mouth closed." He glanced over at Geri, who hadn't stirred.

"What did you do to her?" I demanded.

"She had a change of heart and decided she didn't want you and that nosy Miss Marple taken care of. You've caused me nothing but headaches and heartburn." He tossed the duct tape onto the sofa beside me. "I gave her a little sedative to shut her up."

The way she hadn't stirred since we'd arrived made me

think it was more than just a little sedative. At least it appeared she was breathing. "Geri was in on it with you? Why?"

"You know, I don't think I'll tell you. I'll let you stew on it and drive yourself crazy." Reece cackled. "I'll bet you thought you could outwit me and solve Ian and William's deaths, but you haven't, and you won't."

"But how do you know Geri? And why did she get involved with you?" If I knew that, I might be able to piece together why Ian and William had been killed.

"He's my baby brother." Geri's voice was faint, and it cracked on the word brother. "They were revenge killings."

"Ger, don't you say another word!" Reece's voice held menace as he barked out his command. There wasn't a drop of love in the way he glowered at his sister.

Geri tried to sit up but couldn't seem to find the strength. She slumped back down. "It doesn't matter. You're going to kill me, even if I'm your blood and practically raised you."

"I said, enough!" Reece roared. His eyes were manic, and his gaze roamed the room, seeming to search for something. "I'm leaving, but I'll be back soon. If I find you've tried to escape, your death won't be fast and painless. And believe me when I say that's not an idle threat."

# Chapter 37

The back door slammed shut, and an engine roared to life. Once the sounds of the vehicle leaving faded away, I inched to the edge of the sofa to better see Geri.

"Is there a pair of scissors or a knife in this room?" Not knowing how long Reece would be gone, I didn't want to waste a second on anything but trying to free myself.

"No! Don't do anything foolish." Geri's eyes were wide with terror. "You have to do what Reece said."

"You realize he's going to kill us both, don't you?" I scanned the room, looking for drawers that might hold a sharp implement to cut through the duct tape. "I won't sit around and wait for him to slaughter me without trying to escape."

"He meant what he said about making your death painful." Geri closed her eyes and seemed to draw herself in. "He's always had a cruel streak, even as a little boy."

I couldn't let myself worry about what might happen if I failed. What I knew for certain, if I didn't try, our deaths would happen no matter what. Pushing off the sofa to a standing position, I hopped over to the end table. As I'd hoped, there was a small drawer beneath the top. Thankfully, Reece had at least taped my hands in front of me instead of behind my back. I slid the drawer open.

There was a pack of emery boards. If I had unlimited time, I might be able to use the rough edges to file through the duct tape, but with Reece coming back sooner rather than later, they were of no help. There was also a cheap plastic magnifying glass and a local telephone directory. Were they even used by anyone? The directory gave me hope, though. This was Geri's mother-in-law's home—if she'd been telling the truth—and the elderly woman probably relied on a landline and not a cell phone. My hopes were raised.

"Geri." I raised my voice to get her attention. She looked like she'd fallen asleep. "Is there a landline in the house?"

"What?" Her voice faded away.

"Is there a landline telephone in the house?" I tried to keep the impatience out of my voice but was unsuccessful.

"Yeah…" She closed her eyes, and her mouth went slack. Geri had fallen asleep.

I hopped over and gently shook her shoulder. She didn't wake. I shook it harder and still received no response. I used the back of my hand to not so gently tap her cheek. She didn't stir. My body started shaking like I had a fever chill. Had Geri died? Because of the way my wrists had been taped together, I couldn't position my fingers to find a pulse. It didn't look like her chest was rising or falling.

I had to find a phone and get help. The panic that welled up in my stomach made me clumsy. I hopped to the kitchen, adding bruise upon bruise as I careened into furniture. I fell twice, and it took precious long seconds to climb back onto my feet again. My heart plummeted when I reached the kitchen and found that Reece had bashed the landline into pieces. Hopping to the back door, I thought if I could make it outside, I could scream for help and hop down the street to the neighbor's house for help.

Except the back door had a keyed dead bolt. The dead bolt had been locked, and the key was missing. Reece must've taken it with him. I eyed the small rectangular glass window inserted in the door and immediately discarded the idea of escaping through it. It was much too small. I hopped to the kitchen, grabbed a chef's knife from the knife block with the tips of my fingers, and hopped back to the living room. Geri hadn't stirred.

My battered body screamed as I hopped toward the front door. My breath came fast, much too fast. I felt lightheaded. I didn't even have to reach the door to see it, too, had a keyed dead bolt with the key missing. Time had probably run out for Geri and was running out for me. I needed to move faster.

Clumsily, I dropped into a seated position on the floor. Carefully, I used the blade from the chef's knife to cut through the tape that bound my legs together. It was slow going and I nicked myself a few times. Blood oozed down my calves. Finally, my ankles were free but I could barely feel my feet. The tightly wound tape had practically cut off circulation.

I thought about taking time to try to cut through the tape that bound my wrists but decided finding a phone and calling for help was critical. Reece could be coming back any second.

The only thing left to do was check if any of the bedrooms had a landline. Not that I held any hope of finding one. Reece most certainly would have destroyed the phone if there had been one. Hobbling toward the hallway that led to the bedrooms, I tripped on a throw rug and went down hard. The knife flew from my grasp and slid across the hardwood floor. Pain shot through my shoulder and my right ankle twisted beneath me when I'd landed. Trying to push myself back to standing made stars dance in front of my eyes from the pain. I couldn't do it. Had I broken my ankle or was it only a bad sprain? There was no time to worry. I had to keep moving.

The only thing I could do now was scoot on my hands and knees... something nearly impossible with my hands taped together and my ankle screaming in pain with each movement. But I couldn't, I wouldn't, give up. The first bedroom I peeked into looked like it had been turned into a sewing room. Stacks of fabric were piled on every surface, and a half-completed quilt was draped over a chair. I didn't see a phone amongst the clutter.

My heart stopped when I opened the door to the second bedroom. Lying on the bed in the darkened room was a small, still form. Matted white hair clung to a wizened face. The rest of the body was covered with a colorful quilt. I scooted closer to get a better look. As with Geri, the woman's eyes were closed, her mouth slack. A small wheezing sigh escaped the woman's mouth, and I jumped at the sound. This could only be Mrs. Dalton, William's mother.

I moved to the bed and shook her shoulder. She didn't stir even one bit. The fact that Mrs. Dalton had been heavily sedated yet still lived gave me some hope that Geri might be clinging to life. I hurriedly scanned the room, hunting for a bedside landline, but didn't see one from where I kneeled. There was a stack of books on the far bedside table, so I scooted around the bed to take a closer look. And found no landline.

Exhausted from the effort and pain of scooting and the disappointment of not finding a phone, I rested my head on the edge of the mattress. That's when I saw the glint of matte silver peeking from beneath the thin pillow Mrs. Dalton's head rested on. With great effort, I pulled myself to standing, stretched over the bed, and used my fingertips to edge the device toward me.

It was an old-style flip phone. My hands shook as I opened it, and my breath caught in my throat when it powered on. The battery emblem showed the charge was low, but at least I didn't need a password or a face to open it. I could barely keep my finger still—my entire body quaked—to dial 911. I almost cried with relief when the emergency operator answered.

"What's your emergency?"

"I need police, paramedics, and an ambulance. I and two other women have been abducted and are being held against our will. We're at…" I couldn't remember the address. Refraining from thumping my head against the mattress, I continued. "I don't know the house number, but it's on Rose Hill Lane in Chino Hills. It's a sage-green house with a yellow door. The owner is Mrs. Nora Dalton."

"Emergency personnel will be there soon." Keys clacking filled the phone. "Where is the person who abducted you?"

"He left. His name is Detective Reece, except he was recently fired. Call Detective Gabe O'Neill of the Newport Beach PD. He has all the information and needs to know where I am." Chills swept up my spine at the bang of the back door slamming. "Hurry. Reece just came back."

"Are you safe?"

"No. I've got to hide." My gaze swept the room. There was one small closet, the door slightly ajar.

"Stay on the line. Help is on the way."

Too late, I remembered the knife that had slid in the hallway. I'd left it there when I'd decided finding a phone was more important. Mrs. Dalton's bedroom door had been closed before I'd entered, and it was now open. Reece would know exactly where I was. I dropped to the floor and checked to see if I would fit beneath the bed. Not a chance. There were extra blankets stacked beneath the bed, so I grabbed one and scooted to the door. I almost fell flat on my face several times, trying to scoot while bringing the blanket with me. It was only a matter of a minute or less before Reece found me.

Using the very last reserve of energy in my body while ignoring the shooting pain in my ankle, I stood, unfurled the blanket, and slipped between the door and the wall.

Seconds later, Reece burst into the room.

He stepped toward the bed, pausing as if to give his eyes a moment to adjust to the dimness.

At that exact moment, I threw the blanket over his head, raised my arms as high as I could, jumped on his back, and lowered my arms so they wrapped around his chest. Even though I'd pinned his arms to his side, he was strong. The blanket inhibited his movements, and the duct tape around my wrists made it impossible for him to loosen my hold. Still, my arms felt like they were being pulled from their sockets as he attempted to escape.

He tried bucking me off, so I wrapped my legs around him. Stars danced in front of my eyes as my ankle connected with his torso. The blanket tangled in his struggle to free himself, and he began toppling. There wasn't a thing I could do except topple with him.

As he fell, he twisted one last time then hit his head on the corner of the nightstand with a muffled *crack*. He crumpled to the floor, taking me with him.

Sirens pierced the air, and soon, pounding fists sounded on the front door. I couldn't extricate myself from Reece, so I filled my lungs with as much air as I could and screamed.

# Chapter 38

Still shivering, even though a paramedic had wrapped me in a space blanket, I allowed the medic to tend to the cuts and abrasions from the duct tape and from my clumsy nicks when freeing my ankles. Geri—who thankfully was still alive—had been wheeled out on a gurney, as had Mrs. Dalton, to waiting ambulances.

After handcuffing Reece, one of the paramedics deemed him uninjured enough to be taken straight to jail, despite the nasty bump on his head.

Detective Smith from the sheriff's department sat beside me. "I understand this is part of a case the Newport Beach PD is investigating."

"Yes. Detective Gabe O'Neill is in charge of it."

"I've spoken to him, and he's on his way." He pulled a small notebook and pen from his shirt pocket. "Since this abduction took place in my jurisdiction, and my officers are the ones who arrested Mr. Reece, I'd like to ask some questions."

"Of course. I'll tell you everything I know." By the time I'd finished telling him about Ian and William's deaths and how I'd gotten involved, Gabe arrived. He must have blared his siren and pushed his car to its maximum speed the entire way over.

"Is there any word on Geri and Mrs. Dalton's conditions?" I asked after the two men introduced themselves.

"Geri Dalton is in stable condition, and the sedatives are wearing off. She's still groggy and unable to speak, so we'll have to wait to interview her." Gabe rolled his shoulders. "Did I hear correctly that you told the responding officers she was involved in her husband's death and your abduction?"

"Yes. Reece is her younger brother, and she told me Ian and William's murders were for revenge." I shivered and wrapped the space blanket around my shoulders. "It's about all I got out of her before she fell unconscious. Honestly, I thought she was dead. How is her mother-in-law doing?"

From what I'd seen when they'd wheeled her out on the gurney, she wasn't in good shape.

"She's unconscious, and the doctors are doing everything they can to keep her comfortable and pain free." Gabe's face clouded over. "Her cancer is terminal, and she probably doesn't have much time left. Maybe a week or less."

"How horrible to spend the last few weeks of your life as a captive. I hope she didn't know what was going on."

"From what I gather, she's been on a heavy dose of morphine for quite some time." Gabe glanced at Detective Smith, who nodded. "Physically, Mrs. Dalton looked like she'd been taken care of and hadn't been abused. It stands to reason Geri and her brother kept her on the painkillers to keep her comfortable and to keep her quiet."

"I have so many questions." I twisted a lock of hair around my finger. "Reece taunted me about not telling me why he killed the two men and why he abducted me, and Geri, for that matter."

Gabe clapped a hand on my shoulder. "It's over, Emory. The bad guys got caught, so you can go home and start baking cupcakes again."

Yes, I was happy that the murders had been solved and that, eventually, once it became known I wasn't responsible for the poisoned cupcakes, my business would pick back up. But I hated not knowing the why and the how.

"Stop those little wheels from turning in your head." Gabe chuckled when I stuck my tongue out. "We'll get the answers."

"This is official police business, after all. You need to leave it to the professionals." Detective Smith pointed at himself and at Gabe. "I have your statement and your contact information, so I suggest you head on home."

"There's one minor problem with that…" I gazed at Gabe expectantly. "My SUV is still at the nursing facility."

"We can't let you take your vehicle yet. My team is still processing it and the area for evidence of your abduction." Detective Smith frowned. "If I were you, I'd call a friend or family member to come pick you up. Or you can also call for an Uber."

"And the problem with that is Reece took my phone and my purse." I briefly closed my eyes as I worried about the amount of work it would take to replace my ID and credit cards. "Were they found by my SUV?"

Detective Smith spoke into his radio. It squawked back a moment later. "A black leather purse was found nearby, but it was empty. No one has found the wallet or phone."

"Swell." I turned to Gabe to ask if I could borrow his phone. He was already talking on it.

When he disconnected, he turned to me. "Brad is on his way. He'll also call Brian and Tillie to let them know you're safe."

"Thank you." I was ready for a hot bath, a steaming cup of tea, and a cozy bed. It would all have to wait. Instead, I sank back into the sofa cushions.

"Are you feeling all right?" Gabe's voice held concern.

I gazed up at him. "Yeah. A little overwhelmed but grateful to be alive."

"I understand. Truly." He looked around the room. "Are you okay to wait here? I have to get back to work, but if you really need me, I'll sit with you."

"I'm okay. Really." I flashed him a half smile. "The sooner you find answers, the sooner my mind will find some peace."

He smiled back then looked over his shoulder. Confirming no one was within hearing distance and no one was paying us any attention, Gabe lowered his voice. "I'll let you know the whys and hows of the case as soon as we figure them out."

"You know me too well." This time, I gave him a genuine smile. "I appreciate it."

# Chapter 39

Family and friends surrounded me with love and care as I healed from the minor injuries. Tillie declared we'd have our Sunday dinner, whether or not I felt up to it. When my mother and Lars cut their vacation short to be with me, I felt cherished.

Gabe and Brad came early for the dinner so that Gabe could fill me in on what their investigation had uncovered. He'd been able to pry most of the information out of Reece after offering some concessions on his incarceration. We agreed it would be better to talk privately before my nieces and nephew arrived.

"Reece insists it was he, alone, who killed both Ian and William. According to him, his sister, Geri, knew nothing about what he planned on doing." Gabe looked down at his iPad, checking his notes. "Since she's taken a turn for the worse, we can't confirm."

"I thought Geri was recovering?"

"They found arsenic in her bloodstream. The doctors speculate Reece had been dosing her with small quantities to make her sick and eventually cause her heart to fail. With the large dose of sedatives he gave her, it hastened the job."

Gabe's expression turned somber. "It's not looking good for her."

No one spoke for a moment, a contemplative silence falling over us. My thoughts lingered on wondering how a brother could kill his sister.

"Tell her about the shed at the back of the house in Chino Hills." Brad sat on the edge of the chair, his knee bouncing.

"I'm getting to it, but I want to do this in order." Gabe swiped the screen to close it.

"Did you have too much coffee this afternoon?" I pointed at Brad's jiggling knee.

"No." He clamped his mouth shut and pushed his knee down until his foot was flat on the floor.

I narrowed my eyes at him. "As much as I want to know why and how Reece did what he did, I'm more interested in finding out what you're trying to hide."

"Nothing." Brad shot a side glance at his husband. "Absolutely nothing."

"Liar, liar." I turned my gaze to Gabe. "Spill it. What are you two trying to hide?"

Gabe turned to Brad and huffed out a snort. "We agreed to keep this between ourselves until we know for sure. But no, you're like an overinflated balloon ready to burst if you can't say anything."

Brad cupped Gabe's cheek in his hand. "It's a good thing you love me so much."

"As sweet as you guys are, tell me what your secret is. Now!" I looked from one man to the other.

"Secret? Who's got a secret?" Tillie bustled into the room. "I want to know what it is."

"Fine." Brad held up his pinky. "Pinky promise this doesn't go any further until we are ready to share with the world."

Tillie and I held up our pinkies, and Gabe pushed them down. "I'm not going to make you promise to do something that my husband is incapable of doing, but I'd appreciate it if you didn't say anything for now."

"Stop stalling. What. Is. The. Secret?" I crossed my arms in front of my body.

"Well. Uh." Gabe gulped and looked at Brad. "Okay. Here it goes."

Brad jumped in. "A friend of a friend has a niece who just found out she's pregnant. She's a sophomore at UCLA and has decided to carry to term and give the baby up for adoption."

I squealed and jumped up to hug the guys. "So you're adopting! Congratulations!"

"Not so fast, Em." Gabe, ever the serious one, said. "There's still a lot of ifs before it happens. We're supposed to meet her and her parents next weekend to discuss the possibility. She thinks she'd like to be involved in the child's life on the periphery, which we're okay with, as long as we have the legal rights to be known as the child's parents and make all the decisions for the child's life. If she considers us as the adoptive parents, then there'll be a lot of meetings with attorneys and whatnot."

"How far along is she?" Tillie asked.

"Just eight weeks. We realize things can go wrong, so we're not getting our hopes up." Gabe elbowed Brad. "Right?"

"Yeah. Right." Brad rubbed his hands together. "You'll throw us a baby shower, won't you, Em?"

"You betcha!" Tillie agreed for me.

Gabe ran a hand over his face. "Can we get back to the murders before the rest of the family arrives?"

"Yes, please." I answered.

"We found a tiny tool shed at the back of Mrs. Dalton's property. There were grow lights installed to aid in the growth of several poisonous plants." Gabe checked his iPad again. "The plants were belladonna, hemlock, tansy, and lily of the valley, all of which were used in the concoction that killed Ian

Hesser. A small hotplate with a metal saucepan was found behind the shed as well, and it's being tested for poisonous substances. We surmise Reece, or Geri, boiled the substances outside to keep the toxic fumes from building up inside the shed."

"Were you able to identify fingerprints to see who used the shed and grew the plants?" I asked.

"Yes. They found fingerprints belonging to both Reece and Geri Dalton."

"Which proves Geri had to be involved in the murders." Tillie made a fist and smacked it against her palm. "She's evil."

"It's only my job to collect the evidence and let the prosecutor decide if it can be used against her." Gabe shook his head. "Since she's unable to speak and Reece is saying she wasn't involved, until we can definitively prove it, there's nothing I can do. However, I'm still investigating, so maybe something will turn up. Her brother can claim her fingerprints are there because she cleaned the shed or watered the plants for her mother-in-law or for him and didn't know what they were. Be prepared though. We may never know the full truth."

I pursed my lips. "Did Reece ever say why they killed the two men? Geri said something about revenge before she passed out, but didn't say revenge for what reason."

"Reece claims it was because Ian and William were both frauds, cheating honest people out of their money, making them destitute. He was angry about what happened to his sister and wanted to make them pay for hurting her. She apparently felt devastated over losing her home and social standing. Being dumped at her ill mother-in-law's home and expected to become housekeeper, cook, and nurse made the situation even worse. William had also told Geri that he was filing for divorce, and she'd never get her hands on the money he and Ian stole from their clients." Gabe tugged on the collar of his shirt. "We have a forensic accountant looking into

Reece's accounts, as well as Ian and William's company. We speculate Reese lost a chunk of money to their investment schemes, but it will take time to uncover it. Reece won't admit that he invested with his brother-in-law."

"What I want to know is how he got into Frances's house and poisoned the cupcakes." Tillie's eyes gleamed. "It takes someone with nerves of steel to pull something like that with Frances around."

"I haven't figured that part out, either." I'd racked my brain but couldn't remember seeing Reece or Geri at the party or even before the event started.

"Reece bought a huge bouquet of flowers and the heart-shaped box of chocolates and basically waltzed right in as a delivery person." Gabe pointed at me. "He said you and the housekeeper were running around like chickens with your heads chopped off and didn't question him. There were several boxes of cupcakes still in the kitchen, so he took four, put them on a plate, and hid out in the garage. While waiting, he injected poison from the syringes hiding in his jacket pocket."

I rifled through my memories and vaguely recalled seeing a bouquet being delivered. "I kind of remember someone bringing in a huge bouquet, but honestly, I couldn't even tell you if the delivery person was a man or a woman."

"That's what Reece was counting on." Gabe smiled. "Don't worry. It's human nature to overlook those types of people, especially when you're in a chaotic time crunch. His words, not mine."

"What did he do after hiding out in the garage?" I tried to picture the layout of the house. The garage entry to the house was a hallway away from Frances's office, so it wouldn't have been difficult to sneak back in when people were in the dining room.

"Once the party was in full swing, he carried the flowers, candy, and cupcakes to Frances's office—Geri was able to tell him exactly where it was located—and left the sweets. He took the flowers with him when he snuck out of the office, as a cover in case anyone questioned him, and walked out the back door."

"But why use my cupcakes to poison Ian? Why didn't he come with the chocolates already poisoned?"

"It was easier to frame someone else for the poisoning by using something, like the cupcakes, already at the house. If poison had been found in the candy, there would have been more scrutiny about where the box of chocolates came from."

"No wonder he was so quick to jump all over me and try to prove my guilt." My shoulders drooped, and the corners of my mouth dropped. Reece had ruined my business. It might recover, but it could take a long time.

"What if Frances had eaten one of the cupcakes? She might have died as well." Concern etched on Tillie's face. Frances might be her nemesis, but Tillie would never wish her harm.

"Reece didn't care in the least. He initially thought he could frame Frances for Ian's death if she didn't die first. And if she were the one to die, then he'd have swooped in and arrested Ian." Gabe pointed at me. "You and your cupcakes were in the wrong place at the wrong time."

"Such a disturbed man. I hope he spends the rest of his life in prison." Tillie brushed the palms of her hands together as if brushing off the bad juju of Reece. "Now, if you'll excuse me, I have a few things to do before the rest of the family arrives."

Gabe, Brad, and I put all conversation of murder aside and instead talked about the birth mother and their excitement over the baby and potential adoption. Gabe, as expected, kept cautioning Brad to harness his expectations, but it was no use. When the sounds of happy chatter of kids filtered through the house, we went to join the party.

# Chapter 40

My sisters, Vannie and Carrie, bustled around the kitchen, cooking and baking all sorts of mouth-watering dishes. My twin nieces, Kaylee and Sophie, kept me company and tried to one-up each other in making up the silliest stories. Their brother, Tommy, chased Piper and Missy around on sturdy legs. When the dogs got too tired, Tommy begged to feed them treats.

The only sour note of discordance came from Brian. He'd texted me twenty minutes before he'd been expected to arrive at the house, saying he had an emergency at the restaurant and couldn't make our dinner. I tried to disguise my disappointment, but Vannie, Carrie, and Tillie saw right through my stiff smile.

"Cheer up, Emory. You know he'd be here if it weren't a genuine emergency." Tillie poured an overly full glass of wine and handed it to me.

What she said was true. But it was on top of his lack of being around to provide comfort after my ordeal. He'd come by every night after work, but it was usually midnight or later by the time he'd roll in, and then he'd leave by seven the next morning. He'd even been too busy during the day to talk for more than a few minutes. I felt like our relationship had become disjointed, and I didn't know how to get it back on track.

When my nieces announced they wanted to perform a dance for us before we ate, I shoved all thoughts and worries about Brian aside. This was family time, and I was going to enjoy every single second of it.

My mother helped costume the girls in blue jeans, purple plaid flannel shirts, and purple Converse Chuck Taylor high-top sneakers—apparently their dance had been rehearsed and planned for. Once the girls struck a pose—arms crossed in front of their chests, one leg bent in front of them, and their backs resting together—Tommy ran in wearing a similar outfit and black sunglasses on his nose.

I couldn't help but laugh at the cuteness of it all. Carrie hit a button on a large boom box I hadn't seen brought in, and Alvin and the Chipmunks began rapping. Kaylee and Sophie started their hip-hop routine while Tommy struck a few poses then ran in circles around the girls. The dogs joined in, and I laughed until tears leaked.

The kids, and dogs, received a standing ovation, and then they wanted to do it all over again.

"Let's eat dinner first," Carrie said. "There will be plenty of time later, and you're going to want to show Uncle Brian when he gets here."

My eyebrows shot upward, and Carrie mouthed 'oops' at me. She wasn't usually forgetful, so I didn't know why she'd told the kids he'd be there later. They loved Brian, and I didn't want them disappointed when he didn't show up. It was better to let them know he had to work now rather than later.

"I'm so sorry, but Brian has to work tonight. He said to give you all a great big hug and a noogie." I reached my hands out as if to rub my knuckles over their towheaded tresses. They ran from me, laughing and pretending to be scared, as I knew they would. It was a fun distraction for them and for me.

Vannie, Gabe, and Brad carried in platters and bowls of food from the kitchen and arranged them on the long dining table. Carrie and her husband, Thomas, settled the kids in and fixed plates of food for them. My mother and Lars poured drinks for everyone—I still nursed the glass of wine Tillie had foisted on me. Tillie sat beside me and clinked her glass.

She waited until everyone had taken their seat, then she spoke. "We have so much to be grateful for, having Emory home with us, safe and sound. It's a good reminder to cherish those we love, which is every one of you. Now dig in and enjoy the meal."

My mother, sitting next to me, grasped my hand and gave it a tight squeeze. "Please darling, start those self-defense classes next week. My heart can't handle the worry I have for your safety."

"I'm all signed up and start next Friday." I kissed her cheek. "Thank you for coming home early, but I'm truly sorry you missed out on some of your vacation plans."

"We only missed out on two days and, to be honest, Lars is probably relieved." She giggled, a sound I never would have believed would come from my mother's lips. "The only thing on our itinerary was shopping in Paris."

"Then I'm glad I saved Lars from a huge credit card bill." I winked at her, and her face flushed a pretty pink. My stepdad had the means to spoil my mother silly, and spoil her he did.

Dinner, as always, tasted divine. Carrie and Vannie were excellent cooks as well as bakers, and I loved how well they worked together preparing feasts. The roasted pork tenderloin was succulent and simply seasoned with garlic and herbs. The mashed potatoes were creamy and the perfect vehicle for the roasted-garlic-and-rosemary gravy. Even the simple green salad was fresh and crisp, complementing the pillowy soft dinner rolls. My taste buds were happy.

Tillie and Lars got into a lively discussion about the best season to visit Paris while my two sisters tossed menu ideas about for Easter dinner, only six weeks away. Tommy surreptitiously fed the dogs pieces of his pork beneath the table while his sisters regaled Brad and Gabe with descriptions of the costumes and dances they'd be performing in at their upcoming recital. They made their two honorary uncles promise they'd attend and bring them bouquets of flowers. The girls stressed they needed *gigantic* bouquets and not the tiny single roses sold at the auditorium.

My stomach was full, and my heart nearly burst with love, being surrounded by all this happiness.

Tillie's cell phone trilled beneath the table. She quickly pulled it close to her face and read the screen then returned it to her lap. To say I was surprised would have been an understatement. Tillie was practically adamant that, during family dinners, no phones were allowed. The rest of my family didn't look concerned and went on with their conversations.

"Is everything okay?" I asked.

"I'm just a forgetful old woman." She tsked and shook her head. "It's Mr. and Mrs. Nelson's fiftieth anniversary today, and he bought a special present for her. He asked me to hold on to it so she wouldn't be able to snoop around and spoil his surprise."

"So, what's the problem?" Tearing off a piece of dinner roll, I nibbled on it.

"I was supposed to take it over while they were at dinner and leave it in their house. Unfortunately, I completely forgot. He poured the champagne and went to hand her the gift, and it's not there." She fished around the pocket of her slacks, extracted a key, and handed it over. "Would you be a dear and take the present over to their house? Mr. Nelson said he'll keep her in the garden sipping champagne, so all you have to do is let yourself in and leave the gift on the hallway credenza."

"Sure. Where is this mysterious gift?" I pushed back my chair and stood.

"It's in the kitchen pantry, left side on the top shelf." She patted my arm. "You won't be able to miss it. It's a square box wrapped in gold paper and a large silver bow adorning the top."

"I'll be right back."

"Thanks, doll."

I slipped out of the dining room. It didn't seem like anyone noticed me going, even the dogs. I found the package exactly where Tillie said it would be then headed to the house across the alleyway, just right of my pool house and yard.

As I pushed through the wrought iron gate, flickering candles sitting in hurricane vases lined the walkway. Rose petals had been strewn about. The romantic gesture of Mr. Nelson after so many years together with his wife made me grin. Soft jazz floated on the gentle ocean breeze, and golden candlelight glowed from the windows.

Mr. Nelson had certainly gone all out to celebrate their milestone anniversary. I was curious about the special gift he'd bought her too. I'd have to get Tillie to find out what it was if she didn't already know.

The door easily unlocked, and I pushed it open. I stepped inside the house, prepared to deposit the gift onto the credenza just a few feet from the door. Brian stepped into the foyer from around the corner that led to the rest of the house.

Startled, my hand flew to my heart. "Brian? What are you doing here? Did you cook a private dinner for the Nelsons?"

He took the gift from me and handed me a glass of chilled champagne. The bubbles danced in the candlelight. He led me down the hallway to the great room.

My eyebrows drew together. "Are they having an anniversary party?"

Brian leaned in and kissed me. "No. This is our private party. Just me and you."

"What? How?" I gazed around the room. Vases of red roses were scattered around the room. A bottle of champagne chilling in an ice bucket sat on a marble table alongside chocolate-dipped strawberries.

"I've missed you, and we haven't properly celebrated Valentine's together."

"I've missed you too." I set my flute down and wrapped my arms around his neck. "But this is extravagant. How did you manage to get the Nelsons to loan you the house?"

He chuckled, but I could feel his fingers tremble as he moved his arms from around me. His Adam's apple bobbed as he swallowed, and then there he was, on one knee in front of me, holding a small box.

"Emory, I've been wanting to ask you this important question for a long time." He swallowed, making a gulping sound. He closed his eyes for a moment then gazed up at me. "Would you do me the honor of allowing me to be your husband?"

"Yes. A hundred times, yes." I started to kneel next to him, but before I could, he stood and swooped me into his arms and swung me around while kissing me.

"Oh, thank goodness. I've been a nervous wreck all week long." Once he set me back down, he handed the box over to me. "I think I was supposed to show the ring to you when I asked, but I forgot."

I couldn't stop the giggle that escaped my mouth. Opening the box revealed a single solitaire diamond, set in platinum. It wasn't overly large, under a carat—Brian knew I didn't like ostentatious jewelry. He slid it onto my left ring finger. It fit perfectly.

"If you want another style or a larger diamond, we can go together and you can choose what you want."

"This is absolutely perfect. I love it." I kissed him, lingering in his arms. "And I love you."

"I love you too." Brian pulled away and motioned around the room. "If you can see yourself living here and making this our home, Gram said it would be our wedding present from her and David. Mr. and Mrs. Nelson are planning on selling it to downsize and move closer to their grandkids. But they wanted to give Gram a chance to buy it first since they know we've been looking for a home in this area."

My hand flew to my mouth. The house was stunning and, most importantly, it was right next to Tillie and Vannie. I couldn't think of a more perfect combination. "I love it. But that's too, too much to accept from them."

"Gram knew you'd say something like that, so she said we could consider it an advance on our inheritance." Brian bent over to peer into my face. "If you think you can be happy here, please say yes and accept their gift."

I threw my arms around his neck, my happy tears wetting his shirt. "I can't think of anywhere that would be more perfect."

"Then let's toast with champagne, eat some strawberries, and then go share our news."

I mock slapped his shoulder. "How long have you and Tillie been cooking up this totally awesome proposal?"

"It wasn't just me and Tillie. It was the entire family." His face reddened. "They wanted to sneak over and hide out in the bushes to capture the moment on video, but I nixed that idea. Is that okay?"

"Completely okay with me." I caught his hand in mine and couldn't help but admire the sparkling diamond on my finger. "This is between you and me, and for now, no one else."

"We brought the champagne," Tillie hollered as the entire family rushed through the front door to celebrate our joyous news.

"Family. You gotta love 'em," Brian gathered me in his arms, right where I belonged.

# Recipes

# Chocolate Dessert Buffet

*Mudslide Cupcakes*
*Mudslide Cocktails*
*Mini Chocolate Cupcakes with Fudgy Buttercream*
*Tunnel of Fudge Cake*
*Chocolate Truffle Cake (gluten-free)*
*Mini Chocolate Macaroon Tarts (gluten-free)*
*Chocolate Raspberry Pie (gluten-free and vegan)*
*Chocolate Chunk Cookies (gluten-free)*
*Brownie Cookies (gluten-free and vegan)*
*Chocolate-dipped Strawberries (gluten-free)*

# Mudslide Cupcakes

*Makes 1 dozen cupcakes*

## Ingredients

### Cupcakes:

1-1/3 cups (6.7 ounces) all-purpose flour

1 tablespoon Dutch-process cocoa powder (natural cocoa powder can be substituted)

1 teaspoon baking powder

1/2 teaspoon baking soda

1/2 teaspoon instant espresso powder (or similar to Star-bucks' VIA)

1/2 teaspoon salt

1/2 cup (1 stick) unsalted butter, room temperature

1 cup granulated sugar

2 eggs, room temperature

1 tablespoon vanilla extract

3 tablespoons Kahlúa

3 tablespoons Bailey's Irish Cream

3 tablespoons Coco Lopez (cream of coconut)

1 tablespoon vodka

## Glaze:

1/4 cup confectioners' sugar

1 tablespoon vodka

1 tablespoon Bailey's Irish Cream

## Buttercream Frosting:

1/2 cup (1 stick) unsalted butter, room temperature

5 cups confectioners' sugar

1 tablespoon Dutch-process cocoa powder (natural cocoa powder can be substituted)

1/4 teaspoon salt

2 teaspoons vanilla extract

4 tablespoons Kahlúa

3 tablespoons Bailey's Irish Cream

1 tablespoon Coco Lopez (cream of coconut)

## Instructions

## Cupcakes:

Preheat oven to 350 degrees (F).

Line a twelve-cup muffin tin with paper liners.

In a small bowl, sift the flour, cocoa powder, expresso powder, baking powder, baking soda, and salt together. Set aside.

Whisk the Kahlúa, Bailey's, vodka, Coco Lopez, and vanilla together. Set aside.

In the bowl of a standing mixer, beat the butter until smooth, about one minute.

Slowly add the sugar to the butter and beat until creamy on medium-high speed, about three minutes.

Add the eggs, one at a time, and mix until fully incorporated. Add in the vanilla.

Reduce mixer speed to low and add 1/3 of the flour mixture to the butter mixture.

Mix until it is mostly incorporated then add half of the liquid mixture.

Once the liquid is incorporated, repeat with remaining flour and liquid, finishing with the flour.

Once all flour and liquid has been added, increase speed to medium and mix until batter is smooth, about forty-five seconds to one minute. Don't overmix.

Divide the batter evenly between the muffin liners.

Bake sixteen to twenty minutes until the tops spring back and a wooden skewer inserted into the middle of the cake comes out mostly clean. Don't be alarmed if the cupcake middle falls a bit. The frosting will fill it in.

Allow the cupcakes to rest in the muffin tin for five minutes then remove and place on a wire rack.

Prepare the glaze while the cupcakes rest in the muffin tin.

While cupcakes are still hot, pierce the tops of the cupcakes with the tines of a fork four times, making sure tines reach 3/4 of the way down.

Immediately brush with the glaze, making sure to allow liquid to soak in before applying another layer. Use all the glaze.

Allow the cupcakes to cool completely before frosting.

**Glaze:**

Place the confectioners' sugar, vodka, and Bailey's Irish Cream into a microwave-safe dish. I like using my glass one-cup measuring cup for this.

Microwave on high power thirty seconds. Stir to dissolve the sugar. If sugar isn't completely dissolved, heat in additional fifteen-second increments, stirring each time.

**Frosting:**

Sift the confectioners' sugar, cocoa powder, and salt together. Set aside.

Whisk the Bailey's Irish Cream, Coco Lopez, vanilla extract, and Kahlúa together. Set aside.

In the bowl of a standing mixer, whip the room temperature butter until creamy, about one minute.

With the mixer on the lowest speed, slowly add 1/2 of the sugar mixture into the butter. Mix until incorporated.

Add 1/2 of the liquid mixture into the mixer and beat until incorporated.

Repeat with the remaining sugar and half of the remaining liquid mixture. (A quarter of the original liquid measurement should be remaining.)

Once the sugar and the liquid have been incorporated into the butter, increase the mixer speed to medium high and beat to combine. If the frosting is too thick, add additional liquid mixture, one tablespoon at a time, beating well after each addition, until desired consistency is reached.

If frosting becomes too thin, add additional confectioners' sugar, one tablespoon at a time, until desired consistency is reached.

Generously frost the cooled cupcakes as desired and enjoy!

## Mudslide Cocktail
SERVES 2

### Ingredients

3 ounces vodka
    1 ounce Bailey's Irish Cream
    1 ounce Kahlúa
    1 ounce Coco Lopez

### Instructions

Fill a cocktail shaker half full with ice.

Add the vodka, Bailey's, Kahlúa, and Coco Lopez. Shake vigorously until thoroughly chilled.

Strain and divide between two martini glasses and serve.

# Mini Chocolate Cupcakes with Fudgy Buttercream

*Makes 36 mini cupcakes*

## Ingredients

### Cupcakes:

1 cup (4.8 ounces) all-purpose flour

1/2 cup Dutch-process cocoa powder (natural cocoa powder can be substituted)

1 teaspoon baking powder

1/2 teaspoon baking soda

1/2 teaspoon sea salt

1 cup granulated sugar

1/4 cup vegetable oil

2 eggs, room temperature

1 teaspoon vanilla extract

1/4 cup buttermilk*

### Fudgy Buttercream:

1-1/4 cups (2-1/2 sticks) unsalted butter, softened at room temperature

1 cup confectioners' sugar

3/4 cup Dutch-process cocoa powder (natural cocoa powder can be substituted)

1/8 teaspoon sea salt

3/4 cup light corn syrup

1 teaspoon vanilla extract

8 ounces dark chocolate, melted and cooled until just barely warm

## Instructions

### Cupcakes:

Preheat oven to 350 degrees (F). Line a mini muffin tin with paper liners. You may have to bake the cupcakes in batches.

In a small bowl, whisk the flour, cocoa powder, baking powder, baking soda, and salt together. Set aside.

In a large bowl, whisk together the sugar, vegetable oil, eggs, and vanilla until smooth.

Stir half the dry ingredients into the wet ingredients. Add in half of the buttermilk (or milk mixture) and stir until blended. Repeat with the dry ingredients and buttermilk. Stir until batter is well blended.

Fill each mini cupcake liner two-thirds full with the batter.

Bake for fourteen to sixteen minutes or until a wooden skewer inserted into the center of a cupcake comes out mostly clean. A few moist crumbs are fine.

Remove from oven and place baked cupcakes on a wire rack to cool completely. Repeat with remaining batter.

### Fudgy Buttercream:

Add the butter, sugar, cocoa powder, and sea salt to the bowl of food processor. Pulse a few times to combine then scrape down the sides of the bowl. Process for thirty seconds until mixture is smooth.

Add the corn syrup and vanilla and process ten seconds to

combine. Add the cooled melted chocolate and pulse a few times. Scrape down the sides of the bowl then process ten seconds until mixture is creamy.

Transfer the frosting to a piping bag fitted with a star tip and pipe swirls of frosting onto the completely cooled cupcakes.

Use the frosting within three hours. If making in advance, transfer the frosting to an airtight container and refrigerate for up to three days. Bring to room temperature for at least an hour before using.

**Note:**

*You may substitute 1/4 cup whole milk mixed with 1/4 teaspoon white vinegar. Allow the mixture to sit at room temperature for a least five minutes before using.

# Tunnel of Fudge Cake

## **Ingredients**

### **Cake:**

3/4 cup Dutch-processed cocoa powder plus extra for Bundt pan (natural cocoa powder can be substituted)

1/2 cup boiling water

2 ounces bittersweet chocolate, chopped

2 cups all-purpose flour

2 cups pecans, finely chopped

2 cups confectioners' sugar

1 teaspoon salt

5 eggs, room temperature

1 tablespoon vanilla extract

1 cup granulated sugar

3/4 cup packed brown sugar

1-1/4 cups unsalted butter, room temperature

### **Chocolate Glaze:**

3/4 cup heavy cream

1/4 cup light corn syrup

8 ounces bittersweet chocolate, chopped

1/2 teaspoon vanilla extract

**Garnish Ideas:**
Pecan halves or chopped nuts, chocolate leaves or hearts, chocolate shavings, colorful sprinkles, fresh raspberries

## Instructions

**Cake:**
Preheat oven to 350 degrees (F). Heavily grease a twelve-cup Bundt cake pan then dust it with cocoa powder. Set aside.

Place two ounces of chopped bittersweet chocolate into a small heatproof bowl and pour the boiling water over the chocolate. Whisk until smooth. Set aside to cool to room temperature.

In a large bowl, whisk together the cocoa powder, flour, pecans, confectioners' sugar, and salt.

In a small bowl, beat the eggs and vanilla together.

Using an electric mixer on medium-high speed, beat the granulated sugar, brown sugar, and butter together until light and fluffy. Reduce the mixer to low, add the egg mixture, and beat until combined. Add the chocolate mixture and beat until thoroughly incorporated. Batter may appear curdled, but that is normal. Mix in the flour mixture and beat until just combined. Don't over mix.

Pour the batter into the Bundt cake pan. Bake for about forty-five to fifty minutes, until the edges slightly pull away from the pan and the top springs back when lightly touched. A skewer won't give an accurate measurement of doneness, so don't use.

Remove the cake from the oven and place on a wire rack. Cool in the pan for one to one and a half hours then invert onto a serving plate and cool completely.

**Chocolate Glaze:**

Once the cake is completely cooled, heat the cream, corn syrup, and chopped chocolate in a small saucepan over medium heat. Stir constantly until smooth then stir in the vanilla.

Remove from heat and allow to thicken for about thirty minutes.

Drizzle glaze over the cake. Add garnish if desired. Allow it to set for about twenty minutes before serving.

# Chocolate Truffle Cake

*(Gluten-free)*

## **Ingredients**

### **Truffle Cake:**
    8 ounces (2 sticks) unsalted butter
    6 ounces semisweet chocolate, finely chopped
    6 ounces unsweetened chocolate, finely chopped
    5 large eggs
    1 cup granulated sugar - divided
    2 teaspoons vanilla extract
    1/3 cup light corn syrup

### **Chocolate Ganache:**
    1-1/2 pounds semisweet chocolate, finely chopped
    2 cups heavy cream
    8 tablespoons (1 stick) unsalted butter
    1/4 cup light corn syrup

## **Instructions**

Preheat oven to 350 degrees (F). Heavily grease a 9" x 2" cake pan. Line the bottom and sides with parchment paper—a round for the bottom and strips to line the sides—and grease again.

**Truffle Cake:**

Place the butter and both semisweet and unsweetened chopped chocolate into a heatproof, microwavable bowl. Microwave for one minute at 50% power. Stir. Continue to microwave at 50% power in thirty-second increments, stirring after each cycle, until chocolate has melted. Use caution to not overheat. Set aside and cool until barely warm.

Place the eggs, 1/2 cup granulated sugar, and vanilla extract in the bowl of a stand mixer. Using the whisk attachment, beat on high speed until the mixture triples in volume, about four to five minutes.

While the egg mixture beats, combine the remaining 1/2 cup sugar with the light corn syrup in a small saucepan and heat to a full boil.

When the egg mixture has reached full volume, reduce the mixer speed to low and <u>very slowly</u>, drizzle the hot syrup into the egg mixture. Do not turn the mixer off to do this step, or you may end up with curdled eggs.

Increase the speed to medium and beat the mixture about seven to eight minutes until volume becomes light and fluffy.

Reduce the mixer speed to low and add in half the cooled chocolate mixture. Before it is fully incorporated (there should still be streaks of yellow), stop the mixer, remove the whisk attachment, and fold in the remaining chocolate mixture by hand.

Pour the batter into the prepared pan. Place the filled cake pan into a larger pan, and place on the middle rack of the preheated oven. Before closing the oven door, add hot water to the outer pan, until it reaches halfway up to the filled cake pan. The water bath will assist in the truffle cake cooking evenly.

Bake for forty minutes. The top of the cake should look set but not undercooked. Don't use a wooden skewer to test doneness, as the center should still be fudgy.

Cool the cake in the pan for twenty minutes then invert onto a cake plate or serving platter. Cool completely, remove the parchment pieces, then place in the refrigerator to chill before adding the chocolate ganache topping.

## Chocolate Ganache:

Place the chopped chocolate into a heatproof, microwavable bowl. Microwave for one minute at 50% power. Stir. Continue to microwave at 50% power in thirty-second increments, stirring after each cycle, until chocolate has mostly melted. Use caution to not overheat. Set aside.

Add the heavy cream, butter, and corn syrup into a saucepan and warm over medium-high heat, stirring constantly. Heat just until small bubbles form at the edges of the pan, but be sure to not boil the mixture.

Slowly pour the hot liquid over the melted chocolate, whisking constantly until smooth. Strain through a fine mesh sieve.

Pour over the top of the chilled truffled cake, allowing the ganache to drip over the sides of the cake.

Return the cake to the refrigerator and chill for another two hours or overnight.

Allow the cake to sit at room temperature for sixty minutes to come to room temperature or, for a firm consistency, serve chilled.

Cover leftover cake with plastic wrap and store in the refrigerator for up to four days.

# Mini Chocolate Macaroon Tarts

*Makes approximately 40 mini tarts, depending on the size of your pan*
*(Gluten-free)*

## Ingredients

**Macaroon Crust:**
    1 (14-ounce) packaged sweetened flaked coconut
    2/3 cup sweetened condensed milk
    1/4 teaspoon sea salt

**Chocolate Filling:**
    12 ounces premium dark chocolate, chopped
    1 cup heavy cream

## Instructions

Preheat oven to 350 degrees (F). Line a mini muffin tin with foil liners and heavily spritz with nonstick baking spray.

**Macaroon Crust:**
    In a large bowl, mix together the flaked coconut, sweet-

ened condensed milk, and sea salt until well blended. Mixture will be thick.

Scoop a heaping tablespoon full of the mixture into each of the foil liners. Lightly grease your hands and press mixture into the bottom and sides of each liner to form the crust. A wine cork works well to tamp the mixture down.

Bake for thirteen to fifteen minutes or until the tart crusts are golden brown. Immediately remove the crusts to a wire rack. Using the back of a small spoon or a wine cork, lightly press down the centers of the tart crusts to create a well. Cool completely.

**Chocolate Filling:**

Heat the cream in a heavy-duty saucepan over medium heat, just until small bubbles begin to form at the edges.

Add chopped chocolate to a heatproof bowl and pour the hot cream over the chocolate. Do not stir. Allow the mixture to sit, undisturbed for five minutes. Using a whisk, stir the chocolate mixture until completely smooth.

Scoop the chocolate filling into a piping bag. Snip 1/4 inch off the end of the piping bag, and then pipe the chocolate into the completely cooled macaroon crusts, filling 3/4 full.

Place the mini tarts in the refrigerator, uncovered, for at least an hour, until the filling has set.

Remove from the refrigerator twenty minutes before serving.

Place leftovers in an airtight container and store in the refrigerator.

# Chocolate Raspberry Pie

*(Gluten-free and vegan)*

## <u>Ingredients</u>

### Chocolate Crust:

22 gluten-free Oreos (not double stuffed)

4 tablespoons Earth Balance vegan stick margarine, melted (or similar)

1/4 teaspoon sea salt

### Chocolate Raspberry Filling:

10 ounces premium dark chocolate, chopped (dairy-free and gluten-free, if needed)

5 ounces (about 1 cup) fresh raspberries

1 tablespoon pure maple syrup

1 teaspoon vanilla extract (make sure the brand is gluten-free, if necessary)

3/4 cup confectioners' sugar

1 (12.3-ounce) shelf-stable package firm silken tofu

Optional: 1/2 to 1 teaspoon raspberry extract, or to taste

**Garnish:**

Vegan whipped cream

Fresh raspberries

## Instructions

Preheat oven to 350 degrees (F).

**Oreo Crust:**

In a food processor, pulse the Oreos until they are fine crumbs. (If you don't have a food processor, you can crush them by placing in a Ziploc bag and crushing them with a rolling pin or mallet.)

Transfer the crumbs to a medium-sized mixing bowl and stir in the melted margarine and sea salt.

Pour the crumbs into a 9-inch pie plate and tightly press the crumbs down on the bottom and sides of the pan.

Bake for ten minutes then cool completely before filling.

**Chocolate Raspberry Filling:**

Place the chopped chocolate into a heatproof, microwavable bowl. Microwave for one minute at 50% power. Stir. Continue to microwave at 50% power in thirty-second increments, stirring after each cycle, until chocolate has mostly melted. It will take several cycles but it is imperative that the chocolate not overheat. Set aside and cool until barely warm.

Using a high-speed blender (a food processor or stick immersion blender can be used in a pinch) add the raspberries, maple syrup, vanilla extract, raspberry extract, if using, and confectioners' sugar to the jar. Blend on high speed, scraping down the sides of the jar as necessary, until raspberries are puréed.

Add the tofu and blend until fully incorporated.

Add the melted chocolate and blend until completely

smooth. (If using a food processor or stick blender, the mixture may still contain fragments of raspberry seeds.)

Pour into the cooled prepared Oreo crust and refrigerate at least two hours or overnight.

Serve with vegan whipped cream and fresh raspberries if desired.

Cover leftovers and store in the refrigerator for up to three days.

---

# Chocolate Chunk Cookies

---

*(Gluten-free)*
*Makes about 24 cookies, depending on size*

## **Ingredients**

1 cup packed brown sugar

1/3 cup vegetable oil

1/3 cup butter, room temperature

2 tablespoons honey

1-1/2 teaspoons vanilla extract (make sure the brand is gluten-free if necessary)

1 large egg, room temperature

2 cups (9 ounces) buckwheat flour, or you may substitute brown rice flour

1 teaspoon baking soda

1/2 teaspoon salt

4 ounces premium semisweet or bittersweet chocolate chunks

2 ounces mini semisweet chocolate chips

1/2 teaspoon Fleur de sel or other coarse sea salt (optional)

## Instructions

Add brown sugar, vegetable oil, butter, honey, and vanilla extract to the bowl of a standing mixer. Beat on medium until well combined.

Add the egg and beat until thoroughly incorporated.

Whisk together the flour, baking soda, and salt.

Add the flour mixture to the sugar mixture and beat on low speed until blended together.

Add the chocolate chunks and chips and mix by hand until just incorporated.

Refrigerate the dough for at least forty-five minutes.

Preheat oven to 375 degrees (F).

Place rounded tablespoon-sized pieces of cookie dough on a parchment-lined baking sheet.

Sprinkle a bit of the Fleur de sel over each cookie, if desired.

Bake ten to thirteen minutes until the edges start to brown.

Remove the baking sheet from the oven and allow the cookies to cool on the sheet for five minutes then place them on a wire rack to cool completely.

Store in an airtight container in a cool, dry place.

# Brownie Cookies

*(Gluten-free and vegan)*
*Makes about 30 cookies*

## Ingredients

1/2 cup natural cocoa powder

1 teaspoon baking soda

1 cup granulated sugar

3/4 cup peanut butter (or substitute almond butter if desired)

1/2 cup aquafaba (chickpea brine)

3/4 cup mini dairy-free white chocolate chips plus more for optional garnish (I prefer the Life Joy brand)

Flaked sea salt

## Instructions

Preheat oven to 350 degrees (F). Line a baking sheet with parchment paper.

In a medium-sized bowl, whisk together the cocoa powder, baking soda, and sugar.

Stir in the peanut butter and aquafaba until well combined. Fold in the white chocolate chips. The batter will resemble brownie batter.

Using a 1-tablespoon-sized spring-loaded cookie scoop, scoop the batter and place on the baking sheets. Leave 2 inches between cookies since they will spread.

Bake the cookies, one baking sheet at a time, for eleven to thirteen minutes. Rotate the baking sheet halfway through. The tops of the cookies will crack, and the insides of the cracks should appear undercooked. This is normal, so don't overbake!

Remove from the oven. If desired, sprinkle the extra mini chips on the hot cookies, along with flaked sea salt. Allow the cookies to cool on the baking sheet for ten minutes before removing to a wire rack to cool completely.

Repeat with the remaining cookie dough.

When completely cooled, store leftover cookies in an airtight container, layered between sheets of parchment or wax paper, at room temperature for up to three days.

# Chocolate-Dipped Strawberries

*(Gluten-free)*
*Makes 12 to 15 servings*

## Ingredients

1 pound strawberries (12 to 15 berries), stems intact
8 ounces premium chocolate (milk, semisweet, or bittersweet), finely chopped
2 ounces premium white chocolate, finely chopped
1/2 teaspoon vegetable shortening

1 cup white vinegar for washing the berries

## Instructions

**Wash the berries:**
Soak the berries in a mixture of 4 cups cold water and 1 cup white vinegar for ten minutes.

Rinse with fresh water, drain, and gently pat the berries with a clean towel or paper towels until they are *thoroughly* dry.

**Dipping the strawberries:**

Line a baking sheet or tray with parchment paper.

Place the 6 ounces of chopped chocolate into a heatproof, microwavable glass measuring cup, along with the vegetable shortening. Microwave for one minute at 50% power. Stir. Continue to microwave at 50% power in thirty-second increments, stirring after each cycle, until chocolate has melted. Use caution to not overheat.

Working with one berry at a time, dip into the melted chocolate. Shake the excess back into the measuring cup, and place on a parchment-lined tray. Repeat with the remaining berries, working quickly.

If the chocolate gets too cool and begins to thicken, reheat in the microwave at 50% power in twenty second increments, stirring well each time.

Allow the chocolate to set for fifteen minutes then proceed with the white chocolate drizzle.

**White chocolate drizzle:**

Place the white chocolate in a small heatproof, microwavable bowl and melt using the same method as the chocolate above.

Transfer the melted white chocolate to a disposable piping bag (or use a small Ziploc bag). Snip a small opening into the bag and drizzle white chocolate zigzags over the chocolate-dipped berries.

Refrigerate until ready to serve. Store leftovers in an airtight container for a day or two.

**Tips:**

When dipping the berries, allow them to set for about a minute, then move them to a clean spot on the parchment paper to keep the "puddles" of chocolate from forming and attaching to the strawberries.

Alternately, you can dip the strawberries in white chocolate and accent with dark chocolate zigzags.

*For the firefighters and first responders who put their lives on the line as they respond to devastating and tragic natural disasters.*
*And to those who have endured what Mother Nature has thrown at us this past year.*

## Acknowledgments

It's true that it takes a village to create a book. I'd like to thank my husband, Dan, for reading and editing my manuscript several times. His engineering mind is invaluable in helping to keep my books (mostly logical).

Thank you to Janet Clause for being an early reader of my (very) rough draft. Your comments and suggestions always help in making my book so much better.

To the incomparable and very talented cover designer Karen Phillips, thank you from the bottom of my heart. You always take my ideas and create a cover that is SO much better in capturing the vision of my book.

To all the bloggers who help me spread the word about my new releases and put up with my last-minute requests to review, I owe you a debt of gratitude! Readers and authors alike are fortunate to have you in our community. And to all the readers who take the time to read and review my books—you are appreciated! You're what makes me get up extra early to put my stories on the page. A special thanks to all the lovely people who follow my blog, Cinnamon, Sugar, and a Little Bit of Murder, and share in my love for delicious food and mysteries! You inspire me to create recipes to share with family and friends.

# About the Author

Kim Davis writes the Aromatherapy Apothecary cozy mystery series, the award-winning Cupcake Catering cozy mystery series, and the middle grade fantasy adventure The Board Game Chronicles series. She has also written several children's nature articles published in a variety of magazines.

Kim Davis is a member of Sisters in Crime, Mystery Writers of America, and Society of Children's Book Writers and Illustrators.

She lives in Southern California with her husband and rambunctious mini Goldendoodle, Missy, who has become an inspiration for several plotlines. When she's not spending time with her granddaughters or chasing Missy around, she can be found either writing on her next book, working on her blog, Cinnamon, Sugar, and a Little Bit of Murder, or in the kitchen baking up yummy treats to share.

To learn more, please visit http://kimdavisauthor.com/

CHOCOLATE CAN BE DEADLY

Cupcake Catering Mystery Series Book 7

Cinnamon & Sugar Press

All characters and events in this book are a work of fiction. Any similarities to anyone living or dead are purely coincidental. Kim Davis is identified as the sole author of this book.





ISBN 979-8-9853601-7-2

ISBN 979-8-9853601-8-9

ISBN 979-8-2303138-7-8

Cover Design by Karen Phillips

Edited by Red Adept Editing

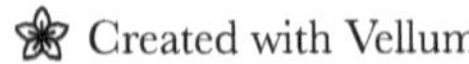 Created with Vellum

Also by Kim Davis

## The Cupcake Catering Mystery Series

**SPRINKLES OF SUSPICION** – Award Winning!

One glass of cheap California chardonnay cost Emory Gosser Martinez her husband, her job, and her best friend. Unfortunately, that was only the beginning of her troubles. Distraught after discovering the betrayal by her husband and best friend, Tori, cupcake caterer Emory Martinez allows her temper to flare. Several people witness her very public altercation with her ex-friend. To make matters worse, Tori exacts her revenge by posting a fake photo of Emory in a compromising situation, which goes viral on social media. When Tori is found murdered, all signs point to Emory being the prime suspect.

With the police investigation focused on gathering evidence to convict her, Emory must prove her innocence while whipping up batches of cupcakes and buttercream. Delving into the past of her murdered ex-friend, she finds other people had reasons to want Tori dead, including Emory's own husband. Can she find the killer, or will the clues sprinkled around the investigation point the police back to her?

### Praise for Sprinkles of Suspicion

"…there is enough action, including a few surprises—plus baking— to maintain a steady momentum. The breezy book concludes with a collection of unique recipes. An engaging cozy best enjoyed with a plate of cookies." – *Kirkus Reviews*

"The mystery, characters, and mouth-watering recipes will charm readers until the very end." – *InD'tale Magazine, Crowned Heart Review*

"You are going to love this delicious new cozy mystery! Kim Davis pens characters who come to life and a story you won't want to put down, not to mention recipes that will make your mouth water. Don't miss this scrumptious treat! – *Paige Shelton*, New York Times Bestselling author of the Farmers' Market, Country Cooking School, Dangerous Type, Scottish Bookshop mysteries, and Alaska Wild suspense series

"Sparkling prose, a deliciously twisty plot, and a colorful cast of characters make this debut cozy a surefire winner!" – *Linda Reilly*, author of the Cat Lady Mysteries, Deep Fried Mysteries, and the Grilled Cheese Mystery series.

"A delightful new cozy with a cool California setting and an imminently likable heroine." – *Ellen Byron*, Best Humorous Lefty Awards winner and author of the Agatha Award winning and USA Today Bestselling Cajun Country Mysteries, The Catering Hall Mysteries, and the Vintage Cookbook Mystery series.

"This story moves along at a great pace and doesn't lag anywhere. There is always something happening, drama, twists, and yes, cupcakes. So well-plotted, I was totally taken in by the entire story and flabbergasted when the real killer was revealed." – *Escape With Dollycas Into A Good Book*

## CAKE POPPED OFF

Cupcake caterer Emory Martinez is hosting a Halloween bash alongside her octogenarian employer, Tillie. With guests dressed in elaborate costumes, the band is rocking, the cocktails are flowing, and tempers are flaring when the hired Bavarian Barmaid tries to hook a rich, hapless husband. Except one of her targets happens to be Emory's brother-in-law, which bodes ill for his pregnant wife. When Emory tracks down the distraught barmaid, instead of finding the young woman in tears, she finds her dead. Can she explain to the new detective on the scene why the Bavarian Barmaid was murdered in Emory's bathtub with Emory's Poison Apple Cake Pops stuffed into her mouth?

With an angry pregnant sister to contend with, she promises to clear her brother-in-law's name. As Emory starts asking questions and tracking down the identity of the costumed guests, she finds reasons to suspect her brother-in-law has been hiding a guilty secret. Her search leads her to a web of blackmail and betrayal amongst the posh setting of the local country club crowd. Can Emory sift through the lies she's being told and find the killer? She'll need to step up her investigation before another victim is sent to the great pumpkin patch in the sky.

### Praise for Cake Popped Off

"This book has all the qualities of a top notch cozy mystery. The characters were entertaining and the whodunit was well written and certainly kept me guessing." – *Karen Kenyon, Reviewer*

"The mystery is top-notch and had me popping from one suspect to another only to have my suspicions lead to dead ends. Surprise after surprise had me enjoying the plot moves and startling revelations!" – *Linda Langford, Chatting About Cozies*

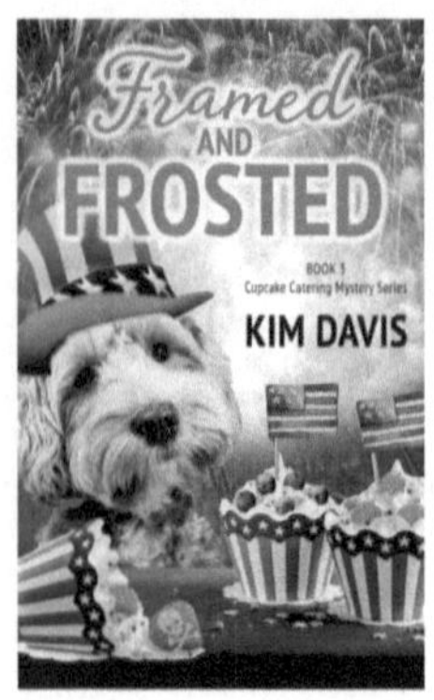

## FRAMED AND FROSTED

Framed and Frosted, the third book in the Cupcake Catering Mystery series, finds cupcake caterer, Emory Martinez, working at a Laguna Beach society Fourth of July soiree, with her sister and their new employee, Sal. With a host who seems intent on accosting both catering employees and guests alike, things go from bad to worse when he accuses Sal of murdering his long-dead son.

As the crescendo of exploding fireworks overhead becomes the backdrop for cupcakes and champagne, a deadly murder occurs. Can Sal and Emory explain why the cupcake the host ate, after shoving a trayful of buttercream-frosted cupcakes onto Sal, resulted in his death? Or will the detective and guests alike believe that Sal is a murderer? Emory and her octogenarian employer, Tillie, whip into action to find out who framed Sal after he was frosted by the victim.

### Praise for Framed and Frosted

"Framed and Frosted" is a fun-filled novel filled with murder, blackmail, manslaughter, theft, and total chaos that will have one flipping through the pages like mad to find out what happens next! – *Belinda Wilson, InD'Tale*

"Kim Davis is an awesome storyteller and her books are amazing treats that should not be missed!" – *Escape With Dollycas Into A Good Book*

"Wow! Once I started reading Framed and Frosted, I couldn't put it down! . . . Davis keeps readers on the edge of their seats as she crafts a suspenseful mystery with plenty of surprising twists and turns." – *Reading Is My SuperPower*

## FROSTED YULETIDE MURDER

Set against the holiday cheer of twinkling lights, costumed carolers, and a festive line of extravagantly decorated boats participating in the annual Christmas boat parade in Newport Beach, California, cupcake caterer Emory Martinez finds that the Grinch has crashed the party. Together with her sister Carrie, Emory is catering a delectable feast of holiday cupcakes and cookies aboard a luxury yacht for the new Mrs. Blair Villman and her guests.

Sparks fly when Carrie comes face-to-face with the hostess, who just happens to be Carrie's high school frenemy, and old grievances are dredged up. Adding fuel to the fire, Blair's stepson brings his mother, the former Mrs. Villman, to the party. Instead of celebrating holiday cheer, someone seems intent on channeling the Burgermeister Meisterburger and shutting down Blair's party permanently. When Emory finds a body aboard the yacht, she needs to discover who iced the victim before the Scrooge ruins not only her livelihood but her freedom as well.

### Praise for Frosted Yuletide Murder

Kim's writing style is very entertaining, descriptive, and with dialogue that solicited lots of emotions. The murder investigations requires "all hands on deck," with Emory having to deflect accusations, navigate roadblocks of lies and secrets, weed through untrustworthy persons of interest, and recover from perilous predicaments. But, Kim always adds those personal stories beyond the cozy mystery with a bit of romance, a bit of friendship, and a lot of cupcakes and cookie talk. – *Kathleen Costa, Kings River Life Magazine*

Makes for a fabulously fun cozy read that is sure to be enjoyable to fans of the genre. A must-read for me. I totally loved it so I give it 5/5 stars. – *Books a Plenty Book Reviews*

## BUTTERCREAM BETRAYAL

Intent on getting their two mischievous dogs under control, Emory Martinez and her half sister, Vannie, join a group dog training program led by Shawn Parker. With a graduation certificate just within grasp and a party to celebrate their hard-won achievements, what could go wrong? For starters, their two dogs have decided to wreak havoc during the party and tempers flare. It turns out not everyone is pleased with the dog trainer and his mother, the condo association president.

Whispers of the mother and son's misbehavior, or worse, fly amongst the barks, whines, and growls of the canines. When Emory finds the body of Mrs. Parker amidst an explosive situation, it becomes apparent there is more truth to the whispers instead of just gossip. Could one of the canine-loving participants be responsible? Or an outsider who hated her heavy-handed rule over the condo homeowners? Emory, Vannie, and octogenarian Tillie must sift through the clues to find out who has been betrayed and who has decided to take justice into their own hands.

### Praise for Buttercream Betrayal

"Davis outdoes herself in this latest caper, including side stories of puppy mills, blackmail, money laundering, theft, and secret alliances. I thoroughly enjoyed this latest episode in the lives of a charming and funny cast, and now I am eager to find out what happens in the next one." – *James Cudney, This Is My Truth Now*

"Davis once again shines with her well-developed characters that always makes me feel like I'm coming back to visit friends. As for the mystery, this book is full of action... There are several red herrings that lead to numerous surprises along the way." – *Kim Heniadis, Reviewer*

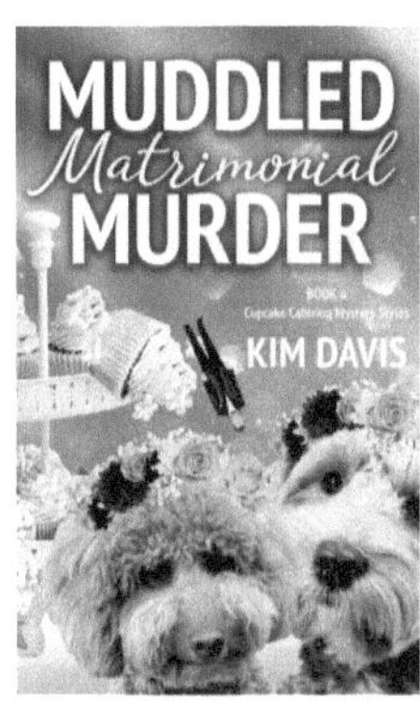

## MUDDLED MATRIMONIAL MURDER – Award Winning!

With only two weeks left to finalize the arrangements for the nuptial ceremony and reception for Emory Martinez's best friend, Brad, and a Thanksgiving feast to plan, she has enough to keep her busy. But when Emory and Brad stumble across the body of his former stalker, with a wedding gift marble muddler lying next to the body, it soon becomes apparent someone is intent on framing the groom before vows can be exchanged.

How did the victim locate Brad, and how did she end up being murdered at the scene of the impending nuptials? Was someone so desperate to stop the wedding that they'd resort to murder? Or was she killed for revenge? As the countdown to the wedding speeds by, it'll take Emory and her family and friends pulling together to pick through the muddled clues to clear the groom's name.

### Praise for Muddled Matrimonial Murder

*Winner of Readers' Favorite Gold Medal and Finalist in the Chanticleer International Book Awards!*

Cozy mystery lovers will want to check out this book. Charming, funny, and lighthearted, Muddled Matrimonial Murder serves as another clever installment in the series and delivers a compelling new mystery featuring your favorite characters. *– Liz Konkel for Readers' Favorite*

I anxiously await each new book in this series and devour the whole thing in one sitting. I totally escape into the book and the rest of the world falls away. Like many others in this series, you will find Muddled Matrimonial Murder on my Best Reads list for the year. Each book in this series is a fantastic treat for cozy lovers and each one tops the last. *– Escape With Dollycas Into A Good Book*

www.ingramcontent.com/pod-product-compliance
Lightning Source LLC
Chambersburg PA
CBHW051309130726

47987CB00004B/1733